Double Entry

Double Entry

Jane Honeck

REVERSING FALLS
PRESS

ISBN: 978-0-9845020-4-2 (Paperback)
ISBN: 978-0-9845020-5-9 (eBook)

Reversing Falls Press, Robbinston, Maine

Also by Jane Honeck:

Fiction

Numbers Don't Lie

Non-fiction

The Problem With Money? It's Not About the Money!

To Wonderful Wayne, eternal supporter for this and all my other hare-brained ideas.

And, for my writing companions—Careyleah, Cheryl, Kit, Lucia, and our teacher and mentor, Jodi Paloni, whose guidance made this journey possible.

PART ONE
PROLOGUE

ELLEN

ANOTHER SLEEPLESS NIGHT—ELLEN HARTMANN has many—and with the Damocles sword of *The Money Dynamic*'s deadline looming over her, she uses her insomnia as an excuse to work on her passion project, the one that will save her from long hours of numbing tax returns and tax laws. Sometimes, her tossing and turning, stirred up by a multitude of troubles crowding her mind, will lead to solutions that she'll put into motion the following day. Other times, her nocturnal musings slip back into her subconscious, never to be resurrected. Tonight, she cannot risk losing any critical thoughts to her own personal Neverland, and she tiptoes out of her bedroom, treads softly down the stairs, and shuffles to her office. Her LL Bean sheepskin slippers muffle her footsteps, ensuring she won't disturb her three sleeping sons.

She slides her hand down the wall outside her dark office, walks her fingers across it to find the light switch, and flips it on. The harsh overhead light assaults her, and she flicks it off. She blinks to regain her night eyes, then sits at her desk, gliding her mouse over the photo of the boys posing at Fort Williams on Maine's rocky cliffs. Her computer screen springs to life with enough glow to access her right-brain creativity but not enough to activate her accountant's left-brain analysis. She won't be using her CPA number-crunching skills tonight, not that she doesn't appreciate how she, as a single mom, supports her family with them.

Tonight, she'll tap into her other expertise—the one that connects deeply with her clients to unlock the mysteries of the human mind, keeping her motivated in the emotionless world of accounting. Tonight, her fingers dance passionately across the keyboard, and she feels a buzz in her chest. Tonight, she feels alive and driven, knowing that her life's purpose isn't to prepare the perfect tax return, but rather to journey with her clients through good times, bad times, and everything in between.

Tomorrow, she returns to Nashville to push digital marketing and creative genius Sam Davis, one step closer to her project's finish line. It's been a long, slow slog trying to corral Sam's abundant ambitions, one especially challenging for a tax accountant who efficiently and effectively meets the steady stream of critical tax deadlines. Tomorrow, although she has loved the invigorating opportunity to break free from the mundane world of numbers and work with Sam, she needs *The Money Dynamic* to be completed.

Ellen isn't aware of the approaching dawn, but Random, her forty-four-pound cream-colored curly companion, is. The pooch nudges her elbow to remind her about their morning walk. She gazes out the window as the shades of purple night sky fade into sunrise pinks and blues. Her tapping fingers become more animated as she wraps up the section she's working on. Then she gives the Wheaten terrier's head a scratch, stands up, and stretches her back. Wearing an oversized sweatshirt over her pajama pants, she slips into her waiting socks and sneakers, clips on the dog's leash, and opens the heavy mahogany door of her red brick home. With Random by her side, she strolls through the awakening streets of South Portland.

CHAPTER 1

HENRY

HENRY'S THUMBS DRUMMED ON THE LEATHER-wrapped steering wheel. Sam was late. In the early hours of the day, Henry had driven Sam Davis over two hundred miles to Atlanta for a critical 10 a.m. meeting. Sam promised that his meeting with investors would be short, not only because he tried to avoid law firms like the plague, but also because everything had been pre-negotiated, and today was about signing on the dotted line. They would make it back in plenty of time to pick up Ellen Hartmann at the airport. Now, it was one o'clock, two hours later than expected, and more than enough time to sign any contracts. Even if traffic cooperated, it would be a stretch to make it to the airport on time.

Henry knew his Atlanta meeting was crucial to Sam, his company Brand & Broadcast, and indirectly, to Henry himself. Over the past ten days, whenever clients called, Sam placated them and assured them their money was well spent and that everything was progressing as planned. He reassigned staff from one project to another, leveraging the company's talent to fill all the gaps. Roxie, Sam's wife, amplified Henry's suspicions with her worried whispers filled with words he couldn't quite grasp. When Sam let slip that these investors could make or break him, Henry's intuition was confirmed.

Today's road trip, aside from the unspoken tension, was normal. Sam didn't fly and admitted to having a strong case of aerophobia. He also didn't drive. An accident in his teens had stripped him of any desire to take the wheel. Henry never asked for details but understood that, as Sam's driver, he was expected to be available whenever and wherever Sam needed him. It was a cushy job that provided him with a stable financial foundation, allowing him to pursue his music career most nights.

He hated being on call, but it came with unexpected perks. It drove Sam crazy to see anyone standing around doing nothing, and when he saw that Henry's primary activity was hurry-up-and-wait, he slipped Henry a few minor acting roles. Henry was a natural, and Sam cast him in videos for clients like Ellen. As Sam's business shifted from marketing projects to TV and movie production, Henry landed the lead role in one of his television series, along with bit parts in a movie. Henry would never have guessed that an acting career would stem from answering an ad for a driver.

He had arrived in Nashville after busking on Richmond's busy street corners hadn't given him enough money to move out of his parents' house. Neither of them wanted him to leave, but his mother's suggestion to give it more time and his father's snarky comments, always ending with *get a job*, motivated him to give it a try in Nashville. Accepting the job with Sam satisfied them both.

He checked his watch. Ellen's plane was scheduled to land at 4:44, and unless Sam showed up soon, they'd be late. He remembered Ellen's frustration with Sam the last time she was here. All of his delays and excuses were wearing thin, and the thought of Ellen waiting on the curb mixed with the growing unease in his belly. Where was Sam? How would he find him?

CHAPTER 2

ELLEN

ELLEN WAITED FOR THE BOARDING CALL FOR her flight to Nashville. Portland International Jetport had an impressive name, but despite being the busiest airport in Maine, it was tiny. Having grown up in a small town in southern Wisconsin, her usual airport had been Chicago's O'Hare, famous for its long walks between security and hundreds of gates, and its neon-lit underground tunnel connecting terminals. Over the years, Portland Jetport had expanded significantly and now boasted a total of eleven gates. Clearly, navigating the airport was a piece of cake.

Speaking of which, Ellen was hungry and pulled out the remnants of the blueberry muffin she had started eating that morning. After dropping her sons off at school, she ordered a coffee and muffin at Dunkin' Donuts, picking at the blueberries during the quick drive to the office. She finished her coffee when she got into the office, but forgot about the muffin until she packed up her briefcase to leave. She stuffed the bag with the uneaten treat along with her laptop and cords. Now, she was grateful for its squashed presence.

The few hours before her flight were filled with brief meetings with staff and a longer discussion with Julie Benoit, her senior accountant, to brief her on the tasks that needed attention during her absence. Julie's competence allowed Ellen to focus on *The Money Dynamic*, and her support allowed Ellen to move from the sterile world of tax accounting into the realm of financial psychology. Utilizing her creativity and empathy to explore the frustrating and confusing world of finances nourished her soul.

Last night, her fingers clacked on the keyboard in her home office as she refined her online, interactive program designed to help people uncover the mysteries of their minds on money. It went beyond other programs that touted the same old solutions: wipe out debt, invest wisely, save more, spend less. Simple advice that was impossible to follow, until one dove into the murky depths of why we make the choices that rule and ruin our lives. *The Money Dynamic* identified hidden anchors that formed the basis for flawed decision-making. The app would liberate users from the cloak of guilt and shame that enveloped them when they failed to adhere to conventional financial advice.

Ellen was convinced that the world needed her program because, over the years, her clients had shown that without awareness, change cannot happen. She refused to believe that anyone woke up in the morning and decided to screw up their finances. Yet, the outcome was always the same. Her program would open their eyes to new solutions that would guide them to a personalized off-ramp from their hamster wheel of financial frustration.

She smirked. Over the past two years, Sam Davis's marketing jargon had seeped into her thinking, and his creative language enhanced both *The Money Dynamic* and her elevator pitch. He was an innovative force of nature, full of groundbreaking ideas and imaginative solutions for apps, websites, and even TV shows and movies. That's why she and Sterling, her former partner, hired him more than two years ago. With Sam's endless delays and inability to finish tasks, Sterling decided to give up, but Ellen was still trying to find the magic formula to get Sam to deliver on his promises.

Would he ever come through? For over two years, she had pushed, prodded, poked, and everything in between until she reached the end of her rope. This trip, she would not take no for an answer.

CHAPTER 3

HENRY

HENRY RACKED HIS BRAIN FOR ANYTHING HE might have overlooked that morning. When he dropped Sam off before ten at Symphony Tower, the forty-one-story skyscraper at 1180 Peachtree Street, Sam told him to grab a cup of coffee and return in an hour. The meeting at Alexander and Cross, a small boutique firm specializing in entertainment law, was merely a formality and would be brief. Henry watched as Sam strode toward the building's glass front. A man in a black suit tapped him on the shoulder, shook his hand firmly, and guided Sam through the door. The unknown man's black suit oozed designer quality, and he wore shoes Henry could only dream of. Both were in stark contrast to Sam's heather gray sweatshirt and running shoes. Sam was clearly running with the right crowd.

Now, three long hours had passed without a word. Why wasn't Sam keeping Henry informed? He was always a step ahead of everyone, liked to be in control at all times, and used his cell phone to keep others tethered to his changing whims. Henry didn't dare call him, but he could make sure he had dropped Sam at the right place.

He activated the flashers, locked the Escalade's doors, and pushed through the skyscraper's front entrance. He strode to the building's tenant directory and examined it from top to bottom. A large law firm occupied the upper floors, with its reception area on the thirty-first floor highlighted. Other professional firms dotted the remaining floors, while the smallest companies filled unused corners on the lower levels. No Alexander and Cross. He scanned the directory again and used his internal voice to read the names aloud to avoid missing any. Again, no Alexander and Cross. He checked a third time. Nothing.

Was the law firm new to the building, its name not yet listed? He searched the lobby for a security or information desk. A muscular man with white earbuds resting in his ears stood silently near the elevator bank. He might be listening to his favorite music, but Henry suspected the earbuds served a greater purpose, and he approached him.

"Excuse me. Can you help me? I'm looking for Alexander and Cross law firm. It isn't listed on the directory." Henry reached out his hand with a smile. Neither was reciprocated.

"There's no one in this building by that name." The man glanced at his feet, and Henry followed his gaze. He wore shoes like Henry's.

"Are you sure? I dropped my boss off this morning." Henry tried to sound casual, hoping to nudge the large man to try harder. The security guard didn't respond.

"He was here for a meeting," he said, his voice shaky with anxiety, and he frowned. "At Alexander and Cross law firm. I'm not sure what to do next."

"Not my problem." This time, the man locked eyes with Henry and didn't look away. "I assure you there is no Alexander and Cross law firm or any other business with that name in this building."

"Damn." He lowered his head and felt his ponytail brush against his neck. Goddamn Sam and his acting gig. Maybe if he had been allowed to cut the damn thing off, and his hair was brown instead of red, the guy might have taken him seriously.

He put on his most sincere look and tried again. "Someone greeted him and led him inside. That was around ten this morning. He was supposed to be finished in less than an hour." He glanced at his watch, flashing 1:09. "Now he's two hours late. Doesn't make sense?" The rise in Henry's voice made his statement sound like a question.

"I don't know what to tell you. He's not at Alexander and Cross, or at least not in this building. Now I'll have to ask you to leave as you seem to have no business here." This time, the man stuck out his beefy hand to bid Henry farewell. Henry's smile quivered. He had no choice but to accept the handshake. The security guard's eyes followed him as he turned away to slip through the door to his blinking car.

Henry stared over the steering wheel at the parade of cars moving down Peachtree Street. What should he do? Where should he go? He sensed the guard's unseen eyes daring him to make a mistake. He turned off the flashers, shifted the giant SUV into drive, and looked over his shoulder to double-check the car's blind spot indicator before merging into the congested downtown traffic. He didn't know where he was going, but the security guard's message was clear. Leave. Now.

Without Sam? A wave of worry surged from his gut and settled in his throat.

CHAPTER 4

ELLEN

ELLEN LIFTED HER GROGGY EYELIDS AT THE sound of the flight attendant's squeaky cart moving down the aisle. It reminded her of Bobby, her favorite office cleaner, who assisted with everything and anything that anyone at Hartmann and Associates came up with. With his broad smile, quick wit, and eagerness to help, Bobby brightened everyone's mood at Maine's first woman-owned accounting firm. From moving files to painting offices and everything in between, Bobby was their go-to guy.

Not too long ago, Bobby assisted Julie, Ellen's right-hand woman, in uncovering embezzlement at a client's office. Strapped by CPAs' rules and ethics, Ellen didn't ask for the gory details from these partners-in-crime but accepted the spoils of their stealth. With their help, she closed the case of a client's son's mysterious death at sea and helped his parents find their way back to each other. It was a bittersweet ending that gave meaning to her life as an accountant. She smiled.

Her clients were second in her heart and mind, right after her three sons.

Her boys were home in the capable hands of their father, her ex-husband. Instead of following the path of messy divorces that tore families apart, leaving children to choose between feuding parents, Ellen and their father worked hard to maintain a civil relationship. Five years later, they had settled into a mutually supportive arrangement: she provided financial support for their children, and he offered emotional support to all of them, including her. Knowing her sons were in the loving care of their dad made leaving much easier.

Ellen placed her small glass of water, no ice, into the circular indent of the tray table and debated between the two snack options offered by the cheerful flight attendant. Pretzels with carbs or cookies with sugar? Sweet or savory. Her stomach rumbled, reminding her that she had skipped lunch, and she grabbed the paltry packet of pretzels, ripped it open, and popped one into her mouth. It was stale. She should've gone for the Biscoff Cookies. A little sugar wouldn't hurt after her lack of sleep last night, and were pretzels that much healthier, anyway?

She guzzled the small glass of water to wash away the musty taste and dropped the empty cup and full pretzel bag into the roving attendant's trash bag. She didn't bother asking for replacement cookies. Gone were the days of complete meals and impeccable service; customer service was slipping, and passengers' duties were now as robust as the stewards'. It confirmed Ellen's insistence that her office not join the downhill slide into do-it-yourself civility.

Hartmann and Associates was in good hands with Katie, its receptionist extraordinaire, keeping clients content, and Julie, her second-in-command, ensuring the work flowed smoothly. Thanks to them, Ellen could enjoy her time away from her mind-numbing CPA tasks. During previous trips to Nashville, she felt rejuvenated after sharing creative ideas and learning about platform building and strategic marketing. However, recently, her trips had ended in frustration, with unmet goals and the endgame slipping further away as Sam demanded more rewrites.

Were Sam's endless revisions a quest for perfection? She had given up on that hopeless goal long ago, and *good enough* was her new mantra. Therapy had taught her that seeking perfection was an excuse for procrastination and a recipe for failure. Ellen hoped that as Sam developed her app, he'd learn from it. *The Money Dynamic* explained how perfection-seeking souls and other emotionally conflicted individuals were stymied, believing that money operated with fixed rules and universal truths, when in reality, money was booby-trapped with emotions that kept financial success at bay. They were left feeling like they were the only ones doing it wrong. Her program would build them a new foundation of hope.

Ellen's golden-brown eyes were unflinching as the crease between her brows deepened. This trip, she'd push through Sam's excuses, leap over his final hurdles, and shove him across the finish line. This time, she'd confront the elusive Sam Davis and demand the launch of her program. This time, she'd shift Sam away from perfection to settle into good enough completion.

CHAPTER 5

HENRY

HENRY FOLLOWED THE DOWNTOWN TRAFFIC flowing out of the city center. He needed a quiet place to think, and a crowded street filled with inattentive pedestrians darting in front of too many cars in too much of a hurry was not it. Symphony Tower faded from view in his rearview mirror as the traffic thinned. He pulled into a Whole Foods parking lot, squeezing the Escalade between two cars more expensive than his. His gut churned. He had missed both breakfast and lunch, but the idea of eating didn't appeal to him. His head was spinning, and he craved fresh air. Stepping out of the car, he looked up at the sky and took a deep breath. He needed to talk to Sam, and for now, the phone would have to do.

Sam was unreliable when it came to a lot of things, but answering his phone wasn't one of them. Even during important meetings or brainstorming sessions, he'd always pick up to tell the caller that he was busy and would call back later. That's why Henry only called in emergencies, but today's call qualified. Henry punched in the number, and as expected, Sam answered on the third ring, but before Henry could explain, the call disconnected. He scrunched his eyes and called right back. It went straight to voicemail. What was going on? Sam never turned off his always-at-his-side phone. Nothing, not even important meetings like this, was ever a reason for Sam to sever his lifeline to clients, colleagues, and family. Uneasiness crawled down Henry's throat and coiled in his stomach.

Maybe the proverbial third time would be the charm? He tried again. It wasn't. What was going on? Did the meeting move? Had the man with the fabulous shoes taken him somewhere else? He didn't have the answers, but Henry wouldn't leave the city without Sam. He would have to track down the law firm, and if that didn't work, call Roxie, Sam's wife. But not yet; he wasn't ready to face her.

Henry walked to the entrance of Whole Foods and pulled his phone out of his back pocket again. Two bars, not great for a connection. Henry's nerves were stretched too thin to handle garbled words or dropped calls. Connecting to the internet would be easier. He scanned for a spot near the door to make the call. An elderly, still-dapper man using a walker had just left a bench. He was toddling over to his helper, who loaded the old gent into the passenger seat of an ancient blue Pontiac after stowing their grocery bags in the trunk. Henry took a seat on the vacant bench and connected to the store's guest internet.

Atlanta was unfamiliar to Henry, and given Sam's aversion to lawyers and Henry's lack of business connections, he turned to what he knew best. He googled Alexander and

Cross. A Scottish politician and an apartment building in Yonkers popped up. He tried Alexander and Cross Atlanta, another apartment building, this time not in Atlanta but at least in Georgia. Alexander and Cross Law yielded a lawyer, but in San Francisco. No matter how many combinations of Alexander, Cross, Law, and Atlanta he attempted, the outcome was the same. There was no Alexander and Cross in that skyscraper or anywhere else in Atlanta.

Henry rested his phone on his knee and closed his eyes. *Relax. Be patient. Sam will call.* He waited.

CHAPTER 6

ELLEN

ELLEN STOOD ON HER TIPTOES AND STRETCHED to reach the overhead bin. A soft let me help you interrupted her, and she looked over her shoulder to see the tall young man squished in the middle seat beside her, coming to her rescue. Carry-on luggage and overhead bins did not work well for a five-foot-three-inch woman, and she appreciated his willingness, youth, and height. She stepped aside with a smile and a nod of gratitude.

She wheeled her luggage down the aisle, through the jetway, and into the terminal. She loved Nashville's airport, where tomorrow's music stars performed, waiting to be discovered. Was her seatmate one of them? His fidgeting fingers might have been the silent practice of a musician, rather than an annoying sign of anxiety. She should have asked; it might have made for a lively conversation.

She paused to listen to her favorite Country song while waiting for Henry's usual text saying he was at the curb. As she listened, she reminisced about the four-hour road trip that introduced her to Country music. After battling with her sons over control of the radio, they settled on Country as a fair compromise between Adult Alternative and Hip Hop or Rap. They all thought they hated it. They were wrong. *Whiskey Lullaby* made her a believer. This airport duo might not be Allison Kraus and Brad Paisley, but their version was just as believable and passionate.

A tear rolled down her cheek, dampening her good mood as she listened to the song's refrain about death by bottle. She always responded this way; the tale was too close to home. But her story had a happier ending. Alcohol was the death of their perfect family, but with its breakup, her ex got sober, and now her sons benefited from a fully present and loving father. What more could she ask for?

She wiped her eyes and checked her phone. Nothing. Henry was late, by a lot. He was never late, and she hated to bother him, so she listened to another Allison Krauss favorite to pass the time. After ten more minutes, the duo took a break, and she texted, *I'll wait for you at the curb*. No reply. She dropped a ten-dollar bill in the duo's tip jar, followed the signs to ground transportation, and steered her wheeled suitcase to curbside pickup.

She searched the lined-up cars for Sam's formidable black Escalade, the beast Henry drove to chauffeur Sam and his guests in style. The giant SUV was not there. She stretched her legs by pacing the sidewalk as other passengers' rides arrived to whisk them out of the airport. Twenty minutes passed.

Are you on your way? she texted. No reply. Henry usually responded quickly. She waited. Where was he? Should she try Sam? He was always in a virtual or in-person meeting, and she didn't want to disturb him with something as trivial as this. She pulled out her phone to check yesterday's email. Maybe she misread it or overlooked something. She hadn't. Sam was clear that Henry would be at the airport. She even reconfirmed the airline and flight number in her reply which ended *see you soon*. There was no confusion. Henry should be here.

On her first trip to Nashville, Ellen was surprised that Sam provided door-to-door transportation. Having a chauffeur was a thing of the past, but she grew accustomed to its luxury. There must be some hold-up, and getting herself to the hotel was the least she could do. She texted Henry: *Taking an Uber to the hotel. Pick me up at 6 for dinner at Sam's. I'll be ready and waiting.*

CHAPTER 7

HENRY

HENRY WASTED THE ENTIRE AFTERNOON LOITERING on the Whole Foods bench, ping-ponging between waiting and calling. Every fifteen minutes, he'd punch Sam's number again. The outcome was always the same. Nothing. After an hour and a half, he changed tactics. Sam despised texting and preferred voice contact over the isolated anonymity of messaging, but Henry tried anyway and scattered text messages for another hour. Still nothing.

With each text, he hoped Sam would feel his anxiety grow in the same way it was brewing in his gut when he thought of Ellen stranded at the airport. Technically, Sam, not Ellen, was his priority, and consequently, Ellen was Sam's problem, but during past visits, Henry started to see Ellen as less of Sam's client and more of his close friend. His loyalties were shifting. Should he text her? No. She was still flying, and even if she wasn't, he had nothing concrete to say. His brain accepted the excuse despite his stomach's protests. He tucked his misgivings away.

When a woman, corralling three small children into Whole Foods, smiled at him again, this time pushing an overflowing cart, he gave up. Calling and texting were not working; it was time to call Roxie. Roxie was level-headed, almost emotionless, but Henry feared whatever lurked beneath her frigid exterior. His index finger scrolled for her number and chose his friend Rhonda by mistake. He texted a hasty apology and tried again. The call went straight to Roxie's full voicemail box. What the hell was going on? He tried again, then texted. No response. He waited another half hour. He was out of ideas. It was time for Henry to return to Nashville without Sam. Two hundred miles would give him plenty of time to think.

During the first hour, Henry hurled profanities into the universe, hoping they would reach Sam wherever he might be. But during the final two hours, his anger shifted to fear. Questions swirled and multiplied as the black Escalade got closer to Nashville. Was Alexander and Cross Law Firm's meeting in Atlanta a ruse to get Sam out of Nashville? Was the man in the black suit friend or foe?

Henry sifted through the conversations leading to their sunrise departure. The trip was planned on the run, no different from any other. Henry's life was filled with unexpected twists and turns as he ferried Sam from one place to another. But this was different; he had never left Sam behind before. And what about Roxie? Where was she? His heart raced, and his fingers turned white from clutching the steering wheel.

The blazing high beams of an oncoming vehicle blinded him, and he blinked hard to restore his vision. The jacked-up pickup truck's taillights faded in his rear-view mirror, and Henry's questions returned. Where was Sam? More importantly, did Sam want to be found?

CHAPTER 8

ELLEN

HENRY'S TEXT CAME IN AT A QUARTER TO SIX as Ellen sat at the desk in her hotel room, where she was finishing one more review of her middle-of-the-night edits. *Sorry I wasn't there to meet you. Something has come up. No dinner tonight. I'll pick you up in the morning.*

She was quick to answer. *No problem. 9 tomorrow as usual?* A thumbs-up emoji was the response. She kicked off her shoes. This might be another of Sam's delay tactics, but tonight she didn't care. A night without responsibilities was a rare treat. Tomorrow morning, at Sam's daily ritual for all of his out-of-town clients, with his standard order of French toast and sausage arriving soon after him, she'd be well-rested and ready to rumble. Nothing would hold her back from pushing Sam to deliver.

She ordered a Caesar salad with grilled chicken from room service, and while waiting, she read through her edits. Editing things to death, knowing it took more than one pass to make words concise and meanings clear, would be her undoing, but Sam had to accept this as the final version. She wouldn't fall for whatever delay tactic he tossed her way. On other trips to Nashville, he'd sandwich her between last-minute filming of one of his TV shows or movies. He used Ellen's curiosity about his many projects to distract her by inviting her to watch the filming and by dining with the actors afterward. She loved being part of a creative community filled with freewheeling ideas and out-of-the-box thinking and never complained. But this time, she wouldn't fall for a brush-off.

This time, Sam promised Ellen that *The Money Dynamic* would be his number one priority. This time, her rewritten and redesigned money program was ready for Sam's eye-catching logos and attention-grabbing taglines. They'd fine-tune the app's exciting and cohesive online presence to capture the attention of anyone wanting to take control of their finances. This time, Ellen's dream of demystifying people's minds on money would become a reality. This time, Sam would come through. Enough was enough.

Ellen hit save one last time and snapped her laptop shut for the night. It was her time to relax. She hoped her mind would let her.

CHAPTER 9

HENRY

THERE WAS NO MOON, AND THICK CLOUDS obscured any twinkling stars. The night mirrored his dark and murky thoughts as he pulled into the parking lot in front of Brand & Broadcast. No cars were visible, and no ambient light from the depths of the office shone through the windows. As expected, no one was there. Last night, Sam told everyone to take the next day off while he was in Atlanta. No one argued. They had been filming for twelve straight hours in an abandoned mental hospital with no heat, and Sam's free dinner afterward hadn't dispelled their grumpiness. Getting the day off did.

He poked his head into Sam's office. A picture of Sam's three dogs flashed on the computer's screensaver, casting a dim light over the papers strewn across the desk, piled high on the credenza, and dotting the floor around them. It was a chaotic mess as always. Henry moved across the hall to Roxie's office. The exact opposite. Her desk was clear of everything, including her laptop. It never varied unless the laptop was open with Roxie pecking away at the keyboard. How did the two manage to coexist at home?

Home. Sam's mother. Henry should call Diane. The rental home she shared with Sam and Roxie was nearby. He checked his watch; it was almost ten o'clock. He knew her routine: Diane retreated to her room after watching her early evening game shows, and he knew better than to disturb her. Profanities tumbled down the stairs whenever Joe or Roxie's phone rang after hours. His heart pounded as he recalled other times he had made that mistake, but Diane needed to know that Sam would not be home tonight. The details could wait until morning, or at least until he knew more about Sam's whereabouts. He punched in Diane's number.

"What!" Diane barked. Henry's heart double-timed, and he switched his phone to speaker mode so his trembling fingers wouldn't drop it.

He sucked in a deep breath and slid into the lilting, friendly tones that Sam had trained him to use in scenes just like this. "Diane, I'm sorry to disturb you this late at night."

"Where the hell is everyone?" Diane growled. "Goddamn Sam won't answer his phone again. It's not like I bug him all day or anything."

Henry knew the opposite was true, but didn't argue. "That's why I'm calling. He got hung up in Atlanta. He won't be home tonight. I'm not sure about Roxie."

"I figured as much, and wherever Sam goes, Roxie goes. God forbid they plan ahead or tell me anything!" Diane's snarl turned to a purr. "But my good son David is coming. I just got off the phone with him, and he's on his way. At least he cares."

"Well, good," Henry said. "I won't dist..." Diane cut him off.

"Goddamn those dogs. Will they ever shut up?" she snarled. "I don't care if they shit all over this house, I'm not going downstairs again."

She was gone before Henry could offer to help.

CHAPTER 10

ELLEN

ELLEN REACHED FOR HER CELL PHONE ON THE hotel's nightstand. 6:36 a.m. It confirmed what her body and mind were telling her. She slept through the night. After an overdue gabfest with her best friend Mo, she slowed her mind watching a few hours of *Ugly Betty* reruns on Netflix. Without much sleep the night before, she was gifted seven uninterrupted hours of slumber. Unheard of. She stepped out of bed, twisted her spine from right to left, and touched her toes. Today would be a good day.

She slipped into her yoga pants, t-shirt, and heavyweight hoodie. It was too early to call her sons, but perfect for a morning walk. Sam had promised a full day of work today, and after a good walk, she'd be ready. Sam was a workhorse when he wanted to be, and when he was, he expected the same of her.

She waved a combination hello/goodbye to Brad, the night clerk with the scruffy beard and beautiful blue eyes, and stepped through the automatic doors. The hotel was off Interstate 24 in Smyrna, and her ears vibrated with the steady hum of early morning traffic. At the first intersection, she turned right, away from the busy highway and onto a road that led to a residential area filled with tiny, red-brick homes, leftover base housing from the former Sewart Air Force Base. Sam was a World War II buff and loved to tell stories about the base's training programs and spectacular crashes, the most recent in 2016. She found it an unusual hobby for someone afraid to fly, but who knows? Sometimes, we're attracted to what we fear most.

Like money. Her mind drifted to *The Money Dynamic* as she walked down identical streets lined with identical homes that were slowly emerging from sleep. Fear played a major role in financial decisions, and until people understood that fear was a puppet master pulling the strings of their financial lives, they were doomed to a life of poor choices. Fear showed up in multiple disguises, and one-size-fits-all solutions didn't work. Fear drove some into a life of scarcity, believing there was never enough. It nudged others to live beyond their means, fearing they'd miss opportunities. Some avoided dealing with money at all, not wanting to become King Midas by forgetting their values. Others dwelt in analysis paralysis, unable to decide until they gathered the right information. Ellen saw every configuration and combination of these in her clients, and *The Money Dynamic* centered on raising users' awareness about their go-to approach to money. Ellen's version of Einstein's advice, *change your thinking, change your life*, was clear: without awareness, there would be no change in people's behavior or their finances.

Sam balked when first introduced to the program. He asked about the program's measurable outcomes. "Our program works with people's strengths, not their weaknesses," Ellen's partner Sterling, a psychotherapist, explained over his office's speakerphone. Ellen nodded in agreement.

"Ok, I get that. Tell me more." Sam sounded intrigued. A marketing professional in Florida whom Ellen had previously used to build her firm's website had connected them.

"Awareness of their strengths will give them peace of mind," Ellen offered.

"Won't work," Sam guffawed, and Ellen turned to Sterling. He cozied back into his leather couch with a smug expression, as if his doubts about Sam were confirmed and the conversation was over.

"Peace of mind doesn't sell, and it sure as hell won't bring in the bucks," Sam ridiculed. "Less debt, more savings, higher investment returns. That, I can sell. Trust me, I know how to make money."

Sterling leaned forward with his elbows on his knees.

Ellen tried again. "That's not what our program is about. We can't promise any of those, but they are potential outcomes of becoming financially conscious."

"Financially conscious, what the hell is that? I can't sell that airy-fairy crap," Sam pronounced.

"Can you say more?" Sterling slipped into counselor mode. He tilted his head, considering Sam's point, his eyes asked Ellen to do the same.

Was Sam right? An accountant like her, struggling to help others exist in a profit-fixated world, and Sterling, a therapist wanting to reach mass markets, were few and far between. But, with Ellen's knowledge of finance and Sterling's expertise in human behavior, they believed in what they had created. But they recognized their limitations and needed someone like Sam to market it. They listened.

After Sam enlightened them with marketing theories, Ellen and Sterling shared their insights in depth. They explained that people cannot implement the nuts and bolts of finance until they understand what influences their decisions. Family history, society, education, and even religion all come into play, and these factors are further complicated by guilt-ridden marketing practices. Lastly, neuroscience and how our brains operate cannot be ignored.

Eventually, they found common ground and agreed that by leveraging their three areas of expertise, they could transform the program, with its fun and informative exercises, into concrete, measurable results that Sam could build a marketing plan around. Now, over two years later, she was skeptical that he would ever deliver. Perhaps Sterling was right when he decided that Sam told a big story, would never follow through, and that they had hired the wrong person.

A car horn blasted as Ellen stepped off the curb without looking. She jumped back, calmed her pounding heart, and headed back to the hotel to shower. She didn't want to be late. During their last call, Sam promised that all of his formidable creativity and expertise would be hers. It was time for the final countdown for *The Money Dynamic*'s launch.

CHAPTER 11

HENRY

HENRY DROVE UNDER THE HOTEL'S CANOPY AND saw Ellen seated by the window at Sam's usual table with a coffee cup in her right hand and her phone in her left. He was worried that she was upset about last night, but relaxed when he saw her giggle into her phone. She was probably thinking of her three sons in Maine, and if anything could put her in a good mood, it was her boys. She shifted to joy whenever she talked about their baseball games, school recitals, or anything else about them. And when they interrupted her with an untimely phone call, unlike most of Sam's clients who were annoyed when children or spouses distracted them, Ellen pushed business aside. Another reason Henry admired her.

The front parking lot was full, and Henry parked the Escalade between a blue and white MINI Cooper and a flashy red BMW. Ellen must've been up early to snag their table by the window. She waved as he approached and greeted him with a hug.

"Sorry I wasn't at the airport. We were in Atlanta, and I didn't get back until late." Henry was intentionally vague.

Henry sat down opposite her, in Sam's usual chair, the one facing the door. Did she notice? He looked down to avoid a questioning look.

Ellen shifted in her seat and leaned in. "For the record, you really don't have to pick me up. It's easy enough to get an Uber."

"I know. But that's why Sam hired me, and it's a good excuse to spend time with you. You're a respite from Sam's chaotic energy, you know." He ran his fingers through his strawberry-blonde hair and wished he had a tie to pull it back. Long hair was not his style, and it always dangled in his eyes. He couldn't wait for his latest TV role to end so he could cut it off.

"Speaking of Sam, where is he?" Ellen asked. "He's not pulling a fast one, is he? He promised we'd launch my program this trip."

Ellen wasn't stupid. Sitting in Sam's chair had been a dead giveaway.

"Well, here's the deal." The agitation in his gut swirled, and his spine stiffened against the back of the chair. "I dropped Sam off at his meeting yesterday, but when I returned to get him, he wasn't there."

"Moved on to the next thing and forgot to tell you?" she laughed. "Where did you find him?" She leaned back in her chair to make room for the server, who dropped two bagels and a cup of hot black coffee for Henry.

He nodded to the server and waited for her to move beyond eavesdropping territory. He was unable to fall asleep until almost four this morning, and his hands shook as he gulped his much-needed first cup of coffee. It blistered the roof of his mouth, and he set it down on the table. "Well, that's the thing. I couldn't find him."

"Couldn't find Sam? He's always glued to your side, or I should say, you're always glued to his. You're a chauffeur and manservant all in one." She shook her head. "Don't take that wrong; it's an honorable role, but it's straight out of the eighteen hundreds. Or like a cartel's bodyguard. I don't know how you do it."

"I know, I know." Henry rubbed his eyes, wishing they were magic lamps that would make Sam appear, demanding his French toast. "That's why I'm worried. I couldn't find Sam, and he didn't answer his phone. Roxie didn't either."

"Not answering their phones. Now, you've got me worried. But at least they're together, I should've said the three of you were glued together." Ellen looked down at the table and then directly at Henry. "I can criticize Sam for a lot of things, and he's heard them all from me, but not answering his phone isn't one of them. He's always accessible, no matter the time of day."

"There's more," Henry said.

Ellen brushed her bangs out of her eyes and rested her right elbow on the table. Her upturned eyes told him to spill.

"I tried to find the law firm in the building where I dropped him off." He paused for a careful sip of coffee. "It wasn't there."

"Got the address wrong, doesn't surprise me a bit. He's always got too much going on." Ellen cupped her coffee in both hands. Most days, Henry found Ellen's optimism charming, but today, it annoyed him. She wasn't taking him seriously. The corners of his mouth tightened.

"That's what I thought at first, but here's the thing: the law firm Alexander and Cross doesn't exist." He gulped down the bile rising in his throat.

"What do you mean it doesn't exist?" Ellen's voice rose in pitch and volume.

"It doesn't exist!" Henry's shout was a surprise even to him, and he toned it down to explain. "There's no law firm or lawyers by that name. Not in Atlanta, not anywhere." The churning in his stomach intensified. "Sam lied to me, or someone lied to Sam. He's gone, and I don't know where. The first time I tried calling him, someone answered, hung up, and never responded again. He's gone, disappeared." Henry's spine collapsed, and he crumpled into his chair.

"Let me get my head around this. You haven't talked to Sam since you dropped him off yesterday morning? Roxie either?" Ellen's eyes narrowed.

Henry swallowed a slug of the cooling coffee. "Neither of them. I wasted all afternoon trying to connect. Eventually, knowing you'd be texting from the airport, kicked me in the butt to return to Nashville. I ranted and raved all the way back to the office. No one was there, and everything looked normal. I called Diane to tell her Sam wouldn't be home, and she was her usual charming self. She hung up on me."

Ellen was silent. She let him finish without reacting.

"I decided to wait to talk with you this morning," he paused and sucked in a deep breath. "There was no one else to talk to, Sam's so damn private." The corner of his mouth tightened, this time not with annoyance. He was ready for Ellen's input. "I could use some of your expertise," he said.

"Of course, whatever you need. Believe me, I want to find him as much as you do." She pushed both sides of her hair behind her ears. "What do you have in mind?"

"I thought we'd go over to the house and talk to Diane. You two get along well, and you can try to keep her calm."

Ellen twisted her left wrist to glance at her Fitbit. "Let's do it now. Perfect timing. We can stop at Dunkin Donuts and get her favorite caramel latte and two glazed doughnuts. That woman loves waking to her favorite sugar fix!"

Henry pushed his chair back and moved behind Ellen to pull hers out. She stood up, then stooped over for one last sip of coffee. Henry's stomach settled down. He was no longer alone. With Ellen at his side, he knew they'd find Sam.

CHAPTER 12

ELLEN

ELLEN HOISTED HERSELF UP ONTO THE FRONT seat of the Escalade. She was anything but graceful and wished Henry wasn't there to watch. Then again, she appreciated his help closing the door. Short arms and not enough push-ups made it challenging to reach and pull the heavy door closed. These ridiculous gas guzzlers were meant for big men and environmentally unconscious women, not her.

It would be a quick drive to the house Sam and Roxie shared with his mother, unless they had moved again. Why did someone like Sam, with a thriving business like Brand & Broadcast, bounce from one rental house to another? Not what you'd expect, but then again, nothing about Sam was. He was a bit of an odd duck despite his creative talents, or maybe because of them. That's why she wasn't as concerned as Henry. But she didn't tell Henry that. His iron grip on the steering wheel said he was still shaken from yesterday's debacle.

Henry pulled into the driveway of the same house she had visited on her last trip. It looked like all the other two-story cookie-cutter houses sprawling around Nashville. Their only differentiating feature was their choice of brick, stone, or stucco facade. Neighborhoods like this made her miss Maine, where antique farmhouses were nestled among ornate Victorians, squat bungalows, and mid-century ranch houses. Maine neighborhoods were a study in history. Here in Nashville, the present seemed to be all that mattered.

Henry shifted the SUV into park and reached over to squeeze Ellen's hand. "I'm glad you're here with me. I didn't have a good feeling about yesterday, and I have an even worse feeling this morning."

The warmth of his hand resurrected the long-dormant feelings that surfaced during their last time together when Henry took her out on the town to share his love of music. She ignored it then, and she ignored it now.

"It'll be fine. It's just Sam being Sam." Ellen patted his hand and immediately regretted it. A mother would've done that, not a middle-aged woman enjoying the company of a good-looking young man. And that was the problem. How could a mother of three boys even contemplate such a thing? She had no intention of being a MILF and cringed that her oldest son Jack had introduced her to the term before he fully understood its meaning.

Henry was silent, and she suspected her placating attitude had made things awkward. When he circled the car and offered his hand for assistance, he dropped it quickly as soon as she was on solid ground. He turned away, and she followed him to the door.

Sam and Roxie's three dogs yipped at the door. Diane barely tolerated the three, and to protect all parties involved, Archie, Kramer, and Little Pup never left Roxie's side. Hopefully, Roxie came home last night to take care of them. Henry knocked on the painted metal door. The dogs stopped barking, and Henry and Ellen waited for someone to come. No one did. He knocked again. Nothing.

Henry rang the doorbell, and a cacophony of frantic barks erupted. Sam warned never to ring the doorbell unless you wanted a pack of nutsy dogs nipping at your ankles. As pound dogs, their training could use a little tweaking. There was no other option, and he pushed the bell a second time. The yapping intensified. With the third ring, little toenails began scraping at the door. No human came to their rescue.

Henry tried the door. It was unlocked. He cracked open the door and called, "Hello? Roxie, Diane? It's Henry. Are you up? Ellen's with me." Ellen stood behind him, ready to grab a bolting dog.

Henry turned to her. "Do you think we should go in? Someone must be there. They never go anywhere unless I drive them. If Roxie isn't home yet, I want to make sure Diane's safe. She hates being alone."

"Of course, we should check on her. Just go in, no one will accuse us of breaking and entering. We've been here plenty of times before."

She followed Henry through the door, making sure no tiny canine escaped. She was counting dogs when she body slammed into Henry and rammed her cheek into his back. He was statue stiff: without breath, without words.

"What! What is it?" Ellen braced her right hand on his back, leaned to the left, and poked her head around to see.

"Oh my god," she whispered. She burrowed into Henry and clung to his narrow waist. After three deep breaths, they were ready to face the horror before them.

Diane's body dangled, not quite able to rest on the turquoise blue and ashy gray mat at the base of the staircase. Her neck was twisted, and her splayed limbs angled unnaturally. Her face was wedged into the spindles of the stairs, and her cheeks, nose, and forehead, once mottled with patches of rosacea, were stony white. There was no need to check for a pulse. Diane was dead.

PART TWO

Three Months Earlier

CHAPTER 13

JULIE

JULIE STARED OUT HER OFFICE WINDOW AT THE bobbing sailboats moored at the adjacent pier. Hartmann and Associates' on-the-waterfront location in Maine's largest city gave Julie one of the best office views around. The October sun slipped in and out of the cloud-filled skies as it descended to the horizon, illuminating the boats' aluminum masts. The winter solstice was coming, bringing gray days, monochromatic landscapes, and tax season. After working on a tax-free merger of two small businesses, Julie's eyes had needed a rest from the slurry of numbers spread across her desk. Someone slumped into the client chair behind her, and Julie whirled her chair around to face Ellen, her boss.

Julie Benoit came to Hartmann and Associates ten years ago when Ellen rescued her from her first job with a conniving lawyer who used his dual status as a CPA/Attorney to entice unsuspecting clients to invest in his own Ponzi scheme. Newly graduated from the University of Maine, Julie arrived in Portland with a French-Canadian, northern Maine naivete that was easily recognized and exploited by the fraudster. When he was arrested, Julie froze like a deer caught in headlights, unsure of what to do. She didn't want to abandon his duped clients, but locked out of the office, she had no choice. One of those swindled clients suggested she speak to Ellen, who instantly recognized Julie's talent and passion for helping clients. Ellen hired her on the spot.

"It's been a long day," Ellen said. "You look as tired as I feel." She dropped her head back, rested her neck on the wooden trim of the chair, and closed her eyes.

"You said it." Julie kicked off her heels, rubbed her right foot, and placed her crossed ankles on the desk. "I should have this analysis for you to review tomorrow. I'm anxious to get your take on it." Julie had hoped to put the finished project on Ellen's desk tonight, but now it would have to wait.

"Okay. I'll look at it in the morning." Ellen tucked both sides of her straight, chin-length hair behind her ears. Julie recognized the move; things were about to get serious. "I'm leaving for Nashville tomorrow afternoon."

"Finally lost your patience, huh? Going to kick a little ass?" Over the last two years, Julie had listened to Ellen's ranting and raving grow rabid. Her pet project wasn't moving forward fast enough. Sam's excuses, ranging from server breakdowns to bad weather and family deaths, were taking their toll. Julie doubted that he'd ever come through, and more than once suggested that Ellen fish or cut bait, but Ellen didn't want to quit.

"You got that right! But this time he promised that I'm in for a mega work session to finish things up. I'm not going to fall for his excuses, not even when he tells me projects like this take time." Ellen massaged her temples. "Maybe they do, but enough already. It's time to make this thing happen."

"Is Sterling going?" Julie asked. Ellen's partner's interest in *The Money Dynamic* had slowly faded over the last two years, leaving more work to Ellen and, consequently, to Julie, who covered for Ellen in her absence, and distraction.

"He is. But it's probably the last time. I think he's going to quit completely. He's been threatening for a while." Ellen lowered her head and rubbed the back of her neck.

Julie took her feet off the desk. "What about you?" She leaned in and waited for an opening. It was time for Ellen to stop racing to a finish line created with smoke and mirrors. Surely she could see this was a lost cause.

"I know, I know. You think I'm a fool for hanging in this long. But I know we have something really good. There's no other program out there like this."

Julie worked with Ellen long enough to know her rising voice was begging Julie to confirm the project's validity and Ellen's decision to continue. Too often, Ellen's optimism and ambition muffled her own best judgments, and getting through to her was impossible if she wasn't ready to hear it. Tonight was not the time, and Julie chose to listen rather than argue.

"No one out there approaches money issues from two different angles like this. That's why Sterling and I are such a great team. I have the numbers side covered; he has the psychological. It makes our take on financial psychology credible. Every other money program has either a psychologist who knows nothing about money or an accountant with no clue about mental health. Luckily, with all the therapy I've been through, I have a little more than a clue, but Sterling is the real deal. I hate to see him quit."

Julie nodded. She heard it before, had other things to do, and stopped Ellen from continuing. "I'll have this analysis on your desk tonight so you can look at it in the morning before your flight. Anything else you need from me while you're gone?"

"Oh, keep an eye on Michael. I have a lot of hope pinned on him. Lots of firms wanted him, and we were lucky to get him and his clients. We'll be a lot stronger professionally and financially with him on board."

"Got it. Consider it done." Julie swept her dark hair off her shoulders, gathered it into a ponytail, and searched for an elastic in her overflowing pencil drawer.

CHAPTER 14

MICHAEL

MICHAEL TURNED OFF THE HARSH OVERHEAD lights and switched on the dim light of his desk lamp to scroll through Instagram. He had a spreadsheet spread across his desk to make him look busy while he waited for Julie to pass by on her way out. Everyone was gone, and it was an opportune time to start building a relationship with the most senior accountant at Hartmann and Associates. He had overheard Katie at the front desk telling a client that Ellen was going out of town for a few days, and assumed that Ellen had gone to Julie's office earlier to pass on instructions for her absence. He expected Julie to leave right after Ellen, but he was wrong. An hour had passed, and Julie was still at her desk. He could wait.

His office, nestled in a corner opposite Ellen's, was the perfect vantage point to keep track of client meetings and staff comings and goings. He was learning a lot about the inner workings of Hartmann and Associates: who led and who followed, who wasted time and who didn't, who liked to impress and who didn't seem to care. For example, no staff approached Ellen when their leader partially or totally closed her door. But when she opened it wide, she was fair game. On the other hand, Julie was perpetually lost in her work, ambivalent to the comings and goings of the firm. No doubt, Ellen hired him to fill the management gaps that Julie was incapable of filling. A slow grin spread across his face. Michael Prescott was in the right place at the right time.

Michael looked at his Rolex; it was almost seven o'clock. Would Julie ever leave? *Patience, Michael, patience. Slow and steady wins the race.*

CHAPTER 15

JULIE

JULIE GATHERED THE COMPLETED ANALYSIS AND placed it in a plastic folder. She tried to organize the papers to make sense, but her idea of organization was far from Ellen's. Their minds didn't work alike, and they used different paths for their analyses. But it worked; their non-conforming routes to arrive at the same destination gave them confidence that the conclusion was valid.

Julie gazed out her open door and across the office's darkened workspace filled with accountants' semi-private cubicles. She must be alone. Bobby, their favorite office cleaner and all-around good guy, hadn't arrived yet for the evening's cleaning. Shooting the shit with him was one of her favorite ways to end her day, but tonight she was tired. She hurried to Ellen's office to deposit the finished merger analysis on her desk, hoping to slip out before Bobby arrived.

"Julie, do you have a minute?" The deep, rich voice startled her. Male voices were rare at Hartmann and

Associates, and this one wasn't Bobby's. She turned to see the new guy sitting in the dim light of his office.

"Mike, it's you. I thought I was the only one here." Damn, she was tired, but she had promised Ellen. "What's up? How can I help?"

His chiseled chin jutted forward, "For the record, I prefer Michael."

"Got it," she acknowledged, and collapsed into the chair across from him.

"Can you look at this?" he asked. "I'm stumped; I must be missing something. I can't get this thing to balance, and it's driving me crazy." He flipped a worksheet around for her to see and raked his fingers through his thick brown hair.

"Been there, done that. Sometimes, it's best to walk away. Do you mind if we pick this up in the morning? I'm toast, and not sure I'd be much help tonight," she groaned.

"Sure. I didn't realize how late it was. Time gets away from you in a great place like this. Everyone here is exceptional, and I truly appreciate your expertise and counsel. You're awesome to work with." His eyes searched hers. She blinked and shifted in her chair.

She was beyond flattered that a CPA with a law degree to boot was saying this to her. Her clients loved her, and Ellen trusted her, but sometimes she wished she had three initials behind her name to raise her credibility with the outside world. But not enough to waste time studying for an exam that wouldn't change the quality or trajectory of her accounting career.

"Thanks, but you may change your mind when I start asking you to help me keep up with all of Ellen's clients. I don't have enough time to give them the attention I'd like. I'll start passing them on as soon as you're ready." Julie relaxed as she mentally listed some of the more bothersome clients she'd be happy to part with.

"I'm your man." His velvety tones reverberated against Julie's chest. "Once I know your systems, I can handle the rest. I've got plenty of experience." He leaned in and smiled. He had beautiful teeth.

"If that's the case, be ready tomorrow morning. We'll tackle your problem first, and then I'll personally fill you in on how we do things around here. Believe it not, we do have a system." She flipped her out-of-control curls over her shoulder and laughed. Their laughter echoed through the empty office as she stood to leave.

Julie heard the telltale squeak of Bobby's trash barrel in the distance. A wave of something wafted through her body when she stood to leave. Was it hunger, or was it guilt?

CHAPTER 16

STERLING

"I PROMISE THIS IS THE LAST TIME. IF SAM DOESN'T come through, I'll end it completely or just be a silent partner." Sterling slid the bowl of Fruit Loops in front of his four-year-old daughter and glanced across the table at Maggie, his wife, buttering their six-year-old's toast. God forbid they should all eat the same thing.

"I hope so," she said. "Between working late every night and filling your weekends with Ellen and the project, I might as well be a single parent."

Sterling recognized the scowl on her face. "I know, I know," he said, trying to stay open and curious, as he instructed his clients. It wasn't easy. "It's been a long two years, but it hasn't been that bad lately, and you wanted this as much as I did. I can work eight to ten hours a day, five or six days a week, but my income is limited by the hours in a day. This project would be a passive income stream that won't be limited by my available hours. The potential is limitless."

His daughters fidgeted in their chairs and stopped eating to listen. He pasted a fake smile on his face to signal to his wife to tone it down a bit.

"I don't want to hear about potential. It's not limitless if it never gets off the drawing board. You've given it enough time. I want my husband back, and the girls want their father. Enough is enough." She turned her back and leaned on the kitchen sink. Sterling waited for more; there was always more. His daughters squirmed in their chairs.

"Consider it over," he said. "I fly to Nashville tomorrow and will end it. When I return, the weekend will be yours and the girls, whatever you want, just don't make it too expensive."

CHAPTER 17

HENRY

"*THE MONEY DYNAMIC* CREW IS COMING IN ON A 4:44 flight today," Sam said. "Pick them up and drop them at the hotel. I've booked two rooms." Henry moved closer to the computer. Sam pushed his black-rimmed reading glasses down his nose and peered up at him. It was Sam's signal for Henry to pay attention.

"Will do. Anything else?" Henry liked advanced notice for the day's activities. Pinning down Sam was tough, if not impossible, but a man could try.

"We're reshooting the scene we worked on yesterday." Sam slid his glasses back in place and moved closer to his computer screen. "No amount of editing will save it. A bunch of crap."

"Wait, wait." Henry was confused by Sam's instructions. "Tony won't be here. I'm taking him to the airport around ten-thirty this morning. He's anxious to get back to L.A."

"Nope, not today," Sam cut him off. "Told him it would be another two or three days. Luckily, he's cheap and available. Big name in the past, but now his schedule is always open. And he needs the money."

Cheap and available. What did Sam say about Henry? Young and stupid? Eager and foolish? He cringed at the options. But, like it or not, Sam was full of opportunities for those willing to put up with him. You couldn't argue with the quality of what he produced.

"Are we going back to the Springwater?" Henry asked. It was anyone's guess how Sam sweet-talked the owner into letting him use the oldest bar in Nashville for the movie scene. "What time do you want him there?" Henry annoyed Sam with his questions, but he had no choice.

"Get him there by three; he knows we'll be shooting tonight. Then you can help set up before leaving for the airport." Sam turned away from his computer screen, slid his glasses down, pushed his chair back, and looked at Henry.

"Change of plans. Drop Ellen and Sterling's luggage off at the hotel and then bring them to the Springwater. Let's give them a little excitement." Sam winked and tilted his head.

"Good idea, a far cry from sleepy Portland, Maine." Henry laughed. He waited for Sam's response. There was none. "What do you need from me now?" he asked.

"What? I don't know. Study your lines or something." Henry was dismissed.

CHAPTER 18

SAM

"MOVE THAT BARSTOOL OVER TO THE RIGHT AN inch. No, an inch. That's too far." Sam fiddled with the string of his gray hoodie. "Tony, put the bottle there. No, no, between the two stools, so you have to squeeze between them to get to the bar. Good. Now step back. Roxie, get the still."

Still shots were essential. Without it, this film would show up in one of those *what's wrong with this scene* blurbs. Brown Budweiser bottle instead of clear Corona, that sort of crap. "How's it compare with yesterday?"

"Almost there. Yesterday, the gin bottle was to the right of the Crown Royal. It's reversed. Everything else looks good to go." The bottles were swapped. His wife was a pro with details, and nothing got past her eagle eye. She'd saved him more than once by fixing some minute detail.

"Good, good. I think we're ready. Quiet on the set. Lights, camera…" Sam stopped. Warm, humid air carried on a beam of sunlight flowed into the windowless bar.

"Hold it, hold it," he roared. "What gives? Didn't Henry put the closed sign on the door?" He covered his brow with his left hand and scowled at the door. The door closed, and the light dissolved into darkness.

"I did. Sorry for the interruption." Henry ushered two other people through the door and guided them over to Sam.

Sam slid his annoyance undercover and put out his hand. "Ellen, Sterling. Long time no see. It's been a while. Good to see you." Ellen stepped forward, and Sam drew her close for a hug.

"Two years to be exact," she pushed back. "Last time we were here, you were videotaping us at that abandoned mall. I'm still wondering what happened to all that."

Sam ignored Ellen's jab. "Sterling, good to see you. I've missed our phone calls. You're great at calming Ellen down." Might as well jab back. He clapped Sterling on the back.

"Good to see you, Sam. Looks like you're up to no good." Sterling teased.

Sam liked Sterling's light-hearted approach but suspected he used his counseling skills for manipulation. "I figured it was too late to work on your project tonight," Sam said, "and being on set would be fun for you. We're shooting a scene from *Artificial Anarchy*, the movie I'm making for that doctor in San Fran." Sterling looked at Ellen. She was smiling.

"Great! I love it," Sterling said. "Did I tell you I studied film in college?"

"Doesn't surprise me," Sam replied. "I can see traces in what you've written for *The Money Dynamic*. You've got an eye for the visual." Sterling's chest puffed out in response. Bingo. Got him. Two can play that game.

Sam turned to Ellen. "I've got a great idea. We need two people to fill those barstools. Wanna do it? You don't have to do or say a thing, I promise." A big grin spread across Sterling's face.

"Come on, let's do it." Sterling grabbed Ellen's hand and pulled her towards the bar. "It'll be fun." Sam waited for Ellen's reaction.

"My boys will kill me if I say no. What's better than telling your friends your mom was in a movie? Even if no one sees it," she laughed.

"Ouch!" Sam grabbed his chest and gasped.

"Oops, don't take that the wrong way, Sam ."

"There's the Ellen I've come to love. I figured you were coming to Nashville to rip me a new one." He pulled out the empty bar stool on the right for Ellen. Sterling climbed onto the other one.

"That's coming tomorrow. You're not off the hook yet." Ellen bellied up to the bar as Roxie lifted an eyebrow and snapped another still shot. It was worth scrapping all of yesterday's shoot to keep Ellen off her husband's ass.

"Okay folks," Sam shouted. "Let's do this. Quiet on the set!"

CHAPTER 19

STERLING

STERLING WAS DRAINED; THE DAY HAD TAKEN ITS toll. It was creeping up to midnight, and although he might still be thirty-something, anything after ten was too late. He scanned the now-crowded Sweetwater Bar for Ellen. She was at a table with Sam and Roxie, red wine for the women and Sam's signature can of Coke. Two small dogs slept under the table.

When Ellen and Sterling first hired Brand & Broadcast, Sam insisted they come to Nashville as soon as possible to shoot promotional videos. They stalled until after the December holidays and rented an Airbnb across from the Opryland Hotel for the first week in January. He had strolled through the iconic hotel's vast complex, its atriums still hung with sumptuous Christmas decorations, and its lazy riverbank overflowing with holiday cheer. It was over-the-top unnatural beauty, and he wished his daughters' awe-filled wonder was there with him, but he was glad Ellen had opted for quieter, homier accommodations that were more conducive for working.

On that first trip two years ago, Sam jam-packed their days filming videos for *The Money Dynamic*, the name Sam crafted for their program. For three weeks prior, while Sterling was busy dealing with clients' holiday angst, Sam and Ellen worked on scripts for eight separate videos and a fake interview called *Money Materials*. Sam explained that a staged interview for a bogus TV show was industrywide standard, perfect for social media and the website he was building. Sam had big plans for *The Money Dynamic*.

Sterling and Ellen originally envisioned a program to train professionals who wanted a better way to talk about money. Sam expanded their original concept from a B2B to a B2C program, terms unfamiliar to both of them. Sam said the business-to-consumer course would be a cash cow for generating income with little or no hands-on work. The business-to-business program would follow and could train others to sell the consumer program. Sterling loved the sound of it and squeezed time into his busy schedule to review and approve the video scripts.

For four days that January, they played the roles of actor, director, and producer. There were endless retakes of *Money Materials* when anything from the white inside pocket of Sterling's slightly-too-tight dress pants peeked out to ruin a scene, the actor/interviewer crossing her legs too high, or Ellen stumbling on a line were reasons to reshoot. Sam demanded perfection. Occasionally, when Sam lost sight of the deeper purpose, they would remind him that, as creators, their directorial input was essential. It was an arduous process, and by the end, Sterling understood why the $30,000 they had each invested with Sam was well spent.

Tonight was fun, but it was time to get real. Sterling had one last trip before he'd have to live up to his promise to Maggie and walk away. He snaked through the crowd to Sam and Ellen's table. "Let's go. We have a lot of work to do tomorrow." Sam nodded to Henry, waiting at the door.

CHAPTER 20

ELLEN

THE SUN SHONE DOWN THROUGH THE LOBBY'S atrium as Ellen poured herself a cup of coffee at the hotel's complimentary coffee bar. She cocooned the cup in her hands, savoring its deep, rich aroma. Sterling was at a table across the room, giggling into his phone. She waited for him to finish.

"Kids start the day off right, don't they? I called my guys, but their dad was rounding them up for school, and I had to cut it short. I'm lucky he's there to take over when I go out of town." She still hated that divorce had disrupted her dream of a perfect family, but at least they co-parented well.

"And why shouldn't he? They're his kids too. Being divorced doesn't absolve him from parental duties." Sterling removed his glasses and glared at Ellen.

"Whoa, take off your counselor hat." Ellen knew that look too well. "I know they're his responsibility too, but not all exes are so accommodating. Let me have this one. You know I don't always find something good to say."

Sterling put his glasses back on. "Sorry about that; occupational hazard. I see client problems everywhere." He moved his glasses up over his eyebrows and rubbed his eyes.

"And I see *money* everywhere," Ellen's dimples deepened with a smirk. "That's why we're perfect for this project. We see life's nuances and want everyone else to see them too. It's all about awareness." She wrapped both hands around her coffee mug. Sterling did the same. Limbic synchrony, or mirroring, as Sterling had taught her.

They met at a weeklong coaching program while both sought ways to expand their respective practices. Ellen wanted skills to help clients cope with money angst, and Sterling wanted to coach higher-paying business executives. He was curious about her money coaching because he knew he was ill-prepared to counsel clients with money anxieties. Ellen was equally intrigued that he wanted to help executives focus on employees' needs instead of the company's bottom line.

One afternoon, while listening to a lecture about personality assessments, Sterling leaned over and whispered, "We could develop one of these about money." During their next break, they resolved to design a tool to help both psychotherapists and financial professionals talk about money. For the next six months, they met every Friday on Sterling's day off. They melded Ellen's knowledge of money behaviors with Sterling's understanding of psychology while debating the motivations behind people's actions. The result was Your Money Style, a fun, twenty-question quiz that categorized people into four styles. It was unlike other money assessments because it was couched in positive terms. No one was labeled a penny-pincher, unrealistic, indecisive, or terrible with money. Instead, they were Practical, Ambitious, Logical, or Relaxed, and all four styles were inherently good.

Your Money Style Quiz became the center of their program, and they crafted in-depth training guides and easy cheat sheets for other professionals to follow. They envisioned training financial and behavioral consultants to use the quiz as a conversation starter and tool for deeper, more meaningful interactions. Then they hit a brick wall. They loved creating, but neither had any interest nor talent for marketing. That brought them to Sam. He promised to do everything they hated, and his sales pitch gave them confidence that with his marketing expertise, their program would reach and teach the masses about money.

"So, the big question is, how do we get Sam to do what he promised—and not in another two years?" Sterling interrupted Ellen's reverie. "I need to see results. Last night was fun, but I think he was trying to distract us."

Sterling's horn-rimmed glasses slid down his nose. The lenses were filthy. He must see the world through shades of dust and grime. "I don't know; I think it was just one of those things." Ellen set down her cup. "Sam was excited about us coming and said he had some ideas to help speed things up. Filming got delayed, the actors were still in town, and he was just making the most of things."

"We're not the ones slowing things down. We take care of anything he asks immediately. Or rather, you do. You've done most of it." Sterling twirled the stem of his glasses in his right hand.

"Thanks for acknowledging that," Ellen said, "but I love working with Sam." She wanted Sterling to understand that Sam's contributions to the program were valid. "Sam and I hammer out revisions and the program feels more fun. Less like accountants and therapists."

"That might be true, but come on Ellen, don't you think two years is long enough?" His glasses twirled faster.

"I know, I know. But I still want to salvage this. We spent a lot of money and won't get it back. We never signed a contract, remember?" Money got Sterling's attention.

"Don't remind me, another bad decision," he muttered as he remembered their hasty decision to proceed without one. "But at some point, we have to cut our losses. Maybe *The Money Dynamic* isn't meant to be."

He put on his glasses, his sign that he was done fighting. Good, she was tired of arguing about it. It might be a losing battle, but she wasn't ready to surrender to the niggling voice inside saying she should. "I'll come back every few weeks if I have to," she said, "but I understand if you've had enough."

Sterling looked across at Ellen. His glasses stayed in place. "Maggie has had it. I promised this would be the end for me. I'm not sure, but..."

"Got it. Then, let's make the most of it. It's time to kick butt." Ellen waved the server over to place an order to go. She was hungry, but it was too late to eat here. Henry was picking them up at nine and taking them to Sam's office.

Her phone pinged with Henry's incoming text. "Shit," she hissed as she read it to Sterling: *Sam got caught up. I'll pick you up at 1.*

CHAPTER 21

JULIE

JULIE SCANNED ELLEN'S REVIEW COMMENTS. IT WAS eight in the morning, and as promised, Ellen had finished looking at the merger analysis before heading to a client's office and then to the airport. Not much to fix based on the review comments, just some minor adjustments that wouldn't affect Julie's conclusions. She'd deal with it later. First, she wanted to follow up with Michael before her brain got too crowded with the day.

She strolled over to his office. His desk lamp was on, his worksheets still waiting, but he wasn't there. She peeked over the interior cubicles to search for him. He was tall enough to spot over the dividers, but she didn't see his dark, wavy hair anywhere. She headed to the front desk.

"Do you know where Michael is?" Julie asked. Katie held her index finger to her lips. She was on the phone with another demanding client who was sharing too much information.

"Let me see if I can find someone to help you, Mrs. Lacey. I'm sure they'll be able to make sense of it for you." Katie pressed the hold button and heard her pass the call off to one of the junior staff.

"Glad I dodged that bullet," Julie said. "She can talk for hours. That's one client I don't mind handing over to Michael. Do you know where he is? He's not in his office." Julie headed to the kitchen to look for him.

"Don't bother, he's not in yet," Katie called after her. Julie pivoted, and her long, tangled tresses swung across her back.

"Are you sure? I promised to help him this morning and then show him the ropes. His office looks like he was waiting for me." Julie leaned on the cherrywood counter surrounding Katie's desk. The half wall was low enough to keep Katie accessible, but high enough so confidential documents were hidden from nosy clients.

"I don't know what to tell you. He's late most days." The phone rang, and Katie punched line two. Mrs. Lacey was still tying up the first.

Julie headed to the kitchen for a cup of coffee. Michael was still adjusting to their schedule, and she wasn't going to worry about him being late. That could come later if he didn't solve the problem on his own. Before moving to Portland, he had worked for himself and was used to running his own show and managing his own work. It would take time for him to adjust to Hartmann and Associates' routines. On top of that, he didn't have much work assigned to him yet, so there wasn't much to keep him occupied. She was about to change that.

"Send him to my office when he gets here," she mouthed as she breezed by Katie's desk. Line three was flashing, demanding Katie's attention.

CHAPTER 22

MICHAEL

MICHAEL WAS LUCKY TO FIND PARKING ON THE busy pier. Hartmann and Associates' unusual location on a former fishing pier was unique, but parking was a nightmare. Clients must hate coming here on blustery days when the pier turned into a wind tunnel. He preferred a suburban office with plenty of free parking. Not as trendy as being on the waterfront, and it wasn't close to other professionals, but it was easier for clients. But that was his former life; at Hartmann and Associates, he wasn't high enough on the totem pole to have a parking spot in the garage, and neither were their clients.

Katie glared at him as he stepped off the elevator; he was expecting it. There was no way to slip by unnoticed; the stairs and elevator both led to Katie, and the secondary fire exit went one way: out. You could exit but never enter. He had tried it. He lowered his head and went straight to the kitchen. Maybe Katie would be busy when he came out.

No luck. "Morning, Katie," he sang as he left the kitchen with a cup of coffee warming his hands. "I brewed a fresh pot if you're interested. Want me to bring you one?"

"Too late in the day for me, and for what it's worth, it's more like good afternoon now." Katie's passive-aggressive comment grated on him. He didn't bite.

"No wonder I'm hungry," he joked. "They didn't offer me lunch, much less coffee this morning. I may have found a new client. Ellen will be pleased." He didn't need to explain himself to Katie or anyone else, but it didn't hurt to placate her so she'd accept that he wasn't just any inexperienced accountant. He had a job to fulfill.

"Julie is waiting to see you," Katie said. "She expected you first thing this morning." She went back to her computer screen. Tough one to crack; he'd have to remember that. Someone in her position held a lot of clout, and he needed to stay on her good side.

"Oops, my bad," he said. "I forgot to tell her I had an early morning meeting, but I think she won't mind when I tell her where I've been. Should I take her a cup of coffee?" Asking Katie for advice might soften her a bit.

"Not this late, but if you want to butter her up, I know she wouldn't mind a glass of water." Michael couldn't tell whether it was another dig but thought it was best to comply. He returned to the kitchen, then hoisted the glass, and smiled as he passed her on the way back to his office.

Ice cubes clinked in the tall glass as he leaned against Julie's door frame. "I heard you might like this?" He flashed a broad smile, his best feature.

Julie pulled herself away from her computer screen. "Thanks. Sure." She shuffled papers until she found a buried coaster.

How could Ellen rely on someone so disorganized? It wouldn't be his choice, even if he were a bit anal and too controlled. From what he could see so far, Julie was the direct opposite. It might be a good match; they could temper each other.

"Weren't we supposed to meet first thing this morning?" Julie gathered her thick hair into a makeshift ponytail and released them to cascade over her shoulders. He blinked hard.

"Guess I misunderstood. I was meeting with a potential client. Haven't quite signed them yet, but I think Ellen will be pleased." He sat down in Julie's client chair, planted his elbows on the desk, and leaned in with his head on his fists. Julie sat back in her chair.

"I haven't had a chance to take a second look at what I was having problems with," Michael continued. "Let me take another stab at it so you don't waste your time. But I'm ready to review office policies whenever you are. I'm sorry I screwed up your morning." He removed his elbows from her desk and placed his hands on his knees.

"Not right now, my head's stuck in the middle of this. How about later today, around 4?" Julie went back to her computer screen. She was distracted but stopped and turned to him. "But here's the thing." She brushed her tangled curls over her right shoulder and lifted her chin. "Make sure Katie knows when you'll be out of the office."

"Yes, ma'am," he joked. "My bad. It won't happen again. I already apologized to Katie." He stood up to leave. Julie had turned back to her screen.

"Hey, here's a thought," he said. "Do you want to do it over a beer? I owe you one. How about that place down the pier? I think it's called J's Bar or something?"

She flashed a beautiful smile, complete with pearly white teeth that matched his. "Now you're speaking my language. How about five o'clock? I never drink before then."

Julie's laugh was slow and luxurious. He'd love to hear it more.

CHAPTER 23

ELLEN

WHERE WAS HENRY? ELLEN TWISTED HER WRIST, and her fitness tracker lit up. It was 1:12, and she was having a tough time keeping Sterling placated. No one had texted or called to say the time had changed, and even a stranger could see Sterling's irritation was ratcheting up. She had learned to live with Sam's changing agenda, but Sterling hadn't, and she hoped this wasn't yet another time Sam expected her to gerrymander their schedule.

"This is bullshit," Sterling slammed his hands on the table. They were perched at a high top in the hotel's reception area that gave them a driveway view. "I can't believe we flew to Nashville to be ignored. Did you try to reach him?"

"Henry's always on time, but Sam can slow him down with ever-changing priorities. I'm sure he's on his way. Besides, he's just ten minutes late." Ellen tried to de-escalate Sterling. "We did good and necessary work without Sam this morning. You have to admit, our time wasn't wasted." She met Sterling's steely look with the smiling eyes you were supposed to use for official, non-smiling identification photos.

"We could've done that back in Portland. It would've saved a lot of time. And money." Sterling removed his glasses and ground his knuckles into his eyes.

"We could've, but we didn't. At least here in Nashville, I have you at my disposal without interruptions." It needed to be said. Getting Sterling to focus on their project was a losing battle. Should she give up and resign herself to finishing this project alone?

"Agreed, but we came here to work with Sam. I don't even know where things stand. Are we even close to a launch date?" He stared at Ellen. His eyes were barely visible through his dirty lenses.

Ellen's phone chimed, and she avoided the question she couldn't answer. "Sam? What's up? We're waiting for Henry." She raised her left eyebrow as if Sam's call answered Sterling's concerns. "Okay, sure, I understand. Not so sure Sterling will. We'll see you tonight for work and pizza. We'll be ready. And please, Sam, don't let me down. I'm counting on you to come through this time." She waited for a reply, but he was gone.

Sterling was pacing and rubbing the back of his neck ferociously. He had caught the gist of the conversation.

"Okay. Sam gave me two choices for this afternoon," she said as he sat back down. "We can write another article for the website and social media, or enjoy downtown Nashville." Ellen brushed her hair behind both ears and waited for Sterling's answer.

"What do you mean another article? There've been others?"

Ellen was surprised at the tack he took. "Yeah, I've been writing articles for various publications. Sam and his team have been great at getting them out there. I write one about every two or three weeks." She waited. Progress was possible if Sterling paid attention.

"Guess I missed that. Maybe I've been out of the loop more than I realized." Ellen was glad he said it first. It was time for him to acknowledge the imbalance in their respective contributions to the project.

"Okay, let's have some fun," Sterling said. He stood up and slipped his phone out of his back pocket. "We'll pick it up tonight over pizza. I'll call an Uber?"

Ellen was tired of orchestrating the project's work life; Sterling could take the lead for a change. Fun wasn't often on their agenda, but today, they could both use some relaxation.

Ellen and Sterling strolled down Nashville's iconic Broadway. In the daylight, it was smaller but flashier than she had imagined. With all the country stars coming out of Nashville, she had expected endless blocks to explore and was skeptical that the driver had brought them to the right area. Then she spied the historic Ryman Auditorium, home to the original Grand Ole Opry, and she reminded herself it was two in the afternoon, not ten at night. They were in the right place. They found a barbecue joint on a prime corner for lunch and relaxed. Neither were big country music fans, but they loved the free music served with their meal and debated whether the artist might someday be famous. She doubted it; he was Portland good, but not Nashville good.

"What next?" Sterling balanced his chair on two legs. He had emerged cool and calm after his morning meltdown.

"I want a pair of cowboy boots," Ellen said. "We're in Nashville. What better place to get them?"

Sterling planted the chair's four legs on the floor and stood up. "Not what I expected you would say, but why not? Ellen Hartmann in cowboy boots, this I gotta see. Your clients won't believe it." He started for the door.

"Wait, I haven't paid yet." Ellen waved the waiter over and handed over her credit card. Being the accountant in their duo, she paid for everything and billed Sterling for his half. Her attentiveness to details offset his absent-mindedness.

"Right." He stepped away from the door, hesitated, and opened it anyway. "I noticed Ernie Tubbs' record shop a few doors down. It's going to close forever, and I don't want to miss it. It's been around for decades. I'll meet you there."

He didn't wait for her answer.

CHAPTER 24

ELLEN

STERLING WAS SILENT ON THE RIDE OVER TO SAM'S. The afternoon was fun, but now he was all business. He glowered beside her as they walked up to the red door of the third house on the right. Its cherry-red door was the one thing distinguishing it from the other houses, and when the Uber driver slowed on their approach, she knew they were at the right place.

"This is it," she said and thanked the driver before stepping out. Sterling followed closely behind.

Ellen stood tall in her new cowboy boots. The angle of the heel added a swagger to her step, and she liked the jolt of confidence that tagged along. After some light-hearted cajoling on their shopping trip, Sterling caved and bought boots for his wife and two daughters. Buy One Get One was hard for him to resist, not to mention that his little girls would love their matching red boots, and Maggie's good side would respond to the pair he chose for her.

"Sam better not stand us up tonight," Sterling muttered. "We've already lost a day." Ellen knocked on the door, and doggy chaos erupted on the other side. She ignored both commentaries.

The door swung open, and two little dogs swirled around Ellen's caramel-colored boots. Their tiny toenails left little white scrapes in the soft leather, the first of many stories the boots would gather. She stooped down and patted the rambunctious beasts circling her. Diane screamed from the kitchen and charged into the room, adding to the chaos. Sam laid his hand on his mother's shoulder and steered her to the kitchen. "I got this Ma," he said, "I'll let you know when the pizza arrives."

"Ellen, Sterling, welcome to our humble abode," Sam said. He ushered them to the sparsely decorated living room where Roxie sat with another little dog on her lap.

"Come see our new addition," Roxie invited. "We just picked him up at the pound."

Did Roxie say *they* picked him up *today*? Did a trip to the pound come before their working today? A slow boil started in Ellen's gut, but she said nothing. Sam would twist her words to his advantage, and Sterling didn't need any further revving up.

Ellen stooped down to meet the pup eye-to-eye and stretched out her hand, palm down, for him to sniff. "What a cutie," she said and scratched his ears. He tilted his head for more.

"I have everything set up for us in the dining room," Sam interrupted. "We got home earlier than expected, and I had time to review things. We gottta change some things, fine-tune others, and then we'll be good to go."

He walked into the dining room and called over his shoulder. "Launch in two weeks?" Sam bypassed Ellen's raised eyebrows and turned to Sterling.

"Sit down, Sterling; let me show you what I've got." He pulled out one of the two chairs on the table's long side for himself. He motioned for Sterling to sit in the other and positioned his laptop between them. Ellen slid into the chair at the head of the table to their left and scooched over to get a distorted view of the screen.

"New website with new graphics." Sam leaned back with a broad smile. He looked at Sterling, glanced at Ellen, and then back at Sterling. "What do you think?" Sterling slid his glasses atop his head and studied the screen.

Ellen leaned back in her chair. "Didn't we finish that a year ago?" Sarcasm dripped, and her bottled-up frustration uncorked. "A new one, now? What did I miss?"

"I know, I know. But things have changed, website graphics have moved on, and we gotta stay up with the times." Sam dragged his fingers across his thinning hair and looked at his wife at the end of the table, fidgeting with the new pup in her lap. She said nothing. The other two dogs lay with their heads resting on their paws under the table.

"And whose fault is that?" Ellen said. "This whole project should've been done at least a year ago, if not earlier." Ellen was sick and tired of accommodating Sam's excuses.

"So, do you want to spend tonight arguing, or do you want to get some work done?" Sam's words were soft and joking, but his eyes told Ellen he was not. "I'm all in on the latter and want no part of the former. We can call it quits right now if you want." He beamed a Mona Lisa smile at Sterling.

"Don't get your undies in a bundle," Ellen replied. "I'm allowed a little impatience." Ellen couldn't resist one last comment. "Two years is a long time."

"The old site was too stodgy, something you'd go to only if dragged there," Sam said. "I finally got what you were saying. *The Money Dynamic* should be light, informative, and fun, a place to learn and change without shame or blame. Reading the opening of Ellen's book, I put it all together," Sam said.

She had sent him her book, *The Problem with Money,* two years ago! The left corner of Ellen's mouth pulled back to reveal one dimple. The other did not join in.

Sam opened a new browser window. A woman stared at a donut, a piece of cake, potato chips, and an apple. "It's all about choice," he said.

Ellen refrained from muttering what she thought and nodded her head.

Sterling removed his glasses and rubbed his eyes. "I don't get it. What does food have to do with money?"

Ellen ignored Sterling's confusion and relaxed her pursed lips. "I think it works, Sam. Easier for people to connect with food choices than money choices," Ellen explained. "With money problems, they think it comes down to spending less, saving more. But they forget all the rest of the stuff that gets in the way of their choices. Family history, social media, brain chemistry, and marketing campaigns, you name it, they influence all of our decisions—food and money included. Without awareness and understanding, there is no choice; we continue to make the same mistakes over and over, ad infinitum." Sterling nodded his head in agreement. Sam winked at Roxie.

The doorbell rang, and the dogs' claws scraped across Ellen's boots as the two lunged for the front door. The new pup burrowed its head into Roxie's elbow.

"Food's here," Sam bellowed. Sam's mother came bustling out of the kitchen, hurling obscenities at the dogs.

Ellen prayed that pizza would not signal the end of their work session.

CHAPTER 25

LITTLE PUP

LITTLE PUP COWERED IN THE LAP OF THE LADY with auburn hair, the one who took him away from the bad place with all the dogs. Her hands calmed his twitching nerves but caused his mottled brown coat to stand on end, making him look crazy. He peeked up into her deep brown eyes and relaxed. Little Pup was glad that the lady with the auburn hair looked beyond first impressions and recognized there was more of him to love inside. Tonight, in her lap, on this couch, inside this house, he felt safe. If he stayed on his best behavior, maybe he could stay with her forever.

When the lady with the auburn hair first opened the door to this new place, he wasn't sure. It sounded like that other place, with its yapping and yipping, toenails scraping, and someone yelling things he didn't want to repeat. But then it got quiet, and he lifted his head from where he had burrowed it into the crook of her arm and looked down. There were two of them, not a room full of cages with lonely eyes, pleading voices, and spilled water dishes waiting to be filled. Two little guys like him were looking at the man with threads for hair. One was white with a fluffy coat like perfect clouds on a perfect day. The other was black and spiky. Little Pup wasn't sure about that one. Everyone ignored the yelling lady standing behind them. He swallowed his fear and followed the pack. They must know what to do.

The two of them didn't move. Little Pup could do that too, and he wiggled a bit, hoping to show them. The man with threads for hair called out their names, and they stepped forward to delicately remove a treat from his outstretched hand. "Archie, good boy," the man said. "Kramer, good boy."

He wished he had a grown-up name like theirs. He may be little, but that didn't mean he was a puppy. But at that other place, he was the smallest, and they thought the name was cute. Him? Not so much, but at least they fed him.

The man with threads for hair patted the other two dogs on the head, and they retreated to their respective corners. Little Pup pivoted his head to look for a corner that someday might be his.

Then he yawned and burrowed his head into the soft tummy of the lady with the auburn hair. It was one lucky day.

CHAPTER 26

KATIE

KATIE WAITED FOR JULIE TO RETURN FROM LUNCH. An hour and a half had passed since she'd left with the handsome investment advisor, but that was to be expected. Julie might be oblivious that these luncheons were becoming more frequent and much longer, but Katie caught the flirty tone of the guy every time he called. A good receptionist picked up on these things and intuited a caller's hidden motive, even when the caller was unaware of it themselves.

The stairwell door slammed open, and Julie burst through. She unbuttoned her coat on the way to the coat closet. "I thought that would never end," she groaned. "I mean—really! Market updates? I can get those online. If he didn't refer so many clients, I'd blow him off." She gripped both hands on the edge of the thick, polished cherrywood counter surrounding Katie's desk. Then she leaned back and smiled. "But a free lunch is a free lunch. Right?"

"You do know why you see him so much, don't you?" Katie said.

"Why?" Julie asked. "What are you talking about?" She leaned in, and her long, dark ringlets draped over the counter.

"Well, I don't think it's about investments. His voice always hesitates, then gets higher before he asks if you're free. It sounds like he's about to ask you to prom."

"That's never going to happen," Julie sputtered. The look on her face said it all.

"You think so?" Julie's innocence was one of the things Katie loved most. Julie was clueless about how her physical beauty affected others.

"Well, if you're not interested, I say pawn him off on Michael. He seems to have plenty of time on his hands." Katie inserted Michael, hoping to share her worries.

"Good idea. I can use the excuse of Michael being new and needing to connect with other professionals." Her voice got softer. "That should work."

"Michael left right after you did. Said he'd be gone for the rest of the day." Katie pulled the focus back to Michael. Someone other than her had to pay attention to what was going on. After six years at the front desk, Katie recognized she was the depository of the good and bad, the public and private, and all the comings and goings of the office. Her panoramic view of Hartmann and Associates differed from the segmented views of others in the firm.

"He must be at a client's office. I guess I missed that when he stopped in to talk this morning. Sometimes I drift off." Julie was doing the same thing now. Her stare toward the back office told Katie she was itching to get back to work. "Ellen wants to give him some freedom to cultivate clients."

"How long is that going to take?" Katie pushed. "Shouldn't we see some results? With Ellen busy in Nashville and you swamped with everything else, I haven't set up a new client for a long time. Should we be worried?"

"It takes time. His clients will start showing up any day. Then you'll worry that there are too many," Julie laughed and walked away.

Julie didn't take the bait, and Katie wasn't ready to share her suspicions yet. Her receptionist's expertise and ability to intuit a caller's real purpose told her something was off. Things were not as they appeared, but she needed more evidence. Something smelled, and it wasn't coming from the lobster pound next door.

CHAPTER 27

ELLEN

"IS MAGGIE PICKING YOU UP?" ELLEN FOLLOWED Sterling onto the only down escalator at Portland International Jetport. Her carry-on suitcase bumped onto the next emerging step.

"Guess not," he frowned at his cell phone and twisted around to look at Ellen. "Can I bum a ride?"

Ellen blinked both eyes and sighed. Sterling didn't wait for her answer. He returned to his phone, assuming she would say yes. Why did couples think a single parent had nothing better to do than fill their gaps? If he hadn't learned from watching her raise her three kids, he should've understood from his own clients that doing it alone wasn't a walk in the park.

"Sure, no problem," she said, rolling her eyes at his back. "The boys can wait a little longer." Their plane had taken off forty-five minutes late, and she wasn't thrilled that Sterling's extra fifteen minutes meant dinner with her sons would be after seven. It was a school night.

Ellen stepped off the escalator and picked up her pace to walk beside Sterling. "When can we talk about the next steps, or are you really done?" He had waffled after last night's work session with Sam.

"Tomorrow's packed, and I can't do it this weekend. I promised Maggie and the girls that I was all theirs." Sterling stopped and faced her. " I don't think there's much to talk about, though. Maggie's had it, and you know what they say, happy wife, happy life."

Ellen didn't laugh. "We need to at least talk about what happens when *The Money Dynamic* launches and starts making money," Ellen said. "You know, it needs to be fair for both of us." Ellen wasn't about to give away what she mostly created alone, yet Sterling was entitled to something. At the very least, he deserved his financial investment back.

"If you say so, but to be honest, I think Sam's blowing smoke." He pushed his glasses to the top of his head. "I got lost in the haze last night, but this morning things cleared." He slid his smudged lenses back over his eyes. "I don't see it happening, at least not with Sam." He headed out the revolving door to the parking garage.

"I'm just not there yet. But we should agree about some things now. It's too easy for money to become a noisy third partner." She didn't want to leave this to chance. Too many marriages and businesses exploded over money. "How about I email a proposal for you to review?"

"Sure." Sterling was tapping away on his cell, and Ellen doubted he had even heard what he had agreed to.

"One more thing, Sterling." At the sound of his voice, he perked up to listen. "Can I still run things by you from time to time? I value your judgment, and even though you're dropping out of the daily details, it'd feel good to have you as a sounding board." There it was again, and she hated it. Why did she constantly second-guess herself? Why couldn't she trust her own judgment, the one that clients paid top dollar for? When would she get beyond it?

"Yeah, sure. Of course, you can count on me."

Maybe she wouldn't be alone with all this, as she feared. Right now, she was a puppet with Sam pulling all the strings. She needed someone with a bigger perspective, someone who could help expand her narrow view. She wanted Sam to be that person, but more and more, she suspected he wasn't the one.

CHAPTER 28

ELLEN

THE HEAVY MAHOGANY DOOR OF HER RED BRICK house swung open, and Ellen's three sons jumped off the concrete porch, running down the walkway to her car. They must have been watching for her. Her face brightened, and the rest of the world faded away. She was home again, where she belonged. She popped the trunk, and her middle son Kevin grabbed her suitcase.

Jack, the oldest, yelled, "I'm starving. Can we get pizza? Dad said you were feeding us. He left already."

When she dropped Sterling off at his house, Ellen texted their father to let him know she was on her way, and he was off duty. It didn't take long for him to leave.

"I had pizza last night." She wrapped her arms around Ethan, her youngest. He was melting into the background as usual. "What do you want? You win the jackpot. You get to choose." She rubbed his short, ginger buzz cut. Jack must have had the clippers out. His brothers didn't have a chance now that he considered himself an expert.

"I don't know, what do you guys want? Is Friendly's alright?" Ethan suggested. His brothers ignored him. It wasn't Ellen's first choice because she had driven past the restaurant when she left the airport, but Ethan's opinions were few and far between.

"Sounds like a plan. Ice cream for dessert. My favorite." She smiled down at Ethan and caressed his head. "It's getting late, but let me change my clothes first. Did you guys do your homework?" Highly doubtful, but maybe their father had stepped up to the plate.

"Dad made us do it," all three groaned as she chuckled. At least she wouldn't have to fight over homework on her first night back.

"Yeah, said you'd be mad if we didn't," Kevin added. "But he forgot to feed Random. I'll do it now." Leave it to Kevin to remember. Random was meant to be Kevin's dog until the Wheaten terrier bonded with Ellen on their long morning walks.

"Meet me in the car in five minutes. And no fighting over who rides shotgun," she reminded them. "You know the drill. And, no, it doesn't matter that I wasn't here for your day Jack." As much as she loved how Jack's mind mirrored hers, she was too tired to wrangle with all his angles tonight.

"Ha, ha. Thursday's my day anyway," Jack gloated. "You lose," he called as he bolted past his brothers.

Ellen climbed the stairs to her bedroom, stripped off her dress pants and blouse, and threw them on the bed. She plucked her jeans and a baggy sweatshirt from the hook in her closet and drew in a deep breath. It had been a long day.

Ready or not, here she comes. Ellen skipped down the stairs and out the door to her waiting sons. A hot fudge sundae with her favorite people would do her good.

CHAPTER 29

BOBBY

BOBBY PUSHED HIS GRAY RUBBER TRASH BARREL from the wood-paneled elevator into Hartmann and Associates' reception area. He flipped on the bank of light switches and illuminated the common areas. After dumping the kitchen wastebasket filled with the day's leftover lunches, he emptied Katie's trash without conscious thought. His nightly cleaning ran on autopilot, and the routine gave him room to think about life's more important things. Tomorrow, Friday, was his day to volunteer in his pseudo-son's first-grade classroom. He would begin reading *Charlotte's Web* at tomorrow's circle time. He loved it, his niece had loved it, and he expected Corbin, his ex-girlfriend's son, to love it too. Keeping his place in the boy's life was the one thing Bobby and his former partner agreed on.

Julie's laughter floated down the hallway. Good, she was still here and must be on the phone. His friendship with Julie deepened when their late-night sleuthing gave them time together outside of the office. Had Julie noticed the shift? Too much time had passed without any opportunity for him to test out what he was feeling. Maybe tonight was the night to see if the feeling was mutual or just his imagination. Forgetting his routine, he pushed his barrel straight to Julie's office.

Two distinct voices reverberated from Julie's office: one deep and resonant. Julie wasn't alone, and it sounded like too much fun for it to be a client. Bobby turned the corner and saw a tall, trim man leaning against Julie's door frame. He turned his head as Bobby tried to sneak away; his squeaky wheel had betrayed him.

"You here for the trash?" The guy towered over him and crossed his arms. Bobby didn't like the way he used his height to belittle him. He may be short, but Bobby could hold his own against anyone.

"No problem, I'll come back. Don't want to interrupt you two." Bobby walked around to the other side of his barrel and started pushing it back down the hall.

"Bobby? Is that you?" Julie called. "Wait. I want you to meet someone."

He wasn't in the mood to meet the condescending jerk, but it was too late. Bobby couldn't resist Julie's come-hither voice.

"Of course, it's me," Bobby joked, "who else would be squeaking his way to your office?"

He left his barrel in the hallway and slid around the towering dude blocking her door. Bobby grabbed Julie's overflowing wastebasket from her outstretched hands and headed to the safety of his barrel. He wanted to dump and run, but Julie had other plans.

"This is Michael, our latest hire." She twirled her long locks, flipped them over her right shoulder, and smiled. "It's nice to have another man around the place. Some brain to go with the brawn, if you know what I mean."

She slapped her right hand over her mouth, lowered her gaze, and peered up at Bobby through thick, black eyelashes. "Shit, that didn't come out right."

Damn. Bobby melted despite Julie's poor choice of words. He looked over his left shoulder and winked. Really? Where the hell did that come from? He turned back toward the new accountant and stretched out his right hand.

"Hey bro," Michael said, "how you doing?" He bypassed Bobby's offered hand and clapped him on the shoulder instead. Bobby shrugged it off. The guy didn't notice. He was too busy flashing his pearly whites at Julie.

"Great. I'm Bobby, by the way. Welcome to the wonderful world of women accountants, Mike. You're going to love it here." A little humor might ease Bobby's pounding heart.

"It's Michael," the guy bared his teeth. "And I already do."

Julie and Michael, not Mike, laughed. Was there an inside joke somewhere that Bobby wasn't party to?

"Don't miss my office," Michael said, "my trash runneth over. I think you missed it last night."

Bobby ignored the comment and handed Julie's wastebasket back to her. He waited for her usual thank you. When it didn't come, he used it as his cue to leave.

"How could anyone want to do that for a living?" Michael whispered, so Bobby could hear. "Nice of you to introduce me, though. It must make him feel important."

Bobby had had enough of Michael, not Mike, and didn't wait for Julie's response. His hands gripped his trash barrel as he moved further and further away. What the hell was up with Julie?

CHAPTER 30

ELLEN

ELLEN SMILED AT THE SOUND OF HER RESIDENT seagull peck-peck-pecking at her sliding glass door. She had missed the bird's daily visit while in Nashville and could have used its interruption as an excuse to draw a deep breath and drop her shoulders. It was good to be back. She loved this time of year. The angle of the bright morning light said it was early fall, and the hot, humid days of summer had given way to cool, crisp mornings. The final October 15th deadline was over, with future ones not yet visible on the horizon. For accountants, it was a period of rest and rejuvenation.

It never took long for the office to drag Ellen back to reality. Not that her trips to Nashville weren't real. But here at her desk in Portland, she lived in analysis; in Nashville, she thrived on creativity. Her door was half open to alert her staff that she needed time to settle in and switch gears. It signaled that it would be wise to save it for another time. Whatever *it* was. This morning, she needed time for her own *it*.

"Ellen, you're back!" Her seagull took flight at the sound of the approaching intruder. She recognized the voice, and Ellen tried to salvage a bit of her calm by dragging in another deep breath. She turned her chair to face Michael. A half-closed door meant nothing to him.

"That I am," she said. "What can I do for you?"

He didn't wait for an invitation and sat down. With arms folded behind his head, he leaned back and spread his long legs wide.

"Just wanted to say hi." Michael was clueless that he wasn't Ellen's top priority this morning. But he was new, and maybe she should cut him some slack.

"How's working with Julie?" she asked. Ellen wanted Michael to build a strong team with Julie instead of with her.

"Great, fantastic. She filled me in on office protocol and has been dumping work on me since. I've barely had time to come up for air." He laughed and ran his fingers through his thick hair. "She doesn't let up."

"Well, that's a new one. I have to arm wrestle her to give up work. Good to hear she's using you. You won't find a better mentor." Ellen picked up a pen and reached for her pad of paper. Maybe he'd get the hint.

"Could be, but I think she can learn a lot from me, too. I have tons of experience, you know." He leaned forward and rested his hands on Ellen's desk.

"Speaking of which," Ellen leaned back into her chair. She hated it when people invaded her space. "How's it going with moving your former clients to Hartmann and Associates? Any progress? I haven't had time to check in with Katie."

"Slow but sure. They need a bit more nudging. They'll come around. I promise you won't be sorry when they come pouring in."

"That's good to hear." Ellen looked at her computer screen and then back at him. She had no inclination or patience to get into this now. She had more important things to do.

She leaned forward and folded her hands on her desk. "Thanks for stopping in. Can we talk later? I've got a lot of work to catch up with today."

Michael flashed a big smile, and Ellen remembered those perfect teeth from his interview. That day, they captured her attention. Today, not so much.

CHAPTER 31

HENRY

HENRY GRIPPED THE STEERING WHEEL OF THE black Escalade. He tried not to eavesdrop, but it was impossible when Sam insisted on using his cell phone in speaker mode, oblivious to its effect on everyone within earshot. Sam might not want to keep his conversations private, but his lavish embellishment and elasticized truths made Henry uncomfortable. It took a Herculean effort not to accidentally share or complain about Sam and his antics.

"Ellen, I can't talk much," Sam said. "We're in the middle of a huge downpour, and I don't want to distract Henry."

Sunshine streamed through the windshield, and Henry cringed. He wanted to protect Ellen and tell her the truth, but he worked for Sam. Henry's job was to stay silent and uninvolved.

"Traffic is tricky, and we're almost to our meeting." Sam continued his untruths.

"I don't need much time, Sam." Henry detected the frustration in Ellen's voice and wished he could help.

"I need an update. A month ago in Nashville, you said we were done, that we'd be launching soon. And guess what?" Ellen's voice grew louder. "Nothing's happened. What the hell is going on?"

"I'm not going to argue with you, not in this storm. When you're calmed down, give me a call. I'll explain everything. But we're close, real close. I promise."

Sam grinned at Henry. Henry hated it when Sam lied. He hated himself more for never having the courage to call Sam out.

"Don't hang up," Ellen said. "Not until we've picked a time when you can give me a full update."

Henry pictured Ellen's one-dimple scowl. He preferred her two-dimple smile but doubted she was smiling now.

"It's been long enough," she said. "You owe me at least that."

"Call me in the morning. Not too early. Try around ten. Gotta go." Sam ended the call and mumbled something that Henry didn't want to acknowledge. He checked his left blind spot instead.

He appreciated Sam and the work he gave him. His talent for writing scripts and directing scenes was the best Henry had ever seen. He couldn't ask for a better teacher. But he wasn't sure Sam was the kind of guy he wanted to work for. Being privy to Sam's inner world made him doubt his own integrity.

He steered the giant Escalade into Sam's driveway, shifted into park, and listened for instructions. He was starting to dislike this hurry-up-and-wait chapter of his life.

"You can go," Sam said. "I won't need you tonight. Roxie and I are going over finances. Nothing you can help with. Unless you want a pay cut?" Sam laughed. Henry didn't. Sam slammed the heavy car door without a goodbye.

So much for the raise he was going to ask for. A little more money might help ease Henry's conscience. But it would make things more complicated. He was better than money and what it could buy. He shifted the Escalade into reverse and backed away.

CHAPTER 32

ELLEN

NINE-FIFTY-FIVE. FIVE MORE MINUTES AND SHE'D call Sam. She wanted answers. She was tired of his excuses, tired of his stalling, tired of everything. Another month was lost, and the slow march to tax season was on. She needed this to be finished now. She couldn't tolerate putting things on hold to prepare tax returns, but that was the name of her game. Life and anything except taxes stopped. Just ask her sons. *After tax season* was their common complaint. Mother's guilt erupted every time they said it.

The clock ticked to ten o'clock. Sam could wait for a change. Her Fitbit timer counted down the minutes: four, three, two, one. At five minutes after ten, she placed the call.

"Are you ready to talk? Still raining?" She couldn't resist. That was his worst excuse yet.

"Ellen, I was hoping you'd call." Had he forgotten they had scheduled a time to talk? God, she was sick of this.

"When can you get to Nashville?" he continued. "We've got some work to do. I figured out what was wrong with the program." Ellen's cheeks started to burn.

"Wrong with the program? What are you talking about?" She swallowed her words with a deep breath.

"You know how the program splits into separate programs for the four money styles? It never was right, too generic, too one-size-fits-all, and way too cumbersome. You were trying to force a round peg in a square hole."

Ellen winced. Wasn't it a square peg in a round hole? She shook her head to focus. "I'm listening." Safe answer. She switched her phone to her other ear.

"If you say all styles are valid approaches to money management, shouldn't the ultimate goal be a balanced approach? Instead of aiming for one hundred percent of their already strong style, shouldn't they be using all four? That makes the ideal score four times twenty-five instead of one times a hundred?"

"I guess so," she mumbled. She remembered their Gestalt training on overused behaviors. How did she and Sterling miss that? It was so obvious.

"Shouldn't people strive for a balanced approach?" Sam continued.

"God, I hate it when you're right." She didn't want to cave to Sam's opinions when she had planned to be a hard-ass. Her conviction faded, and she gave in. "Sterling and I struggled with that part of the program. Missed the forest for the trees, I guess."

Why didn't Sam point this out a long time ago? She swallowed the lump in her throat and confronted Sam with this truth. "Couldn't you have come up with this a year or two ago or even last month?"

"I'm going to ignore that," Sam said. "It won't get us anywhere. The program will be better, stronger, more meaningful. Trust me. This is going to be big!"

Ellen focused on the idea, not her anger with Sam. She soft-pedaled into her agenda. "How do we move this forward?"

"Get to Nashville. We'll start the rework together. We don't have to trash everything. It's a small blip. We can rearrange, spruce it up, and come up with a different ending. You know how we work together. When we're in the same place, we're on fire." Sam's suggestion was valid.

"My calendar's pretty empty this time of year," she said. Sam's excitement filtered through her frustration, and her creative juices censored her analytical mind. She was so in love with this project and how it would change people's better understanding of their money woes that she left the red flags trying to catch her attention flapping in the wind.

"Give me time to arrange for my boys. What works for you?" she asked.

"For you, Ellen? Any time. You name it and it's yours."

She wasn't going to fall for that this time. The last trip with Sterling was a disaster. This time, she'd make sure Sam was available.

"How about next week? I'll fly in on Tuesday and leave on Friday. Mark those days on your calendar. They're all mine. Promise?"

No response. Sam was gone, escaped again without a straight answer. Why did she expect otherwise?

CHAPTER 33

STERLING

STERLING WAITED FOR THE ELEVATOR IN THE lobby of one of the old brick buildings that filled The Old Port. Once a working waterfront with ship chandleries and banks, it was now filled with shopping, restaurants, and professional offices. He was fortunate to have found office space with other therapists, and his business clients appreciated that he was conveniently located nearby.

His office, located on the fifth floor, had four expansive windows with panoramic views of Portland's waterfront. Clients stared out the window as they bared their souls to him. At first, he snagged the view for himself, but after a client caught him daydreaming, he switched places. Better them than their therapist.

"Tough parking. Had to go to the parking garage." Ellen slipped through the adjoining Starbucks door, one of the perks of this building. From the note he read on her cup, she held her usual French vanilla decaf with almond milk. He carried his travel mug from home.

"You didn't walk?" he asked. Walking was Ellen's nod to easy exercise.

"Spent some extra time with the boys this morning." She smiled at him. "See, I do listen to you." Sterling had cautioned Ellen to slow down more than once.

The elevator doors opened, and Ellen leaned against its mirrored back. He stood next to her. "Thanks for meeting with me on such short notice. Sam's got some new ideas for *The Money Dynamic*, and I need your input. It pains me to say this, but I think he's right."

Sterling's head snapped around, but she missed it. She was staring straight ahead. "Really. New ideas? Now? What's he up to?" The elevator dinged five times, and the doors opened. Sterling headed down the hall to his office. A blast of heat tumbled out as he unlocked the door. He stepped aside to let her in.

"God, it's hot in here. How do you stand it?" Ellen stripped off her coat, threw it on one of the cushy client chairs, and plopped into the other.

"At least I'm not paying for heat. I keep the windows open." He slid up the bottom pane of one of the big windows facing the harbor. "The fresh air keeps me awake. It's not easy listening to clients eight or ten hours a day. If only *The Money Dynamic* could've saved me."

"I hear you, and I'm still hoping it'll come through. I could use the extra money too. You know I can't count on help from my ex, and college tuition is looming on my horizon."

Sterling agreed. He was lucky to have a few more years and a father who would help. He sat on the saggy leather couch he nabbed at a consignment shop. "So, what's Sam selling you now?"

"Don't go there, please. I get it." Ellen reached into her red bag for a notepad. She grabbed a pen from the table next to her. "It would've been nice to hear this two years ago, but I don't think we can ignore it now. He makes sense."

Sterling hid his annoyance by adjusting his glasses and crossing his legs in classic counselor style. "Tell me more."

"You know how we struggled with focusing on a user's dominant style and trying to figure out how to use it to their advantage? Sam thinks the program should be about finding balance with all four money styles."

Sterling pushed his glasses up onto his head and rubbed both eyes. "Geez. That's so obvious. How'd we miss that?"

"So, you agree? I thought you would. We, I mean I, need to change it, but I wanted your perspective. You know me, I'm always ready for a new, bigger horizon to shoot for. I didn't want to jump the gun without taking time to think it through."

He loved how *The Money Dynamic* concepts worked with more than money. It also helped with differences in other matters. In the lingo of their program, Sterling was practical, slower to make decisions, while Ellen was ambitious, more pie-in-the-sky. Together, they found a balance that took them to the right solution. It was exactly what Sam was suggesting. Duh.

"Then you agree. I have to rewrite the program?" Ellen looked for his approval.

"I do." He dropped his glasses back onto his nose. "But I worry you're going to get derailed."

"Derailed? I'm not following. We're on the right track. What am I missing?" Ellen reached behind her to reposition the pillow in her chair.

"You're on the right track, but is Sam the right person? Don't you think it's time to find someone else?" Sam might be talented, creative, and right this time, but he was not trustworthy. Ellen needed to face the truth.

"We're so close to finishing. I can't stand having to start over with someone else." Ellen slid her notepad into her bag. "The truth is, I can't afford it. I have to make this work with Sam." She stood up to leave.

"Just be careful. You don't want to waste more time and energy and end up in the same place." He wanted to say, *don't be an idiot, move on*, but his counselor self wouldn't let him.

"I've got to give it one last try. I'm going to Nashville next week and lay it on the line with drop-dead deadlines for Sam to meet. This time, I'll make it work."

Sterling walked over to the window and closed it. There was no more to say. Until she trusted her own instincts, Ellen would do what Ellen would do.

CHAPTER 34

ELLEN

ELLEN STARED AT THE IMMENSE TV HANGING over the fireplace in Sam's house. After isolating herself for the remainder of the week, she had rewritten much of the program, and to Sam's chagrin, she had returned to Nashville with a finished product. Sam and Roxie had disappeared upstairs as soon as they arrived, barely acknowledging Sam's mother Diane, who sat in her favorite chair, tuned into her nightly fix of *Wheel of Fortune*. Ellen could have used some time to unwind after a long, intense day of work, but Sam insisted there was no time for a break and demanded she come to his house so they could continue their work. Typical Sam: hurry-up-and-wait.

Instead of fuming, Ellen chose to make the most of the free time. Little Pup poked his cold nose into her ankle, and after scratching his ears, she picked him up to let him curl into her lap. Archie and Kramer slept under the coffee table at a safe distance from Diane. Ellen had watched Diane swat or kick one of the dogs if they veered into Diane's territory, and that, along with Sam's and Roxie's screams and profanities that followed when they saw it, was all the training the dogs needed to stay away. Mother, mother-in-law, and son had a strange relationship at best. Loving and respectful some of the time, barely tolerable at others. Kind of like the dogs.

It was Thursday night, and the next day, Ellen would fly home after two and a half days of hard work. She missed her boys desperately, but Sam had come through, and her trip to Nashville had been well worth it. Tonight, she was ready to relax next to Diane on the cushy sofa with a cuddly dog in her lap. Ellen hadn't slept well for days, not before leaving Portland and not even on the plane, where burying her head in a mindless novel during take-off usually put her to sleep. This trip, she was primed for problems, and her mind wouldn't stop swirling with anxiety, fearing that this trip would be a lost cause, along with Sterling's and her own investment.

Ellen slid off her shoes and gently lifted her feet onto the footstool so she wouldn't disturb Little Pup. He opened one eye and then cocooned back into himself. Ellen did the same. She closed her eyes and reviewed the week's activities. It had been a whirlwind since her arrival on Tuesday afternoon. Sam rearranged their original content into seven sections with appealing titles. Gone were the stodgy accountant/therapist headlines threatening boredom. In their places were catchy phrases that pried open users' minds with humor. It took two years to find the side of Sam they hired, but it was better late than never. She felt vindicated that she wasn't a fool for waiting for him to come through.

For two days, she and Sam searched online for graphics and photos to spice up the new app and website. Accountant Ellen disappeared, creative Ellen stepped in, and Sam engaged his entire office to help. Roxie made a comprehensive list of sections for Ellen to rework. The IT guy Jordan, created a new landing page for an updated website. Stacy discussed the social media campaign she'd launch for Ellen. Even Henry set aside his role as chauffeur to rehearse for the promotional trailer. Ellen was blown away. Finally, finally, finally, *The Money Dynamic* was happening.

Sam's voice erupted above them, followed by a loud crash. Ellen's heart jackhammered, and Little Pup flew off her lap to race to the bottom of the stairs with the other dogs. Their ears perked up as a loud, garbled diatribe continued. Then came footsteps and Roxie's calm voice murmuring unintelligible words. Ellen looked at Sam's mother.

"Mystery Novel, you idiots!" Diane shouted. Sam's mother hadn't skipped a beat.

Ellen joined her in her indifference. Sam could be a loose cannon, and tonight, Ellen didn't care.

CHAPTER 35

ROXIE

"ROXIE! GET IN HERE!" SAM BELLOWED FROM across the hallway.

The dogs didn't budge. Archie was asleep to the right of Roxie's monitor, Kramer to the left. She picked up Little Pup from her lap, tucked him under her arm, and made her way to Sam's office. Two thumps and the click, click, click of eight little feet followed behind.

"Shut the door," Sam growled.

Sam was in a mood and had been for at least a week. After fifteen years of marriage, she learned not to ask why. When he was ready, he'd let her into his inner sanctum. Today must be her lucky day. She waited.

"What's the cash look like?" Sam barked.

Straight to the point. No pleasantries, no platitudes. That said, it made Sam easy to live with. No hidden agendas. She placed Little Pup on the floor with the others, then tucked her dancer's legs underneath her to sit. She framed her long neck with a raised right arm in fourth position and stared at Sam. She could have been a ballerina.

"Not enough to make payroll next week," she said. "Time to make some tough decisions." Roxie wasn't worried. Sam always pulled something out of his butt. A new project, a new investor, a new loan from someone she never asked about. Her job was to keep track of things and not ask questions. She was good at that. In the meantime, she'd feign interest. She swallowed a yawn as his voice droned in the background.

She met Sam in Las Vegas. She was a dancer, not good enough for the flashy venues on the ever-expanding Strip, but skilled enough to shine as a star at Sin City's iconic Tropicana, where Sam had been a regular. Now, their fateful meeting place was set to be torn down for a stadium, and both were relieved they weren't there to witness its downfall as the city aimed to transform itself into family-friendly territory. Kids were not Sam and Roxie's style.

"OK. I'll make some calls," Sam said. "How much to get us through until the big guy comes through? Twenty Gs?" Money was one thing Sam trusted her with. He had his place; she had hers.

"I'd go for thirty, or we'll be talking about this again in another two weeks. Thirty will keep us going unless there's a big expense coming up that you failed to mention?" Archie's spiky fur brushed against Roxie's well-toned calf. She bent down to scratch his head, twisted her neck, and smiled up at Sam.

"No, you know it all," he said. "The movie's on hold, the last episode of *Imperfect President* is in editing, and *The*

Money Dynamic's sitting tight for now. But we need to cover rent and payroll. Time to pull in some money, or we'll have to start laying people off."

Sam ran his fingers through his thinning hair, then patted it instead. She missed the thick black waves that had first caught her eye.

"Any possibilities?" She rolled her shoulders and arched her back.

"There's always possibilities." Sam watched her unfold her legs, stand up, and walk over to him.

"Of course there is." Roxie leaned over, kissed his head, and followed her dogs across the hallway to her office.

CHAPTER 36

ELLEN

"SAM ON LINE ONE," KATIE ANNOUNCED. ELLEN resisted the urge to kick her door shut and nudged it instead. There was no point in starting gossip with a loud bang or the string of obscenities threatening to spill from her mouth. She had tried to have a meaningful conversation with Sam all week, but as soon as they got started, he'd cleverly shut her down whenever she asked something meaningful. He was too busy, too late, too whatever. She was not pleased.

"What's going on, Sam? I've been trying to have a real conversation with you all week. I sent those edits two weeks ago; I need to hear something. Anything. No more damn excuses. Since I saw you a month ago, I've done everything you've asked to get this project finished. What the hell is going on!" She held back, knowing that once she got started, she might say something worse, much, much worse.

"Whoa there, Ellen. Calm down. Let's try to have an adult conversation."

Sam's slow, accusing voice deflated her. God, she hated how he did that. He knew exactly which buttons to push to make her inner judge start whipping her for being too strident, too impatient, too much of an angry woman.

"Right," she muttered, staring above the empty client chairs, through the sliding glass doors, across the deck speckled with bird droppings, and out to the flowing water. It was high tide. She took a deep breath. She was ready to listen. Maybe.

"I got great news. We have a celebrity endorsement!" Sam's voice, exuberant, almost joyous, put her on guard.

"I didn't know we were looking for one." Her voice was flat.

"The name of the game is finding an influencer. These days, if you don't have one, you're going nowhere." Sam's mansplaining annoyed her. She sucked in a deep breath.

"Like we are right now?" She couldn't resist. She was pissed.

"Are we going to do this or not?" Sam said. "I'm not playing this game."

Ellen's inner critic took over, and she fell quiet. She blinked her eyes to refocus on the calming waters outside her window.

"Alright, I'm listening." Her voice softened to a sickly-sweet, singsongy tone. "I'm sorry, but I don't remember you ever saying anything about working with a celebrity."

"I didn't want to get your hopes up."

Ellen was silent.

"Amanda Littleton has signed on."

"Who?" Ellen's jaw clenched. "I don't know who you're talking about."

"Oh, that's right, you're not part of the country scene. Trust me, she has a huge online presence and is on her way to a Grammy. Ask any Gen-Z or Millennial."

Ellen was aware that her New England accountant mentality might distance her from the rest of the world. She had built her accounting practice on an impeccable reputation and traditional word-of-mouth referrals. Perhaps it was time to embrace the real world—if a world driven by social media and artificial personas could truly be called real.

"Well, that sounds great, I guess. If you say so," she offered.

"It's going to take a little bit of cash, but she's giving us a sweet deal," he continued.

"Sam, I need those edits back, not a celebrity endorsement. This is coming right out of the blue." Her voice grew louder in volume and higher in pitch as panic began to seep in.

"Settle down, Ellen," he placated. "Let's not get hysterical."

"How much, Sam? You know I don't have anything left to work with now that Sterling is out of the picture." She had confided in Sam that running a business and being the sole support of three kids kept her finances on edge. She mistakenly thought it would motivate him to finish.

"Ten thousand. Five for Amanda and five for promotional costs. You can pull that off, can't you? That's nothing for a successful accountant like you." Sam managed to push another of her buttons.

Ellen swallowed. It should be. But at this time of year, with the slow season over and tax season waiting to start, the firm was low on funds, and she didn't dare put the office at risk. She'd have to find it elsewhere. She understood how endorsements worked and that to make money, you had to spend money. Her shoulders crept up to her ears as her breathing grew fast and shallow.

"How soon?" Her voice was quiet as her resolve yielded.

"End of the week. I want to get it to Amanda fast. Everyone wants a piece of her since her last release. You got her for a steal."

Ellen said nothing. Her mind was off searching for money.

"Send it the same way you always do," Sam said. "You still have my wire transfer information, right?"

Ellen sighed. "Yup. Got it." She'd make it happen; she always did.

CHAPTER 37

JULIE

JULIE DETOURED TO ELLEN'S OFFICE ON HER WAY back from her client meeting. Ellen's door was open, her desk was clear, and she was staring out the window—a perfect time to talk.

"Got a minute? Thought I'd catch you up on a few things," Julie began.

Since her return from Nashville, Ellen had been hard to reach. Although she was back physically, mentally she was still unavailable.

"For you? Always." Ellen turned her gaze from the window. Her mind didn't seem to follow.

"Are you okay?" Julie asked.

"It's this damn project as usual. Just got off the phone with Sam. Not your problem. I know you're as sick of it as I am." She sat motionless, closed her eyes for a long second, before continuing. "What's up?"

"Not enough; slow time of year. Not much work to spread around. I know I was supposed to keep Michael occupied, but finding stuff to pass on to him has been tough. I wanted you to know that I wasn't shirking my duty." Julie perched on the arm of one of Ellen's guest chairs. She didn't intend to stay long and sensed that Ellen didn't want her to either.

"Interesting." Ellen's voice faded. "Michael said you were giving him plenty to do. Guess he has a different idea about what a lot of work is." She smiled. "Unlike you. We both know there's never enough for you." Ellen gazed over Julie's head. "I'm not worried; neither should you."

"Okey dokey, I won't."

But Julie was worried. She needed, no, wanted Ellen back at the helm. She was tired of carrying everything alone. Ellen and she were a team; they did things together. Julie had supported Ellen's Nashville distraction for long enough; it was time for Ellen to confront the reality that Julie had recognized months ago. Sam was, at the very least, incompetent; at most, he was a fraud. Julie didn't care which. Either way, *The Money Dynamic* was dead in the water, and it was time for Ellen to resume her role as the leader of Hartmann and Associates. Julie was done.

CHAPTER 38

ELLEN

ELLEN COULDN'T SLEEP. AGAIN. NOTHING UNUSUAL, but tonight felt different. It wasn't a difficult tax return or a tricky financial plan that kept her awake. It wasn't worrying about finding time to grocery shop, clean, or spend quality time with her boys. It wasn't even that the office's financial cushion had lost its stuffing waiting for tax season's influx of funds.

Instead, she replayed the last two years' battle to save *The Money Dynamic*, hoping to resolve her dilemma about Sam's latest request. She relived the excitement that she and Sterling shared during the program's creation. They were elated, almost astounded, when they discovered someone to market it. With Sam's impressive experience, they felt confident they were on their way. Could they have been wrong?

She navigated every twist and turn on the long, winding road to today: the lengthy conversations with Sam about the complexities of producing and programming their online project, the blog and articles she wrote, the revisions of the old program, and now the new one. Was it all for nothing?

Sterling's words echoed in her head. *Is Sam the right person?* Was he? She wasn't sure, and there was even more that she was unsure of. He might not be the right person, but they could still pull this off as long as he wasn't the wrong one. If she fired him now, would her passion project die on the vine? Who would replace him? Where would she find the time to start over? How much money would it take? She couldn't even come up with ten thousand dollars; starting over would be double or more. Her brain began its arduous overanalysis, searching for the answer. One thing she knew, she wasn't ready to give up.

She picked up her phone from the nightstand. Since she wasn't sleeping anyway, she might as well take action. She opened the Chase credit card app and navigated to Manage Account. She selected Transfer a Balance, then chose Transfer to checking account. A five percent fee and zero percent interest would give her a ten-thousand-dollar loan with fifteen months to repay it. That should be more than enough time for Sam to finish. It had to be.

CHAPTER 39

HENRY

HENRY'S THUMBS DRUMMED ON THE STEERING wheel, keeping time with the beat of his latest earworm. Waiting did nothing to ease his anxiety, and he hoped Ellen would arrive soon. The airport security guard watching the curb was giving him the evil eye. Her monthly visits to Nashville and their trips to and from the airport were becoming the highlights of his job. It was one thing he could thank Sam for. He tried to suppress the twinge in his gut urging him to come clean to Ellen. Keeping Sam's lies a secret made him a liar, too. Could he consider himself a friend if he remained silent? Would breaking that silence jeopardize his job and his opportunities as an actor?

His thumbs hovered midair when he saw Ellen approaching the pickup area. It was December, and Nashville was experiencing colder-than-usual temperatures. Ellen didn't seem to notice. Everyone else was bundled in puffy jackets, woolly hats, and bulky mittens. Not Ellen. As if to announce *I'm from Maine*, her brown hair blew across her face in the gusty wind. Her bare hand brushed it away and tucked it behind her right ear. She walked—no swaggered—toward him, and Henry smiled at the toes of her new cowboy boots peeking out from beneath her jeans. An unbuttoned, oversized corduroy barn jacket covered her off-white sweater, and hoop earrings dangled from her ears. All was right in Henry's world. Ellen was here.

Henry noticed Ellen's calming presence the first time they met. Something clicked that day on their ride from the airport. Unlike many of the other professionals he picked up for Sam, Ellen was easy to like. She was genuinely interested in getting to know Henry. Her questions opened him up, and he revealed more of himself than usual. No matter how he responded, she wanted to know more, and he found himself sharing things with Ellen that he had never shared with anyone. His stomach twisted as he remembered what he still hadn't shared.

"Ellen, you're back! Can't keep away from me?" He threw his arms around her. She didn't seem to mind his longer-than-usual hug, and how her head leaned against his chest.

"Who could? A good-looking cowboy like you? I like the ponytail. Looks good on you." She pulled away to get a better view. "But I'm partial to red hair. Jack and Ethan have red hair, and they always tease me that I want them to grow it long for a ponytail. Instead, they've opted for shaved heads."

Henry loved how she laughed, playful yet hesitant, deep-toned yet light. He wished he could hear it more often. "Tell them to keep it short. This is a real pain, and it makes my red hair stand out more. I bet they hate it as much as I do."

As a child, he cowered when people pointed out his hair. He wanted to be like the other boys, not the one in a hundred who stood apart from the rest.

"They've never said that, but I suppose they do. When I tell other red-headed kids how much I love their hair, my boys cringe." She stared out the window. "I'll have to give that some thought."

Ellen was always willing to reconsider her behavior. The world could use more people like her. The twinge in his stomach pinged as he thought about Sam's lies. He opened the bulky door of the Escalade and reached out his hand to help her get in. Did she hold his hand longer than necessary?

They released their grasp, and her hand brushed his again as she reached for her seatbelt. No mittens on a cold morning; a good thing.

CHAPTER 40

ELLEN

THE ENTIRE DAY WAS INEFFICIENT AND unproductive from the moment Henry dropped Ellen off at Sam's office. With barely a hello, Sam launched into his request for a physical workbook to accompany *The Money Dynamic*'s online program. Ellen thought users could print it themselves; Sam insisted that users should receive something tangible for their money; Ellen said they were getting plenty of intangible benefits. But when Sam reminded her that nobody used printers anymore, she relented, although she suspected it was just another delay tactic. By four o'clock, she was toast. She needed a break. Six-thirty and tonight's session at Sam's house were approaching quickly.

Henry was busy being videotaped for one of Sam's other projects, so she took an Uber back to the hotel. The fifteen-minute drive allowed her to gaze out the car's window and clear her mind. Today, Sam had made her doubt herself. But tonight, she needed to be clear-headed and strong-willed, and she promised herself that she would hold Sam to some SMART goals. She hated the acronym, and goals in general—god knows why—but with Sam, a Specific, Measurable, Achievable, Relevant, and Time-bound goal was the one thing that might work.

After time in her room crafting specific tasks with deadlines, she rewarded herself with a twenty-minute nap. She was refreshed, re-grounded, and staring at the ceiling when Henry's text came in. *Pick you up at 6:15.*

She missed Henry's playful banter this afternoon and responded quickly. *Come early. Have a drink first.* Where did that come from? Her fingers typed what she was trying to ignore, and now it was too late. The message was sent. She sat up on the edge of the bed, waiting for Henry's response.

Sounds good. ETA 5:30. Ellen spread-eagled on the bed and smiled.

Five-twenty and from a cushy chair in the corner of the hotel lounge, Ellen studied her glass of house Cabernet. She needed a moment of calm. At least, that's what she was telling herself. A soft touch on her shoulder stopped her from delving further.

"Henry, I didn't see you pull in. Zoned out for a minute, I guess." She returned to examining her wine. He slipped into the chair across from her.

"I don't know your drink of choice," she said, "and for that matter, I don't even know your last name?" Ellen's face grew warm, and she looked away.

"Henry Allard. Nice to meet you." Henry turned to the waiter, following him to the table. "Bring me a ginger ale."

He turned to Ellen and smiled. "Precious cargo, you know. Besides, I'm still on duty."

Ellen's face grew warmer. "Thanks for coming early. I needed a break and a drink, and I don't believe in drinking alone." She tucked her hair behind her ear, relieved it was too short for a flirtatious flip. "I know Sam won't be serving any booze tonight, and today was grueling." She took another sip of her wine. This was about a drink, not about Henry, she lied to herself.

"I hear you. Days with Sam aren't easy. I try to ignore it. Not much else to do." Henry was right. She could use a little of Henry's restraint. He was a bit of an old soul, and sometimes Henry seemed fifteen years older than her instead of fifteen years younger.

"Enough about Sam. I'll have my fill of him and the pizza tonight. Tell me about the scene you were shooting. Why wasn't Sam directing?" She leaned in and cupped her face in both hands. His fresh-from-the-shower scent was captivating. She blinked to stop her wicked thoughts. She had been single too long, and this was not the time or place. She sat up straight.

"It was a preliminary run-through before the final taping. Roxie handled things." Their eyes met across the table, and they both looked away. "But we're talking about Sam, and we said we wouldn't." He played with his thick, red ponytail. "Tell me what's new back in Portland."

"Well, the boys are great, getting ready for Christmas and

trying to be on their best behavior. They pretend they still believe in Santa, but I think they're scamming me for more presents." Henry's laugh was every bit as captivating as his scent. She blinked.

"I remember those days. I kept my mom and dad going for years."

Ellen gulped. It was not that long ago for him. She changed the subject.

"Tell me about your music. I know your acting career is tied up with him-who-shall-not-be-named. Do you have any time for it?" she asked. Music had been an instant connection between them from day one. A singing scholarship launched Ellen's college career until her practical side switched to accounting.

"It's tough finding the time, but I try to spend at least an hour every day playing or writing, even if it's after midnight." Henry's eyes twinkled, and he sat up taller. Clearly, music was his passion.

"Tell me more." Ellen leaned in. Henry's stories of songwriting, complex chord progressions, and busking on street corners were music to her ears. She urged him to sing the refrain from his latest song *From Two Different Worlds*, and she was impressed, very impressed. This was a side of Henry she didn't know. She liked it; she liked it a lot.

"I have an idea," Ellen said, "Let's forget Sam tonight. I've had enough of him for one day. I'm sure you have, too." She wanted Henry to step out of his daytime role to learn more about him. One night away from her project wouldn't hurt. She deserved it.

Ellen punched Sam's number into her phone. "Hey Sam, I'm beat. Let's pick it up tomorrow. I'll text Henry to be here at nine tomorrow morning. I have his number. Can I tell him he's done for the night?" Ellen didn't give Sam time to disagree; she had learned from the best.

She drained her wine glass and stood up. "Ready? Let's find some music." Henry's half-empty glass of ginger ale clinked on the glass tabletop. She took his arm, and together they left the hotel.

CHAPTER 41

JULIE

JULIE TURNED OFF THE LIGHTS AND HEADED TO the elevator. Five minutes after five, and she was the last one in the office. Everyone left early this time of year. With sunset at four o'clock these days, they wanted to get home to hibernate. Soon enough, they'd be glued to their desks and fail to notice winter turning into spring. Now, they could go home, enjoy some family time, and curl up with a good book—or TV. Neither was Julie's style, and she wasn't looking forward to returning to an empty house.

She took the elevator, skipping the stairs for the short ride down to the parking garage. Even though it was just one floor, she wanted to make sure the elevator's access to that level was secure. Leaning against the back wall of the elevator, she couldn't help but think about the gym. Not tonight had become her mantra over the past few months, and it was going to remain the case this evening. But come January, those early morning trips to the gym would become her secret weapon to energize her for the long hours at her desk. No need to rush things right now.

Julie's hand hesitated on the handle of the door to the garage, and instead of using it, she turned and pushed open the front door. A bait truck, rusted out and dripping fish guts, clunked on the wooden planking and passed her on its way to the lobster pound next door. Who would've believed it possible, a girl from the potato fields of Maine, here on the Portland waterfront? And an accountant to boot, not to mention one trusted to run the office in Ellen's absence. She headed down the pier to J's Oyster Bar, her favorite watering hole.

The horseshoe-shaped bar was almost empty, and her favorite barstool waited for her. This time of year, lobstermen used every excuse not to fish. Lobsters were too far offshore, and the demand for them was too low. While pulling their traps for the season freed up their schedules, it did nothing for their finances. Lounging at the bar became a luxury rather than a necessity. A few couples sat at the tables circling the expansive bar, and one or two other lost souls dotted its circumference, staring into their drinks.

"Hey Julie, where've you been? We've missed you," J called. The bar's owner still wore her usual summer garb of tight jeans and a tank top, but had added a ratty cardigan as a nod to the season. She was fifty-something, but her customers still liked to look.

"It's been a while. Don't worry, soon you'll be sick of me," Julie said. "Tax season's right around the corner, you know. Thought I'd better practice a bit. Wouldn't want to forget how to do this."

J poured Julie's usual dark beer. "Don't remind me." J placed the mug, dripping with icy suds, in front of Julie. "The two things you can count on are death and taxes. Sometimes, I think I prefer death," J laughed.

"Tell me that in April, and I might agree." A blast of cold air rushed in through the open door, hitting Julie's back.

"Ah ha, another partner in crime! A little early for you, isn't it?" J teased.

Julie twisted her neck to glance over her shoulder. A silly grin spread across her face, and she began to play with her long, dark curls. Why did he affect her like this?

"Bobby! Taking a break?" Stupid comment and so, so wrong. She wasn't monitoring his cleaning. Try again. "Not that I mind. Pull up a stool," she said.

"There's that smile I live for," Bobby said as he sat down on her left. J placed his beer in front of him.

"What's up?" Julie asked.

He leaned his left elbow on the bar and glanced at her. She tried not to stare at the toned abs beneath his tight white t-shirt, but it was impossible. Their eyes met, and Julie's heart thumped. Her evening was looking up.

CHAPTER 42

BOBBY

IT WAS TEN O'CLOCK, AND HIS WORK WAS WAITING for him. He wouldn't be finished until at least two in the morning, and tomorrow he'd be dragging. But he didn't regret a minute spent with Julie, how her long curls unfurled against her voluptuous chest, and how her endless smile brightened his day. Their trash-pickup moments were constantly interrupted by that new guy, Michael, and seeing her walk into J's as Bobby turned onto the pier made it an easy choice. Cleaning could wait; time with Julie couldn't. It was a wise decision. Julie was her old self again, and after finding their groove with some playful teasing, their conversation flowed effortlessly. They never failed to discover new ways to connect. He paused for a moment to reflect, then pushed his eternal trash barrel down the dark hallway.

A deep voice interrupted his daydream. He was not alone. Michael. Not his favorite person, but was he Julie's? She mentioned him a few too many times tonight. Worse, she was kowtowing to Michael's experience and grandiose opinion of himself. He hated Julie doubting herself; it wasn't a side he recognized. Michael seemed to have a spell over her.

Bobby left his trash barrel and crept closer. Michael was talking on the phone.

"It won't be long. The clients are starting to line up, just like I promised Ellen, except they're not lining up for her. It's coming together just as I planned."

Bobby couldn't hear the response, but the voice was female. God. Don't let it be Julie.

Michael signed off, and Bobby scurried down the hall. Julie or not, he heard enough to sense that something was off. He didn't know what, why, or who was involved, but one thing was certain: Michael was every bit the snake Bobby believed him to be. Why didn't Julie see it?

CHAPTER 43

ELLEN

AFTER A LATE NIGHT WITH HENRY, ELLEN SKIPPED her morning walk to catch up on sleep. As a single mother of three boys, she had forgotten what it felt like to enjoy herself after ten at night. She stepped off the elevator and checked her watch: 8:54. Still early. She scanned the lobby, searching for Henry. She spotted him, but he wasn't alone. Sam and Roxie were at their usual table by the window. It hadn't been the plan to meet them here, and the two of them rarely showed up unannounced. Henry was at a different table. Sam waved her over to theirs. After last night, she had hoped for some time alone with Henry. Now, that wasn't going to happen.

She diverted her gaze and mumbled a quick hello as she walked by Henry. She trusted Henry to know that last night's little white lie needed to stay between the two of them.

"Sam, Roxie, you're here? I thought I was meeting you

at the office." Ellen hoped they'd chalk up her less-than-perky look to last night's excuse of being too tired.

"Get yourself some breakfast. Mine is on the way." Sam barked at Ellen, and Roxie shrugged her shoulders and tilted her head to excuse his behavior. Some days, Roxie filled in for Sam's calm side. Better than nothing.

"Coffee and a bagel. Not toasted, with plain cream cheese on the side," Ellen told the waitress who had followed her to the table carrying Sam's French toast and Roxie's muffin. "Black coffee too, please." She sat down across from Sam.

Roxie slid her chair a bit closer to Sam.

"Hope you're ready for a full day. Lots on the agenda, and we have an event tonight. You can come along," Sam turned his head and glared at his wife. "Roxie is getting an award."

Sam's lack of enthusiasm was astonishing. What was that about? Most would be proud of their spouse's accomplishments. "Really? That's great!" Ellen turned away from Sam to beam at Roxie. She wanted to fill Sam's gap. "Tell me all about it."

"No big deal." Roxie's voice was soft, and Ellen leaned closer to hear. "Just a newcomer award from Nashville's Women in Film and Television, not much competition." Roxie turned to Sam. He was busy with his phone.

"An honor, nonetheless. From what I've seen, you'd win even in a huge field of contenders." Ellen extended a congratulatory handshake. Roxie's hand felt cold and lifeless, unimpressive at best. She needed to work on that if she wanted to succeed in the business world.

Sam scowled at Roxie, then turned to Ellen. "Anyway, I've got things to tell you. We can talk while you wait for your food."

Roxie had crossed some imaginary line, and whatever it was, Sam didn't like it.

CHAPTER 44

SAM

"WHAT CAN I TELL YOU ELLEN? IT IS WHAT IT IS." Sam and Ellen sat at the worktable in Brand & Broadcast's office. To an outsider, it was a mess, but to Sam, it was a work of art. He could put his finger on anything he needed for all four projects he was working on. Ellen should appreciate how her tiny project amounted to nothing for him. There were much bigger things in the works.

Even though they had worked together all day, Sam waited until now to tell Ellen that Amanda Littleton was a no-go. He prepped her for this moment by spending the day guiding her through the updated website, a copy of the new workbook, and *The Money Dynamic*'s new social media accounts. She still wasn't satisfied. Women. Or maybe it was accountants. Bad choice to work with.

"But I gave you ten thousand dollars!" Ellen's face flushed with anger, and her voice trembled. She was riled up.

"Settle down. I've still got the money. What do you want me to do? Amanda changed her mind. I can't force her to sign with us." Sam's best defense was to avoid joining Ellen in her escalating emotions. Staying calm and carrying on worked best for him.

"Bring it down a notch, please," he continued. "We can't work together if you're going to act like this." Sam glanced across the hallway to Roxie's office. It was empty. She always high-tailed it when things started to get intense.

"I get it. But I need the ten thousand back. I borrowed that money on a credit card."

"I know. You told me last night. Don't worry, you'll get it back." Sam smiled. Anything to keep her happy. He was under a lot of pressure and didn't need more from Ellen.

Ellen remained silent. He handed her a generic marketing plan that he used with everyone. "Can we get back to work? We have to leave soon for Roxie's thing."

Keep her moving. "Let's go over this revised marketing campaign."

Ellen glanced at the marketing campaign. "Right." She was pissed; he knew that voice. Women and drama. The two always go hand in hand.

"Next time you're back, we'll be launching." That'll shut her up.

"Right, and Santa Claus is real. You promise this time?" Ellen didn't let up.

"Merry Christmas to you, too," he snapped. No need to say more.

CHAPTER 45

HENRY

HENRY WANDERED THROUGH THE BANKER'S Alley Hotel after dropping off Ellen, Sam, and Roxie at the front door. This was the place everyone talked about, and now he understood why. The hotel had a storied past, first as a nineteenth-century warehouse, then as an art museum, and now as a boutique hotel on the National Registry of Historic Places. Works by local and regional artists, some of whom were Henry's friends, filled the lobby and hallways, and its art galleries were used for gatherings of all sizes. The concierge mentioned that Roxie's event was in Gallery One. Henry wasn't sure if the guy spoke to him to confirm he had a legitimate reason for being there or if he was just being nice. Either way, he pointed Henry in the right direction.

The trip downtown was interesting. Sam, quiet for a change, didn't acknowledge Roxie and Ellen in the back seat. But that didn't stop the two women from enjoying a Sam-less conversation. Roxie, a woman of few words, was surprisingly talkative about tonight's gathering. Sam interrupted to ask how many people would be there, and she assured him it would be small. As Henry entered the gallery, he wondered if Roxie had only said that to placate him.

Gallery One was arranged for a cocktail party, with high-top tables draped in long white tablecloths, perfect for mingling. A bar occupied one corner, and to its right, a long table overflowed with appetizers. By his count, twenty tables times three or four guests, along with space for standing around and in between, indicated that the room was set up for nearly one hundred people. He chuckled. One night with Ellen, and he was thinking like an accountant.

He made his way to the back corner, across from the crowded bar, where Sam stood. He didn't acknowledge Henry as he approached. From this vantage point, Henry could survey the crowd and keep an eye on Ellen. He noticed how her quiet confidence and easy conversation carried her around the room filled with fellow businesspeople. This was her scene. It wasn't Henry's, and it didn't seem to be Roxie's either. She trailed behind Ellen, fidgeting as she watched Sam scowl from the back of the room. It was clear that it was Sam, not the event, that made her anxious, and he wished he had the guts to tell Sam to lighten up and support his wife.

A woman with flowing blonde hair, wearing a white pantsuit and red stilettos, zigzagged through the tables to reach the podium at the front of the room. "We're about to begin the program," she announced. "Gather around, please."

People moved away from the food table and bar to get closer to the speaker. They filled available spots at the high tables and set down their drinks and plates. Henry and Sam remained alone in the back of the room.

He needed to move; Sam's foul mood draped over everything and everyone around him. He examined the buffet from a distance. The once-elegant food table was a mess, but some good pickings might still be available. His stomach grumbled. He hadn't eaten since breakfast.

"I'm getting some food. Want something?" Henry asked.

Sam snarled something in response but didn't move. Henry didn't ask him to repeat it.

Henry filled his stomach as the program carried on. He was dipping a giant shrimp into cocktail sauce when he heard Roxie's name, followed by Brand & Broadcast, and Sam Davis. Roxie walked up to the podium, and Henry stopped foraging to listen. He scanned the back of the room for Sam. He was gone. Henry's opinion of Sam ratcheted down another notch. What a jerk.

Roxie's acceptance speech was short and sweet, and Ellen was the first to congratulate her as she stepped out from behind the podium. Henry dropped his plate at the nearest open high-top and joined them up front.

"Congratulations." Henry extended his hand. "You deserve it, Roxie. If nothing else, for putting up with Sam," he teased. She didn't laugh or acknowledge him.

"Come on, let's go. Sam's waiting outside." Roxie walked away from her celebration. He and Ellen exchanged a glance of confusion.

The party was over. Henry did as he was instructed and followed the two women out of the room. Whatever.

CHAPTER 46

ELLEN

THE RIDE BACK TO SMYRNA WAS TENSE. SAM SAT in the front seat, glaring out the window. His message was clear to everyone: keep quiet. Roxie sat behind Henry's seat in the back, seething. Neither spoke nor acknowledged the other (or anyone else). Sam muttered something under his breath that Ellen couldn't quite hear. Was it *shouldn't have been there*? She tried to catch Henry's eye when he glanced over his shoulder to make a right turn, but he focused on driving.

"Drop us first," Sam said.

It made no sense, but who was Ellen to argue? Henry drove past the hotel's driveway to Sam's house. Sam wasn't civil enough tonight to say a proper goodnight, but dropping him first meant she'd have time with Henry. She swallowed her smile.

Henry pulled into Sam's driveway, and before he had shifted out of drive, Sam jumped out and hurried to the red front door, with Roxie trailing behind. Their moods matched the color of the door, and as Ellen had anticipated, there were no goodbyes.

Henry draped his arm over the front seat and twisted to look at Ellen as he backed out of the driveway. "Well, that was fun," he smirked. "What the hell was that all about?"

"All I can say is Sam did not want to be there. I can't imagine why. It was good for Brand & Broadcast, and for both of them. You'd think Sam would like the publicity." She tucked her hair behind her ear as she pondered.

"Yeah, you'd think so, but Sam isn't always what you think." Henry's voice sounded strange, a mix of fatigue and something else. She let it pass; he was probably just as tired as she was.

"Tell me about it. He's a chameleon for sure, one I can't seem to capture long enough to get this damn project finished." Ellen's voice faded. It was a telltale sign that she was overtired. But it was worth it. Last night, the music and the company energized her. A flush of heat traveled up from her chest to her cheeks.

Henry pulled the Escalade under the hotel's canopy and twisted around to look at Ellen. "Do you want to have a nightcap?" His eager face was hard to resist.

"As much as my heart says yes, the rest of me is saying no. I'm beat. Guess I'm paying for last night."

Henry's clear blue eyes lost their light, and his chin dropped, but if she gave in to the feeling enveloping her, she'd regret it tomorrow.

She opened the car door and waited for Henry to come around so he could take her hand and help her out of the vehicle. The warmth of his hand traveled up her arm, and she couldn't resist. She pulled him close into an embrace.

"Another time then," Henry whispered into her soft hair.

Her heart thumped in agreement as she walked away. Fearing she might change her mind, she didn't look back.

CHAPTER 47

SAM

IT WAS EARLY, BUT NOT TOO EARLY TO CALL Ellen. Instead of detouring to the hotel to eat breakfast or pick up Ellen, they went straight to the office. As far as Sam was concerned, she was already gone. There were too many things to do, and appeasing Ellen wasn't one of them. She failed to notice that others also demanded his attention. Next week, the investors in his latest TV creation were flying in from California, and he wasn't ready, not even close. He needed to show them something for their money.

Sam stared out the office window, waiting for Ellen to respond. A light dusting of snow had fallen late last night, making the view almost pretty. By noon, it would be just a memory. "What time's your flight?" he replied to Ellen's hello. He had one reason for his call, and it wasn't chit-chat.

"Give me a minute," Ellen said, "I just got out of the shower."

A minute was too long, but she was gone before he could protest. She better not be like his wife, who stretched a minute into ten.

"I'm back."

Quick, of course, the accountant in her.

"My flight leaves at one-twelve this afternoon. Henry and I should leave for the airport around eleven-thirty. That'll give us a couple more hours to work together," she plowed ahead.

"No can do. Got other things. Finish up that list I gave you yesterday at the hotel. Needs to be done fast if we're going to launch this thing in January." That should keep her out of his hair. He patted the few strands that remained.

"Ok Sam, that's fine. Thanks for the time you gave me. I really appreciate it, you know. These trips to Nashville are definitely worth it."

Ellen was something else, always the lady, even after all the shit he'd been dishing out to her. Nevertheless.

"If you say so, who am I to argue?" Sam looked at Henry, who was setting a fresh cup of coffee on Sam's desk. "One more thing, can you get a ride to the airport? Henry's going to be tied up." Sam waited for Ellen to respond.

Henry walked away instead of waiting for his morning orders. What's up with him?

"Not a problem," Ellen replied. "I never expected his services in the first place. But it's a nice perk."

Henry stopped at the door, looked back at Sam, and then walked out. He got the message: Henry worked for him, not Ellen.

"Don't hang up yet, Sam. There's one more thing."

With Ellen, there's always one more thing. This time, he was prepared for it, not like the other night.

"And that would be?" Sam was good at playing dumb.

"When can I expect that refund?" Ellen asked.

Bingo. He was glad Henry missed this part. God, she was annoying.

"I'm working on it, Ellen. You know I'm good for it," he lied. "Give me a few days to transfer funds so I can write a check."

"How about doing a wire transfer? It'll be faster. I'll send you my bank information."

She never let up. "Gotta go, Roxie's yelling for me. We're leaving for a shoot."

Sam clicked off and leaned down to scratch the soft brown ears of Little Pup sitting at his feet. The dog knew the drill and jumped onto Sam's lap to settle in for a day of computer work.

CHAPTER 48

ELLEN

ELLEN SAT IN HER HOME OFFICE, HAPPY TO BE staring at her own computer screen instead of Sam's. She had slipped into her home office intending to catch up on emails, but instead found herself daydreaming about Henry and the lost opportunity of their trip to the airport. Next time. Her heart thumped. Next time would likely be their last time together, and perhaps it was better that they had missed each other today. There wasn't any point in pursuing something that didn't make sense on so many levels. She leaned back in her chair.

The Uber ride and flight home were uneventful, and her ex surprised her by having dinner ready for her and the boys. Nothing fancy, but she didn't care. Pulling chicken nuggets and fries out of the oven wasn't gourmet, but it saved her the energy of preparing a proper meal, and she was too tired to go out. Her ex didn't ask to join them; he understood. He had his time with their sons, and she had hers. She told the boys she had a few emails to take care of and then she'd join them for some TV. She was all theirs this weekend. She had been away too much these last few months, and it was almost Christmas.

She sighed. Instead of working on Sam's list of things to do this morning, she had called Sterling for his perspective. It was an embarrassing conversation, but she needed to come clean to someone. Her inner judge wouldn't shut up, and she needed another voice to enter the debate. Who in their right mind sends ten thousand dollars to Sam after all of his other crap? How stupid could she be? Sterling's long pause confirmed her inner judge was right.

He never said those exact words, but he listened. Ellen confided in him completely: how Sam had made real progress this time and that the program was finished, polished, and ready for the world. The launch was scheduled for her return to Nashville in January, but she was still worried. Sterling asked probing questions: what if the program didn't launch or she didn't get her money back? The same questions swirled in her head, but Sterling's inquiries made them feel more tangible. Money or not, it was time to confront reality. One way or another, January would be it. She and Sam had run their course. She switched off her monitor.

"Mom, are you coming? *Jeopardy's starting.*" Kevin flipped off the overhead light and wrapped his arms around her shoulders. It was time for her boys.

"Ready to get trounced?" Ellen spun around and hugged him. She loved their friendly competition, and tonight she needed it. Jack and Ethan cracked up at their trash talk and tried to squeeze in an answer. But it was mostly a special time for Ellen and her middle son. Kevin didn't expect her to let him win, and she didn't. He was still an easy mark, but she knew it wouldn't be long before the tables turned.

She followed her son, newly cloaked in the pudge of pre-adolescence, to the family room. *Time flies whether you're having fun or not.*

PART THREE

Present Day

CHAPTER 49

LITTLE PUP

LITTLE PUP WAS WAITING, WAITING SINCE THE night skies were as dark as the dreaded cement kennel with the lights turned off. He whimpered and waited while Archie and Kramer sniffed the no-longer-yelling lady. He waited, too afraid to move from his perch on the fourth step of the forbidden staircase. He waited as the darkness faded and fuzzy morning light filtered through the windows. He waited for them to come home. The lady with the auburn hair and the man with threads for hair would know what to do.

From the fourth step, he saw the big black moving machine pull into the driveway. They were home, and he and his friends could go out for some relief. It had been a long night. He wiggled in place and waited. The doors opened, and a man and woman stepped out. It was not them, but he recognized them. He had snuggled on the woman's lap and remembered his ears being scratched by the man. Little Pup sat taller and stretched his neck, waiting for the two that he loved to get out.

The doors slammed, and Little Pup wiggled in place, waiting for Archie and Kramer to get out of their beds. They perked their ears, recognizing the sound, and stretched to wake, but didn't bother to move yet. Their masters were home, and soon the door would burst open with hugs and kisses for everyone. But they were mistaken.

Something was off. Little Pup felt it in his chest, squeezing tighter with fear. He felt it in his quaking paws, unable to carry him from his perch. Most of all, he felt it in his heart. It slammed shut like the doors in that cement prison. Something bad was coming.

CHAPTER 50

ELLEN

ELLEN ABSORBED THE SCENE BEFORE HER. TIME slowed as her senses heightened. She saw but didn't see. She heard but didn't hear. Yet she could feel. Color drained from her face, and deep red blotches bloomed on her cheeks. Her stomach tightened, and bitter bile rose in her throat. She swallowed, then swallowed again. She pushed down her internal horror to make room for the external chaos at her feet.

Diane's body hovered above the gunmetal gray tufts of an area rug designed to cushion the floor at the base of the staircase. Her plump figure angled to the left, and her neck, the connection between life and death, was kinked like a garden hose. Her right foot and ankle, caught in the railing halfway up the staircase, twisted her left knee, preventing her body from resting on the soft landing above. There was no blood.

She heard the dogs scrabbling around her ankles, begging to be picked up, to be reassured that everything was okay. Tiny paws clawed at her calves in confusion. She nudged them away and turned to Henry. His face matched the color of the dead woman's. Ellen searched for his hand for reassurance, support, or comfort; she wasn't sure which. All she knew was that she needed him.

Henry intertwined his fingers with hers, pulled her clutching hand to his chest, and spun her away from the scene. He held her closely, and she allowed his strong arms to shelter her. At another time, in another place, she would have resisted. She had imagined and dreamed of being held by him, afraid of how it would end. Henry was off-limits, regardless of the strength of their mutual attraction or her wish that they were geographically closer. There was so much more holding her back than age and distance. But now, in this moment, she was overwhelmed with brutal emotions, and it didn't matter.

This was not a daydream, and Ellen didn't have the luxury of logic and careful choices. Her jangled brain and twitching nerves chose for her, and she buried her head in Henry's chest. She felt the pounding of his heart, heard the whooshing of his blood, inhaled his scent. Unchecked emotions coursed through her body. She waited for good sense and sound reason to return.

With time, Henry's embrace cleared her brain and calmed her nerves. His strong arms grounded her, and she shifted beyond raw emotion back to her rational self. She started to pull away, and he held her tighter. His arms around her gave Ellen permission to slow down. There was no rush. Diane was not going anywhere.

CHAPTER 51

HENRY

HENRY HAD NEVER SEEN A DEAD BODY, NOT EVEN at a funeral after it was cleaned up and turned into a sleeping version of its former self. It wasn't Diane's contorted body that showed him she was dead; there was something else. A void filled the space where Diane once lived. A void that erased a woman, replacing her with an inanimate doll. Death carried a finality Henry hadn't expected. He was young and foolish. How could he not understand death? And, in this innocence, how could he claim to know life?

He clung to Ellen for ballast and thought of his father. As a child, his father explained that new word to him and how using cement blocks as a weight gave the truck more traction during the rare Nashville snowstorm. Now, Ellen was his ballast and would help tether the emotional balloon threatening to float him away.

As he settled, accusing whispers berated him. How dare he imagine someone like Ellen in his life? She deserved a man, not a child. He pulled her closer so she could rely on him, keeping her oblivious to his neediness, trying to be the strong man his father was. Someday, the whispers said. He understood. Sometimes, age did make a difference.

Still, he clung to Ellen; he had no choice. He needed more time to feel his physicality, to get his feet on the ground, to rein in his emotions. He needed to pack away his childish thoughts and help, not hinder, whatever was next. He held her tighter, and she relaxed into his arms. Time was immaterial. Whatever was next could wait.

CHAPTER 52

ELLEN

THE SLAM OF A CAR DOOR SEPARATED THEM. Ellen stepped back to see Henry's face. His confusion matched hers. Together, they turned to the open door and peered out. A white sedan was parked behind the Escalade, and a tall man approached them. He was buttoning his tailored suit, and his slim waist and broad shoulders suggested that he worked out regularly. Even from a distance, he seemed out of place in Nashville. Ellen wondered if his car was a rental.

"Who are you?" the stranger snarled. "What are you doing here?"

No introductions, no soft-pedaling. A man on a mission. Ellen stepped forward.

"Ellen Hartmann. I work with Sam. And you would be?" She ignored his abrupt greeting and tried to be a little more welcoming. It wasn't easy.

"I'm Diane's son. Where is she? Where's my mother?" The stranger glared at them.

"She told me you were coming," Henry stammered, then turned to Ellen. "I forgot to tell you. Diane said he was coming when I called her last night."

"Damn right I'm here," the unknown man said. "Unlike Sam, I care about my mother."

The exchange was brief but long enough for Ellen to catch her breath before the man had to face his new reality. Life as he knew it was over. His mother was dead. She remembered the pain of being shoved up life's ladder without the foundation of parents. She wanted to slow him down and prepare him for the emptiness that, after ten years, she was only beginning to accept herself.

"Diane's your mother? I didn't know Sam had a brother. It was never mentioned." Ellen's mind was jumbled as her words tumbled out. Should Ellen believe him?

Henry said nothing, but he squeezed his hand as if to confirm what the man was saying. "You must be Sam's brother, David, from LA," Henry's words were quiet and tentative.

"Half-brother. We try to ignore the fact. Now, where's my mother?" David pushed into the foyer.

"Wait!" Ellen cried out, but her movements were trancelike and too slow to stop him. She couldn't have softened the blow anyway, but she would've liked the chance.

"No! No! No!" David's tortured scream tore at Ellen's soul. He shook his head violently and clutched his throat. "Oh my god, oh my god," he bawled. He clutched his stomach, collapsed on the gray rug, and stared up into her dead face.

"No, no, no, this is all wrong." He knelt at the bottom of the staircase and gently removed his mother's face from where it was pinned to the railing. The movement unloosed her wedged ankle, and Diane and her son slid down the final steps of the deadly staircase onto the gray rug. Two bodies lay in a heap, one dead, the other dying with grief.

"Oh, Mom. What did you do?" David's muscular torso covered her twisted body, and his deep-throated sobs echoed off the walls. Ellen cowered in anguish, and Henry clutched her hand tighter. Archie, Kramer, and Little Pup nosed into the heap of emotion.

"Goddamn dogs!" He swatted at them like annoying gnats. "You did this to her." The dogs nosed deeper, not understanding.

"She hated you." He pushed them away. "But Sam never cared; what Sam wanted, Sam got. It was always about Sam." David wept.

Ellen grabbed Archie and Kramer under her arms, carried them to the kitchen pantry, and closed the door. She ignored the frantic scratching; ruined woodwork was the least of her worries. Little Pup followed her to the pantry and back to the front hall. He sat and watched from a distance. She let him be.

"Mom, mom." David's words grew quieter, softer. "Why didn't you listen to me? I told you not to go."

Ellen stepped closer to hear. Henry stayed back.

Sam never cared, but I did; I always did. When you called last night, you knew I'd come—that I'd always be here for you. I love you, Mommy." His voice faded into a whisper.

Ellen's gut clenched when he said Mommy. David would always be Diane's little boy, just as her three would always be her. She should've tried harder to stop him; no son should have to face a scene like this. But she hadn't, and now was not the time to interrupt or comfort him. David needed time to release his emotions, just as Henry and Ellen's embrace had released theirs. There would be plenty of time later to piece together the events of the last twenty-four hours.

CHAPTER 53

KATIE

IT WAS SEVEN IN THE MORNING, AND KATIE was already at the office. A freshly brewed cup of coffee warmed her hands as she stared out the bank of windows in Hartmann and Associates' reception area. She liked to arrive early, settle in, and prepare for the day. January mornings like this, with sea smoke lifting from the harbor, the rising sun warming the frigid air, and its brilliant rays bouncing off the aluminum masts of the marina sailboats, were her favorite. From her seaside window, it was easy to forget that this magical scene occurred only when outside temperatures plummeted. But she still felt the tingling of her frozen cheeks and the metallic stiffness of her fingers on the steering wheel from this morning's drive. She inhaled the fragrant coffee fumes. January, the lull before the storm. Tax season was looming.

"Another early riser, I see. We're two of a kind."

Katie winced at the sound of Michael's voice. Didn't he see she was enjoying her time alone? She had enough of him throughout the day, with his probing and prying into matters that didn't concern him. Didn't he realize she didn't like him?

"Good morning, Michael." Katie didn't move. She wouldn't give up this precious moment for anyone, especially not him. She sipped her coffee.

"Ellen gone again?" Michael asked.

Oblivious. Always oblivious. Michael was so self-absorbed that he couldn't even recognize a brush-off. She turned around and faced him.

"Only for a few days, and mostly over the weekend. She'll be back in the office on Monday." She turned back to the window and took another sip of her coffee.

"I've heard that before." His snicker was uncalled for. Katie refused to acknowledge it; she was better than that.

"Don't you ever get tired of covering for her? She's not here much, and when she is, she's unavailable." Michael's voice grew louder and more grating as he approached her at the window. Katie side-stepped to her left, distancing herself from the irritating bastard.

"She's had a lot on her plate. Trust me, Ellen's here when we need her. She never does anything half-assed." Katie's annoyance slipped into her speech. She'd have to clean it up before clients arrived.

"If you say so."

Katie didn't respond. She said what she felt; there was no need to say anything more. He walked away, and she heard the door to the kitchen open. Michael finally got the hint.

CHAPTER 54

JULIE

BY THE END OF THE DAY, JULIE'S FEBRUARY calendar was filling up with meetings. Each year, the same overzealous clients made their tax season appointments as soon as the new year arrived. These were the organized ones, the ones who planned ahead, the ones who set up a *Tax Return* folder amid late December holiday preparations to collect the year-end statements and tax documents arriving in January. These were the perpetually prepared. Like Ellen, they were efficient and effective with systems that kept them on track. Unlike Julie. Her home mail piled up in stacks that were sorted through only when a deadline loomed that could no longer be ignored. Oh well, to each their own. Whatever floats your boat.

January was an accountant's time to prepare for the next ten weeks before the pace of work shifted from a steady drip to a rushing torrent of tax returns. It reminded Julie of late spring in the potato fields of Maine's Aroostook County, where she grew up. It was a slower time when fields were readied for planting, anticipating more work in the future. Quality preparation and planting ensured a successful crop.

January at Hartmann and Associates was a time for mental and physical preparation. Physical meant resurrecting the internal structure for a tax return's journey from start to finish with as few hiccups as possible. It also meant getting your body in shape for long hours of sitting. Julie had returned to the gym in the dark of the morning after New Year's Day. She had a month to transform exercise, at first an unsavory chore, into a habit, and then, as overtime hours accumulated, a lifesaver. Without her morning workout, tax season was unbearable.

Mental preparation was easier, and she loved having a singular goal that brushed aside life's distractions. Except for exercise, this was not a time to take up new hobbies, make new friends, or start a new relationship. This was a time to keep on keeping on. *Lache pas las patate.* Her French-Canadian roots said it best. *Don't drop the potato.* Unless an activity fell into the categories of eat, sleep, or work, it would have to wait.

"Ellen on line one." Katie's announcement interrupted Julie's thoughts.

She pressed the button on her phone to connect. "Ellen, how are things in Nashville? Didn't think I'd hear from you on this trip. I knew it was going to be a short one. Everything's fine here. Ready for you to return on Monday and lead the charge." Julie supported Ellen's decision to end things with Sam. She needed her back.

"God...I don't know where to start." Ellen's voice was soft, and her words were hesitant.

Things must be bad; soft and hesitant were not her style. Julie took a deep breath to process what was happening and to give Ellen time to choose her words, but her impatience got the best of her. "Ellen, what? You're scaring me."

"It's scaring me too," Ellen murmured.

Julie slowed down and listened. This sounded serious.

"We found Sam's mother, Diane, dead. This morning. Henry and me. It was awful." Ellen's voice crackled with emotion.

"Wait—what? What the fuck? Sam's mother is dead? Why did you and Henry find her? Where the hell was Sam?" Julie's mind raced. Leave it to Sam not to come through even at a time like this. She never met Sam in person, but she hated him just the same. He'd been twisting Ellen into knots too long.

"That's just it. We don't know where he is, and he's not answering his phone. He's not here, and his half-brother showed up out of nowhere. It was weird. There's something about him I don't trust. Something feels off about this whole thing."

Ellen sounded bewildered. Take-charge Ellen was gone. Julie had lots of questions, but she waited. Ellen needed Julie's support, not her questions. She was struggling, and her missing take-charge self needed to be replaced with take-charge Julie.

"What do you need me to do? How can I help?" Julie could learn the details later. Right now, she needed to nudge Ellen, refocus her, and bring her back to herself to make some decisions. Her question was self-serving, but she wanted Ellen back now, not later.

"Do? I have no idea. Keep doing what you always do. Hold down the fort. I can't leave. I have to help sort things out." Ellen started to babble. "I know I won't be back on Monday. Other than that, I can't say for sure. Please take over. I'll keep you updated."

"Got it." Julie gulped. She was tired, had been in charge for the last three months, and she wanted—no, needed—to get back to her work. She didn't enjoy being a leader; she was a supporter. She loved working for Ellen, but she also loved her own work and didn't want to leave her clients behind. But now was not the time to whine. She pulled up her big girl panties.

"I'll tell the staff you'll be gone another week. They rely on your leadership, but we can do this. We've got your back." Julie hoped she was right. The staff felt abandoned because of Ellen's project and was eager for tax season to start when she'd be one of them again. Now they had to wait. "Let me know if things change."

Julie envisioned Ellen tucking her hair behind her ear, a habit of hers when thoughts wouldn't come fast enough.

"What?' Ellen stuttered. "Right. Okay. I'll keep you informed."

Julie wished she had the words to convince her to let go of Nashville, Sam, and whatever was happening now, once and for all. This was not Ellen's problem. It never was, but that didn't mean Ellen wouldn't do everything she could to help whoever's problem it might be.

"Thanks, Julie. I appreciate you and all you do."

"Right." At that moment, it was all she could think of saying, and Ellen hung up before Julie could come up with anything better.

CHAPTER 55

MICHAEL

MICHAEL STOOD UNNOTICED OUTSIDE JULIE'S door. The call ended, and he moved into the doorway as Julie raked the fingers of both hands through her dark corkscrew curls. She clasped her hands behind her head and massaged the base of her skull. Somehow, her face had collapsed into itself; it was lifeless, and her eyes had lost their sparkle. This wasn't the Julie he knew, and he doubted others in the office knew it either. Was it anger, frustration, or fear coursing through her?

"Ellen's gone again, isn't she." It was a statement, not a question. He sat down across the desk from her.

Julie's hands fell into her lap, and she lowered her head and sighed. Then it was over, and she slipped back into her feisty, good-natured self, but this time without much energy, and he could tell there wasn't much fight in her. It was the perfect time to advance his agenda. He waited for her to lead the conversation.

"She's been held up in Nashville. Not coming back for a while, and she wants me to carry on without her," Julie explained.

"Not much to do this time of year anyway, is there?" Michael feigned innocence. Julie needed to see for herself what she'd be carrying for Ellen. If he pointed it out to her, she'd fight against the reality of it.

"Not much?" She planted both elbows on her desk. Her fight was back. "You've got to be kidding me."

He leaned closer but kept his mouth shut.

"We need to get client organizers in the mail. They should have been ready by the time Ellen left, and now they're late. I'll have to write this year's letter so they can go out next week." She rubbed her eyes. "Ellen's the accountant with the English degree. Not me. Not a letter of mine goes out without Ellen rewriting it. An accounting degree doesn't give you many writing skills."

She groaned, then continued. "And what about staff training and the walk-through? You may be the only new staff person, but that doesn't mean the rest of us don't need a refresher. Moving returns through this office doesn't happen on its own. In the meantime, all my work comes to a crashing halt unless I start overtime now, which I refuse to do."

Michael nodded. He didn't know what a walk-through was, but now was not the time to ask. He'd let her keep sputtering until she ran out of steam.

"I'm so sick of doing this alone. It's not what I signed up for." Julie leaned back in her chair and sighed. It was the opportunity Michael was waiting for.

"Wow, I didn't know there was so much to do. In my little firm, I didn't worry about any of that preparation. Life was much simpler with two or three of us." He planted a tiny seed. "I guess Hartmann and Associates is more complex. Makes me wonder if it's worth it."

Julie's smile told Michael that this rare side of Julie was slipping under cover again. But if he saw it once, he could find it again.

"Don't mind me, I'm just blowing off steam." Julie brushed her long hair away from her face and smiled.

He didn't argue or debate. Today was about greasing the wheels with a little bit of commiseration.

"Ellen's expecting an awful lot of you." He paused to let it sink in. "I can help, you know. I'm a decent writer. If you show me last year's letter, I'm sure I can come up with one just as good. You don't have to do this alone. I'm here. We can work together."

Michael dropped another seed. He would let it germinate in Julie's subconscious. Ellen was making this far too easy for him. He shortened his timeline. It wouldn't take long now.

CHAPTER 56

ELLEN

ELLEN AND HENRY WAITED IN THE LIVING ROOM while David finished with the coroner and the police. She held Henry's hand, and no one questioned the couple watching in the background. Diane's son, Sam's half-brother, was in charge. From the outset, he made it quite clear that as next of kin, this was his show. Ellen was relieved to have the take-charge businessman step in. After David explained to the police that he was Diane's son, that she and Henry were not family members, and that all three had arrived and discovered the body simultaneously, the officers weren't particularly interested in what Henry and Ellen had to offer. David's little white lie was close enough to the truth, and the three or four minutes that Henry and she were alone with the body hardly counted. Or so Ellen told herself.

But why did he ask them to keep quiet about Sam's disappearance? Something was off. David told the police that his half-brother was out of town on business and that his mother had asked him to visit while he was gone. It made perfect sense to the police. But not to Ellen. Had Sam planned his disappearance? If so, why hadn't he cancelled her trip, and why did Diane wait to call David last night? What did she say that made David drop everything to come running? Asking too many questions now would put him off. Ellen would have to earn David's trust. He was her one link to finding out the truth.

David closed the front door after watching the coroner's van pull away with his mother's body. Ignoring Henry and Ellen, he trudged to the living room and collapsed onto the overstuffed couch. Pillows tumbled around him, and he tossed them to the floor. Little Pup quivered on his bed, too frightened to move.

Ellen and Henry separated hands and sat down, Ellen in an armchair and Henry on its matching ottoman. They both avoided Diane's favorite chair. David might not have known which one it was, but they did. Ellen waited for David to speak. It took him a while.

"The coroner said preliminary cause of death was a fall. He'll have to do an autopsy because it was an unattended death, but he didn't see anything inconsistent with an unfortunate accident." David leaned his head back as if searching the ceiling for answers. Ellen was glad he didn't blame the dogs.

"I'm so sorry David." Ellen didn't say anything more. She knew less was better at times like this and that she'd learn much more by listening than by asking questions.

"I knew something was wrong when she called last night." He covered his face with his well-manicured hands and wiped his brow. "I call her on Sunday nights—it was our thing—every Sunday night. She'd tell me about the week's happenings, and those damn dogs and Sam." David stared at the floor, shaking his head.

"I'm sure she loved hearing from you," Ellen said. Her mind fast-forwarded to her three sons, and she hoped she'd be fortunate enough to receive weekly calls unless she hit the jackpot and they were living nearby.

"But it was Wednesday, not Sunday, and she was upset," David continued. "Sam was always gone during the day, occasionally at night, but never overnight. I can thank him for that much. At least she never woke up to an empty house." He shook his head as if trying to dislodge their worrisome conversation. "She was frantic last night; he hadn't come home and wasn't answering her calls. I told her to get some sleep, that I'd see her in the morning. That calmed her down, and I thought she'd go to bed and wait for me to get here."

David glanced up at the ceiling, then rubbed the back of his neck. Ellen waited for him to speak again.

"But now I wonder. She wasn't wearing her nightclothes. Either she never made it to bed or got up early." He wiped his eyes. "Getting up early wasn't her style."

"I noticed that too." Ellen thought it was time to slip in a question. "Did the coroner have a time of death?"

"He didn't say, except that it had been a few hours. She was a night owl, though. Maybe she stayed up too late and tripped on her way up to bed. Oh God, why wasn't Sam here?"

David turned to Ellen as though she had the answer. Now was her opportunity.

"That's a question only Sam can answer," she said. "We should try to call him again." Ellen wanted David to think of the three of them as a team. She needed Sam answer his questions and hers.

"I already tried; his phone is still switched off." Henry entered the exchange. "Same with Roxie's."

"I wonder if there's a clue at the office. Do you think we should head over there and see if we can find something to point us to where he might be?" Ellen wanted David to believe that rummaging through Sam's office was his idea, not hers. "I'm pretty good around a computer. Maybe there's a hint in his email or something."

David stared at her. His face was a mask of conflicting emotions.

What was he thinking? Would he trust this woman he didn't know, someone who worked with Sam, his half-brother whom he didn't seem to like, much less trust? Would he let Ellen do what she did best? Could Ellen uncover the answers about Sam, his disappearance, and Diane's death?

"Okay," David croaked. "I'll follow you."

CHAPTER 57

HENRY

HENRY WAITED FOR THE RED LIGHT TO CHANGE and studied David in his rear-view mirror. He looked nothing like Sam. Or Diane, for that matter. But something about his demeanor reminded him of his half-brother, something secretive and withholding. Was Diane the common link that turned her sons into men to be wary of? Was Diane a pleasant, innocent bystander, or did she call David in a panic last night because she knew more than she let on? The man in the mirror nodded his head up and down and scowled. Was that Henry's answer?

Ellen rested her hand on top of Henry's on the console and squeezed it. "Well, I'm having a good time. How about you?"

Henry was confused, but when he saw her smile, he understood. Her penchant for black humor had surfaced. "Oh, for sure. After our night out the last time you were here, I thought you'd like some excitement. Did I deliver or what?"

"That you did, young man, that you did," she laughed.

Henry flinched at her choice of words. He didn't need a reminder of their age difference; Diane's lifeless body had taken care of that.

"I'm so glad you were with me." Ellen squeezed Henry's hand tighter. "I would've lost it without you, and David would've written me off as irrelevant."

Henry glanced at his rear-view mirror again. David's car was still tailing them. "I'm surprised he's coming with us to the office."

"Well, if he wants to keep the police out of this, he needs someone like you to let him in the office. You're the important link here, Henry, not me." Ellen had a way of making Henry feel more like a man, helping him see himself as more than just a chauffeur or a struggling musician.

"I can get you guys into the office, but without some direction, I'm not sure I'll be much help." Henry slid his hand out from under Ellen's to take a sharp right turn.

"There's plenty you can help with," she said. "For starters, it would be best if the office were empty. Can you call and send everyone home for the day? Make up some excuse?"

"I doubt there's anyone there, but I'll call and see if anyone picks up." Henry touched the phone icon on the SUV's media screen. "We're all at Sam's beck and call: freelancers. He told everyone, except me, to stay home for the rest of the week because he'd be devoting all his time to you."

Now that he said it out loud, Sam's intentions sounded suspicious. He never cleared his schedule for anyone. At the time, Henry believed what Sam said, or at least he wanted to believe. He knew how important this visit was to Ellen, that it might be her last, and Henry didn't want to lose her. But now he wasn't sure. Had Sam tricked them again?

Henry placed the call and hung up after the eighth ring, shaking his head. His back-and-forth nod cleared his cloudy thoughts and informed Ellen that the office was empty. Now was the time to reveal the truth.

Sam was a liar, and wishing otherwise was a fool's errand.

CHAPTER 58

DAVID

DAVID FOLLOWED THE BLACK ESCALADE INTO the parking lot of a boxy industrial-style building. His breath was shallow, his hands ached from gripping the steering wheel, and his ass felt like he had bench-pressed five hundred pounds. He needed to pull himself together. He pictured his wife and took a deep breath. He thought of his daughters and smiled. He couldn't focus on the welcoming door of their family home, but he could concentrate on the building in front of him. This was the routine his wife demanded of him after he ruined too many evenings bringing his workday tension home.

The fake bricks covering the building's front wall indicated that someone had attempted to make it seem more impressive than it really was. Across its brick facade were five long sidelights flanking five metal doors arranged like little soldiers. The sidelights were the developer's attempt at design. It didn't succeed. It remained a warehouse among other warehouses dotting a sprawling industrial park. It was precisely what he would've expected from Sam.

Henry's giant SUV dwarfed David's rental car as he pulled into an adjacent parking spot in front of the door with *Brand & Broadcast* stenciled on its sidelight. Sam was either trying to impress, or maybe he planned to stay. It was two years since Sam moved their mother from Vegas to Nashville for what David thought would be a temporary stop. Why his younger brother returned to Nashville was a mystery. David never pretended to understand anything about Sam. Or his mother. When it came to Sam, nothing ever made sense.

David waited for Henry to unlock the door, finally acknowledging that Henry's office key suggested he was close to Sam's daily life, making him someone valuable to know.

"No one's here today. I called ahead to be sure." Henry fumbled with the key. "Sam told the others to take the rest of the week off so he could work with Ellen."

Work with Ellen. Others. What was Sam up to? David followed Ellen through the open door and said nothing.

Henry flipped on the light switch to the right of the door, illuminating the windowless space. David scanned the area and noticed that the inside mirrored the outside. Someone was trying to make a silk purse from a sow's ear. The furniture in the makeshift reception area was flimsy, Walmart-quality paperboard that looked good on day one but gradually collapsed to reveal the truth. Typical Sam.

"Where do you want to start?" Ellen was looking at David for a response. She asked him as if he had a clue. He didn't.

David rubbed his temples and slicked back his thick waves. This morning's gel was starting to dissipate, and he could feel his hair breaking free. His mother loved his wild, unruly hair, but it didn't work in the business world. He'd give anything to hear her complain about the uptight look she hated. He gulped and pictured his daughters again.

"Let's slow down a minute." David's exhale was slow and exaggerated. "My brain is still fried from this morning, and honestly, I never did comprehend who you two are and what you have to do with my brother."

Ellen sat down in one of the uncomfortable chairs. David did the same. Henry continued to stand at a distance.

"Totally understandable," Ellen's voice was kind. "It was one hell of a morning. Let me give you the quick answer. This is Henry Allard, actor, musician, and Sam's driver."

Sam's driver. Of course, Sam wouldn't have a driver's license.

"And I'm Ellen Hartmann from Maine. Sam's been helping me launch an internet program about money."

"You're Sam's client? Interesting." Another long sigh escaped David's tight chest. "But can you help? How much do you know about Sam's business?" He didn't want to waste time with Ellen if she had nothing to offer. On the other hand, did he really want to get more involved in Sam's life? This might be an opportune moment to wash his hands of Sam forever.

"I've worked with him for a while, too long if you ask me." She looked at Henry. "But it's long enough to know what his business is about." She tucked her hair behind her ear.

"More importantly, I know the inside of a lot of businesses. I'm a CPA. It's kind of what I do."

Ellen piqued David's interest. Like it or not, he was stuck in the middle of Sam's mess, and she might be able to help. And what was going on between Henry and her? There was something he couldn't quite put his finger on.

Ellen interrupted his thoughts by clapping her hands on her knees and standing up. "But you're probably starving; I know I am. How about we put this on hold and get something to eat? I'll fill in the gaps over food."

An intestinal grumble filled the small space. David grabbed his stomach. "I guess you know what you're talking about. My stomach agrees. Who am I to argue?"

He stood up and walked to the door. "Let's go," he said, looking over his shoulder. "Henry, you drive. Ellen, sit in the back seat with me and start talking. I'm all ears."

David left the building.

CHAPTER 59

ELLEN

AFTER DINNER AT SAM'S FAVORITE LONGHORN Restaurant, David returned to the house. He hadn't been impressed with his meal, felt tired, and would see them tomorrow. Ellen and Henry headed back to the office alone to do some sleuthing. Now, after two hours hunched over Sam's computer, Ellen closed her eyes and savored the moment. Henry's strong fingers kneaded her tight shoulders, knowing exactly what she needed. Lost in computer land, she didn't see or hear Henry enter the room, or she would have resisted. She should have. But she didn't. Nothing was ordinary about the day, and today's events muted the eternal *shoulds* that plagued every step she took or didn't take.

"Thanks. I needed that." She resisted the urge to groan with pleasure.

"Thought you might. You haven't looked up since we got here."

Ellen shrugged Henry's hands off her shoulders and

turned around. Enough was enough. She was tired, and her defenses were weak. She motioned for Henry to sit next to her in the chair she used when Sam scrolled through photos for her website. Sitting next to Henry was much more pleasant.

Ellen tucked her feet under her and leaned away from Henry. She didn't trust herself to be too close to him. "You've been busy yourself. Did you find anything interesting?"

"Not really," Henry said. "Not much paper in this place. Everything is digital. However, I went through all the paper files I could find. There was nothing I saw that we'd want to keep from David."

They hadn't compared notes earlier, but something in Henry's words confirmed that he was wary of David just like she was.

"I don't know why, but I'm having a hard time trusting David." Ellen sighed, leaned her elbow on the arm of the chair, and rested her chin in her hand. "He pumped us for information but didn't reciprocate. It feels like he's holding something back, something he's not telling us."

Henry's face flushed. This was not the reaction she expected. Ellen untucked her feet, set them on the floor, and searched Henry's eyes.

"What? What's going on?" she asked.

"There's something I need to tell you." Henry's voice was soft and hesitant. "Something I should have said a long time ago, but I could never find the right time. I'm sorry. I hope you'll forgive me." Henry dropped his head and placed his hands over his eyes. A split second later, he straightened his spine and locked eyes with her.

Ellen was confused. This was not the Henry she knew. What could cause Henry this much distress? But he was a man on a mission, and she didn't interrupt.

"Sam's a liar. I heard him lie to you over and over. Little white lies to get out of tough spots, but lies just the same."

She felt fear drain the color from her face and reached for Henry's hands. It had been a tough day for both of them, and no matter what he was about to tell her, they both deserved some compassion.

CHAPTER 60

JULIE

JULIE RUBBED HER EYES, TURNED FROM HER computer screen, and stared at the boats in the nearby marina. All of her was tired and bored. Reviewing tax season's internal checklists, procedures, and letter templates drained her. How Ellen tolerated all of this behind-the-scenes crap was beyond her. But a client's financial mess, one she could dig into and unravel to set right, was right up Julie's alley, leaving her energized and ready for more.

Stuck in Nashville, Ellen had asked Julie to prepare the office for the approaching tax season. Julie owed her that much. Without Ellen, she would have no accounting career, and she would've been tied forever to the dishonesty of her first boss. But Ellen, intuitive Ellen, saw beyond that. Julie's commitment to clients was all that mattered, and she hired her on the spot. Others would have hesitated and taken Julie only as a last resort. Filling in for Ellen was the least she could do, but it still annoyed her, and she hoped Ellen would return before her irritation showed.

"Do you have a minute?" Michael's distinctive voice filled her office. Men's voices were few and far between at Hartmann and Associates.

"Of course." Julie turned away from the window and brushed her dark curls from her shoulders. "What do you have?"

"Katie gave me a copy of last year's letter to the clients, the one that goes out with the tax organizers. I thought you could use some help with it. See what you think." Michael slid the letter across the desk and sat down across from her.

"Geez, thanks. I was saving the good stuff for tomorrow," she laughed. "Not that I'm complaining. Glad you tackled it. I did nothing but regulatory checklists and all that other boring shit today." She picked up the first page and began to read.

"We don't have to do it right now—plenty of time tomorrow." Michael folded his arms on her desk and locked eyes with her. "I was hoping you'd join me for a drink at J's. In another month, we won't have any time."

Julie blinked. She had nothing planned for the evening, and with the winter's late-afternoon sunset, it felt like bedtime. She needed something or someone to fill the long hours ahead. Eight o'clock bedtime was not an option.

"Okay, I'm in." Julie twisted her hair around her index finger and smiled. "I could use a beer."

"Meet me at the front desk in five minutes?" Michael unfolded his tall body from Julie's chair, flashed a toothy smile, and walked out.

Julie shuffled the papers on her desk into a semblance of order and placed the draft letter on top of the pile for her approval first thing in the morning. As she circled around her desk to leave, the last sentence of Michael's letter caught her eye: *If you are a new client or usually work with Ellen, please get in touch with Michael Prescott at our office. You will be working with him this year.*

Tomorrow, she'd read the whole letter to make sense of it. Right now, she needed a drink.

CHAPTER 61

BOBBY

BOBBY'S TRUCK RUMBLED DOWN THE WOODEN planks of Portland Pier. He was early tonight in hopes of catching Julie. As much as he tried to ignore it, he missed her. He missed their sleuthing, the beers at J's, and the casual conversations they'd shared over all the years he'd been emptying her waste basket. Lately, they'd hardly managed to say hello, and when they did, Michael came sniffing around to interrupt any laughs they might have had.

He pulled into one of the five parking spots labeled Hartmann and Associates. Parking spaces on the pier were scarce, and the office was fortunate to have these few. It was beyond him how a distracted client hadn't ended up in the water when they missed their brakes or accidentally put their car in drive instead of reverse. A six-inch-high board separated the parking spot from the water, and it wouldn't take much force to break through it. But, avoiding the pier's frigid wind tunnel this time of year made nearby, if somewhat sketchy, parking spaces well worth it.

Satisfied that his truck was in park and safe to vacate, he glanced in the rearview mirror and saw Julie stepping out of the front door of 50 Portland Pier. Her long, dark hair blew across her face, and she brushed it away as she looked down the pier towards J's. Bobby grinned. Maybe they could grab a beer or supper together. He put his hand on the truck's door handle but stopped when Julie looked over her shoulder and laughed.

With perfect white teeth and a tall, flawless body, Michael followed Julie out the door. He was laughing too and placed his hand on her shoulder to guide her down the pier. Damn. It didn't take a rocket scientist to know where they were headed. Bobby deep-sixed his plans for the night and watched the two joking their way down the pier. They were oblivious to anything but each other.

Michael's hand lingered on Julie's shoulder and ignited a slow boil in Bobby's gut. He didn't like it. He didn't like any of it. And he didn't trust Michael. But right now, he couldn't trust himself either. The familiarity, the possessiveness of Michael's touch, filled Bobby with rage. Who the hell did he think he was? And why didn't Julie tell the guy to buzz off?

CHAPTER 62

KATIE

IT WAS ANOTHER ICY MORNING DESPITE THE sun's sparkling rays, and Katie prepared for the day by enjoying the view from the office's bank of windows. In a few weeks, she wouldn't have this luxury and would race staff and clients to be the first in the office. Julie's car rumbled down the pier and pulled into the garage. Katie moved to her desk. This conversation couldn't wait, and since Michael was likely to be late as usual, now was the perfect time. She took a deep breath to settle her nerves. No one ever accused her of being high-strung, but Michael didn't even need to be in the room for her nerves to start pinging.

"Julie, do you have a minute? I need to talk to you." She hated to grab her as soon as she walked in the door, but Julie could get lost in her work, and Katie needed her full attention.

"Give me a sec to get rid of my coat. Damn, it's cold out there." Julie hung her puffer jacket in the closet and rubbed her hands together.

She rested her right elbow on the cherry counter surrounding Katie's desk and cupped her chin in her hand. "Whatcha got for me? Good news, I hope. When's Ellen back?"

"No, nothing like that." Katie stood up and slammed Michael's letter down in front of Julie. "It's this!"

"Relax. It can't be that bad." Julie recognized the paper. "Oh, Michael's letter. I see he gave you a copy, too. I didn't have time to read it last night, but I did catch that last paragraph. What'd you think?"

"What do I think?" Katie was fuming, and her nerves were vibrating at full speed. "I don't like it; I don't like it at all. Who does he think he is, moving in on Ellen's clients like that?"

"Whoa, slow down! It's not that big a deal. This is why he's here." Julie stepped back from the counter.

"Not a big deal? I doubt she'll see it that way." Katie sat down and pushed her chair back to give them both some space. She wanted to slam Michael, not Julie.

"Chill. It's a draft. I'll check it out with Ellen." Julie handed the letter back to Katie.

"What's there to check about? She won't send that out to clients. Why would she?" Katie wanted to pop out of her chair.

"Because that's what she hired Michael to do, to take some of the client load off both of us and to bring in new clients." Julie's voice was quiet and rational, unlike Katie's.

"Right, new clients. I haven't seen even one." Sarcasm dripped from Katie.

"It takes time. Trust me, I know from experience."

"Okay, but now you know how I feel about it. And about Michael. I do not like or trust him. Not even a little bit." Katie was riled up. She hated the effect that Michael had on her.

"I hear you. But until his clients start coming in, the least he can do is help with Ellen's." Julie's voice remained cool, calm, and collected. "I'll settle this by the end of the day. Just get the rest of the client packets ready to be mailed, and I promise I'll have a letter with Ellen's approval ready to go."

The elevator dinged. Someone was coming, and they both stopped talking. Katie smoothed her facial features into her professional receptionist look. It was Michael.

"If we don't hear from Ellen by late afternoon, I'll give her a call." Julie wrapped up the conversation. "You should have an answer tonight." She ignored Michael's arrival and headed back to her office.

Michael watched her walk away, but inserted himself into the scene and asked louder than necessary, "Nothing from Ellen again? What a surprise."

Julie kept walking.

Katie wanted to slug him. Instead, she turned to her computer screen and pretended to be working.

CHAPTER 63

JULIE

JULIE GLANCED AT THE TIME IN THE LOWER right corner of her monitor. It was 3:34, and still no call from Ellen. Last Friday, Ellen called to say she wouldn't be returning for a while; since then, there had been nothing but radio silence. Three days later, there was still no update, and now it was time to make good on her promise to Katie. She swiveled her chair to look out the window, hoping the swaying masts of the nearby marina would calm her. She punched in her boss's number, and Ellen picked up just before the call went to voicemail.

"Julie, I'm sorry I haven't called. God, what a mess. Still no Sam or Roxie, and his brother David, has been useless. Henry and I are caught in the middle." Ellen's sigh was weak and tired.

Ellen's fatigue showed in her voice first, and grilling her would add to it, but Julie had to ask. "Caught in the middle of what?"

"Everything. Sam's projects, his employees, even the dogs. David might as well not be here; he's just in the way." Ellen's frustration resonated through the phone.

"But why? Why is this even your business to begin with? Just because you were in the wrong place at the wrong time, not to mention working with the wrong person, doesn't make it your problem. You owe them nothing. What makes you think you do?" Julie didn't wait for Ellen's response; she already knew the answer. This is what Ellen did. She never left anyone stranded, even if it came at her own expense.

"There's no one else here to help. And, unfortunately, this is what I do. You, of all people, know that. You'd do the same." Ellen confirmed Julie's thoughts.

"Touché. But we need you, too. We miss you and want you to take charge of tax season like always." Even Julie herself thought this was a shitty excuse, but why did taxes take priority over everything else?

"I know, but you've got this, Julie. I know you hate the mundane, behind-the-scenes stuff, but I need you to fill in for me. You know the drill, and I have total faith in your judgment."

"Thanks for that. But..." Ellen interrupted Julie before she could finish.

"I don't feel comfortable leaving yet." Ellen's voice got quieter. "Something else is going on, and until I get a sense of what it is and where Sam might be, I have to stay. I don't understand why David won't report Sam missing. They might have different fathers, but they're still brothers. He won't even discuss it."

"What the fuck! He still hasn't reported him as missing? *Tabernac!*" Julie slipped seamlessly into her native French-Canadian slang and wished she could be on the next plane to help. Anything, even something for asshole Sam Davis, would be better than office administration.

"It makes no sense. None of it does," Ellen explained. "I need to get David to open up to me, and I can't leave until he does. Give me a few more days. I'll be back next week at the latest. I miss my boys. Phone calls don't cut it, even if they are having a grand old time with their dad. Or maybe because of it. Mommy-me is getting jealous. I'll be back as soon as I can, I promise."

"Good. I get it, and if you need my two cents' worth to speed up the investigation, you know where to find me. Just ask; you know I can't resist a good mystery." Julie's mind started tunneling through the possibilities for Sam's disappearance and his brother's lack of concern.

"Don't worry; I will. I'll be in touch as soon as I know what's up."

Ellen disconnected, and Julie remembered why she had phoned her in the first place. Julie would have to make this decision herself. Ellen said she had total faith in her. She pulled out the draft of Michael's letter and reworked the final paragraph.

Providing exceptional client experiences is our goal at Hartmann and Associates, and Ellen Hartmann understands she can be difficult to reach. Please don't hesitate to contact our new associate, Michael Prescott, for assistance.

There. That should keep everybody happy.

CHAPTER 64

DAVID

DAVID POURED HIMSELF A SCOTCH. FORGET ABOUT two fingers; tonight, he needed at least four. He found his mother's secret Cutty Sark in the same place he found it when he was thirteen: the back left corner of her closet. Some things never change, like her abominable taste for cheap scotch. Whenever he tried to convert her to the smooth, smoky flavors of the high-end brands he enjoyed, she'd denounce them as crap. *Give me my Cutty Sark; keep your hoity-toity brands and leave me alone.* David blinked back a tear, longing to hear her scold him one last time.

Earlier at dinner, Ellen mentioned that Sam didn't drink, and he wondered if she knew that for certain. If it were true, David might almost admire him. But not quite. David watched and learned to drink from his older brother, just as Sam first learned from his own father, and then from their shared mother. Diane said Sam's dad was a functional alcoholic; David's was a teetotaler. Their mother was a dysfunctional alcoholic, and even after marrying David's dad, she never gave up her hidden stash. It was the family secret, and his dad never questioned her perpetually minty breath. He died pretending they were an alcohol-free family.

Family. Was that what he and Sam were? They might have the same mother, but as far as David was concerned, his family died with her. No need to pretend anymore, she was gone. And so was Sam. Did he owe his half-brother anything? David wanted to leave Nashville and return to his life in LA, and if that meant not searching for Sam, he could live with it.

But how could he get rid of Ellen without telling her about Sam's past, even though it had nothing to do with the present? He feared she'd never leave if he didn't clarify the situation, that she'd snoop more if she knew the truth. He was tired, and the thick waves covering his aching head had long since escaped the confines of their morning gel. He wiped them back and off his brow.

Tomorrow was another day, and he didn't need to decide tonight. Tomorrow, he'd start cleaning out his mother's house, and if that meant getting rid of Sam and Roxie's things, so be it. He doubted they'd return. With luck, by the time he was finished, the coroner's report would be ready, and he could go home and forget all about Sam and his shenanigans.

Ah, family. Who needs them? David drained the acrid scotch and poured himself another.

CHAPTER 65

HENRY

"ELLEN, WE NEED TO TALK. WE CAN'T KEEP ignoring this." Henry parked Sam's Escalade near the hotel's entrance, but not right at the door. He didn't want Ellen to leave without addressing the elephant filling the room since he had confessed to knowing Sam was a liar. Days had passed, bringing with them a growing haze that clouded their connection. He couldn't ignore it any longer.

"Henry, I can't." Ellen's voice was soft and shaky, her emotional turmoil evident. "Not tonight. I'm exhausted, my head is spinning, and I need time to process all of this." Henry leaned closer, and she moved the other way. She placed her hand on the door handle, ready to open it. But she didn't.

"I know you, Ellen." Henry used his gentlest tone, the one he reserved for love songs and ballads. "You won't sleep if we don't talk. Let's get it over with now."

He waited for a response. None came, and he tried again. "I'll start. Let me try to explain."

Ellen took her hand off the car door, shifted in her seat, and rested her head against the window to look at him. She closed her eyes for six long seconds and whispered, "Okay."

"There's no excuse other than I'm young and foolish." There he said it, his voice tinged with regret. "At first, I thought I was hearing things wrong or that I misunderstood. Then I got used to it. My friend Brad always lied for no reason I could figure out. I guess I thought Sam was a pathological liar like him. Brad's lies never hurt anyone, so I assumed Sam's wouldn't either. I dismissed Sam's lies like I did Brad's, convincing myself it was just what they did."

Ellen tucked her hair behind her right ear. Henry called it her thinking mode. It was excruciating to wait, but he gave her time.

"I had a friend like that, too." She closed her eyes. "Judy. She made up incredible stories, and I never understood why." Ellen's voice dropped in tone and volume, and Henry leaned closer.

"One time, she even told us she had a serious kidney infection. She didn't. We asked her mother how she was doing, and she laughed at us like we were idiots. We never believed anything Judy said after that. But I saw how she suffered when we discovered her lie, and I never called her out again."

She shifted in her seat and placed her hand on top of Henry's, which he had conveniently rested on the console between them. She squeezed it, and he felt some relief from his angst. "I fell into the same trap you did. Some part of me knew Sam was lying, but I ignored it too. We're two of a kind, aren't we." Her weak smile suggested they would be all right. He picked up her hand and kissed it.

They moved closer, and Ellen tilted her head up to look at Henry. He dropped his eyes to look into hers. No words were spoken; there was nothing to say. He gently touched her cheek at the same time she reached for his. After too many harsh and unsettling days, their first kiss was soft and gentle. They lingered in its tenderness, and Henry prayed it was just the beginning.

CHAPTER 66

ELLEN

ELLEN SLUMPED AGAINST THE DOOR OF HER hotel room. What had she done? It had been five long years since she'd been kissed, and she didn't know whether to laugh or cry. Henry might be younger, but even he would shake his head at her kiss-and-run behavior. She was acting like a middle schooler after her first kiss. She giggled at the absurdity of it all and let her laughter bubble up. Then, in the blink of an eye, her emotions shifted. Full-throated, deep-bellied sobs erupted as she hugged her belly and slid to the floor. Tears flowed like a river escaping its banks. They gushed from much more than the shocks of the last few days or tonight's kiss. They had been waiting, unshed, since the deaths of her mother, father, and sister. All the grief from a failed marriage and the end of its storybook dream poured out. Exhaustion from running a business, a family, and her life had made tears a luxury until now. Henry's presence made her vulnerable, and she released the emotions she had kept buried for far too long. She let them flow until she was finished.

She surveyed the empty hotel room, needing someone's help to pull herself out of this funk. Calling her sons would cheer her up, remind her of her priorities, and strengthen her resistance to Henry's pull. The bedside clock glowed 9:36; her boys were in bed. But her best friend Mo was a night owl, and she'd be awake. Calling her was risky, but she needed someone to talk to, even though she could guess her response. She grabbed her cell phone and called Mo's number.

"Ellen, what's wrong? Are you all right? The boys?" Mo's voice was frantic, and Ellen regretted not warning her with a text first.

"I'm fine, everybody's fine, I promise. I just needed to talk." Ellen snickered. Sure, she was FINE: fucked up, insecure, neurotic, and emotional. No one would argue with that.

"Don't do that to me," Mo said. "My heart is pounding! You never call this late. Give me a minute; I need to catch my breath." Mo's microwave pinged in the background. "I was getting a cup of tea. Let me get settled. It must be something good if you're calling me this late." Ellen imagined her cozying into her dark green recliner, hands cupped around a mug of tea.

"Okay, go. You have my uninterrupted attention." The footrest of Mo's dark-green recliner thumped into position.

"I kissed a guy, and he's fifteen years younger than me!" Ellen crowed like a thirteen-year-old. Heat rose in her cheeks as it had during their first kiss.

"Finally! It's been way too long!" Mo giggled. "I was afraid you were becoming a born-again virgin!"

"But it was stupid." Ellen gasped for logic and dismissed Mo's playful jab. "He's here in Nashville; I'm in Portland. He's barely an adult, and I'm the mother of three children. It'll never work."

"Well, probably not, but who says it has to? There's such a thing as casual sex, you know." Mo threw common sense out the window.

"Yeah, yeah, so you tell me. But it's not my style. You know me, before I undress emotionally and physically, I need to feel something real, something lasting. No offense." Ellen steered reason back into the conversation.

"None taken. But are you sure you're not being a coward? A twenty-something you'll never see again? It's a perfect opportunity. Come on, what do you have to lose?" Mo didn't back down.

"Don't even go there. It's easy enough to forget my responsibilities here in Nashville. And he's so damn cute. He's hard to resist," Ellen pleaded.

"Then don't." Mo was serious. "Give yourself a break; be young, be foolish. Enjoy the moment. Take it from someone who's been there—you won't regret it." Ellen could see the twinkle in her eyes from twelve hundred miles away.

"I'll take it under advisement." Ellen was tempted. After all, what harm could it do?

CHAPTER 67

BOBBY

BOBBY WHEELED HIS SILENT TRASH BARREL DOWN Hartmann and Associates' hallway. A dose of WD-40, and voila, the squeak was gone. He didn't want Michael, or anyone else, to know he was lurking. Lurking, a strange but fitting word, ever since Michael arrived on the scene. More than your typical office cleaner, Bobby's loyalties lay with Ellen and Julie, and if lurking was his means of protecting them, then lurking it was.

Julie's harsh overhead lights were off when he parked his truck, and the soft glow of her desk lamp made her even more drop-dead gorgeous. Another cliché, he was full of them tonight. But who could resist her ready smile, quirky curls, and French-Canadian charm? Bobby was hopelessly smitten that first night they sleuthed together, when she stretched her sexy curves after hiding under the desk. Since then, he'd been content to let their relationship unfurl at its own speed with their occasional after-hours conversations.

But now, with the perfect Michael horning into his territory, he couldn't sit idly by. His feelings for Julie were one thing, but Michael had insinuated himself into every nook and cranny of the accounting firm. There was something rotten in Denmark, and Bobby had started sifting through Michael's trash, looking for evidence. Evidence of what he didn't know, but whatever it was, Bobby intended to find it. Tonight, he was going to enlist Julie's help.

She didn't hear Bobby approach because her chair was turned, and she was staring out the window. The streetlight from the pier shone through the windows, bathing her in soft light and accentuating the romantic glow of her lamp. He lost himself in awe and, for a moment, forgot his mission. Then he shook himself free and announced his presence.

"Working late again? And alone? No Michael tonight?" Bobby wished his whining hadn't leaked through.

"Holy Shit! You snuck up on me! What happened to your squeak?" Julie's sexy laugh enveloped him, and Bobby's cheeks flushed.

"WD-40 works miracles. Working for a high-class accounting firm like this, I needed to up my tools of the trade." Bobby took a seat across from Julie. "So, what's new? It's been a while." He'd let Julie bring up the topic of Michael.

"Not much. same old, same old." Julie leaned back in her chair and stretched her arms over her head. Her white shirt pulled out of her slacks, and a sliver of skin caught Bobby's attention. His cheeks flared with heat.

"Big changes with Michael this year." Bobby stepped into the fray. "Seems like he's taking charge."

"What is it with you and Katie?" Julie's response was quick and fiery. "He's trying to help by doing what Ellen hired him to do."

"Sorry, didn't mean to strike a nerve, didn't want you to get pushed out." What just happened? It was not like Julie to jump down his throat.

"I'm a big girl and fully capable of caring for myself." She grabbed her long hair and twisted it around her fist.

"Of course you are. I didn't mean it that way. You know I don't. I've seen you in action, remember?" She wasn't herself, and a little humor might change her mood.

"I'm just tired. It's been a long day." Julie stood up, grabbed her bag, and walked out.

Bobby and his barrel followed twenty paces behind. That went over like a lead balloon!

CHAPTER 68

KATIE

KATIE SLID THE ZERRIEN'S ORGANIZER INTO another Kraft envelope. She had spent the day stuffing twelve hundred eighty-seven envelopes from A to Z and was fuming. Her anger over the cover letter grew with each packet she stuffed, and she hoped her distrust of Michael was tagging along with each one. How does someone like Michael, new and unproven, get his name included in this vital tax season mailing? Even Julie, the savior of the firm as far as Katie was concerned, didn't get special treatment. It just wasn't right.

She stood at the work counter behind her desk and stared out the window. An ugly scowl reflected back. The sun had set three long hours ago, and after arriving before the 7:14 sunrise, she resented that today, with its few short hours of sunlight, had been wasted on this. Her cheeks ached from feigning smiles for clients and staff, her throat chafed from holding back her words, and her back was sore from carrying it all. But the task was over, and tomorrow morning, on her way to the office, she'd drop off the packets for mailing. She slid the last packet through the postage meter and dropped it into the box with the other twelve hundred eighty-six envelopes.

The elevator rose from the first floor below and settled on her floor. Without a thought, Katie's lips lifted into a welcoming smile. Then she remembered that she had locked off the floor at five o'clock and that the doors would only open for staff with a key. She relaxed, and her scowl returned.

The elevator doors slid open, and Katie tensed, anticipating that Michael, the slimeball, would appear. His late-night snooping was notorious because he was foolish enough to leave a trail. It was her responsibility to stay vigilant; even a misplaced paperclip had a story to tell.

"That frown could sink ships." Bobby's teasing was a welcome respite. "Must've been a rough day."

"Oh, it's just you." Even with Bobby, Katie didn't have much energy left to engage, and she hung back at the counter, finishing up.

"Yep, just me. Not your first choice, I take it." Bobby pulled Katie's wastebasket from underneath her desk.

"I thought it might be that asshole, Michael." Katie tidied up her workspace.

"What'd he do now?" Bobby fished out the returnable water bottles before dumping the contents of the reception area trash can into his barrel.

"Weaseled himself into some place he shouldn't be.

Again. No one sees it but me." She turned to look at Bobby. "Is everyone else fooled by his big teeth and fake grin?"

"Not me, for sure," Bobby commiserated. "But that explains why Julie jumped down my throat when I asked a simple question about him earlier. Said I was being like you and walked out. End of discussion." Bobby brushed his hands together as if wiping off something distasteful.

"I don't get it." At last, Katie had someone to compare notes with. "It's so obvious that he's sucking up to Julie, but she doesn't see it. And now, I'm sending out a letter asking clients to contact him, not Ellen, not Julie, but him! I don't like it at all. If it were up to me, he'd be gone yesterday." Katie stopped to take a breath.

"Whew! Glad I'm not alone; I thought I was the only one. I don't trust him as far as I can throw him! I've been going through his trash, trying to find something. Nothing so far, but I know there's something." Bobby paused. "When's Ellen back? Julie seems lost without her."

"Not soon enough. I'm afraid by the time she is, it'll be too late. These client packets are opening the door for Michael and his dirty deeds. It sounds stupid, but I'm usually right about these things." Katie sighed deeply, feeling utterly drained. She had nothing left to give.

"It's not stupid, not at all, I'm right there beside you." Bobby's sincerity lifted Katie's spirits. "You're exhausted, I can tell. Go home, put your feet up, pour a glass of wine. Bobby is on duty."

"And all is right with the world." Katie laughed, wanting to believe it was true.

CHAPTER 69

JULIE

WHAT THE HELL? JULIE SHIFTED HER CAR INTO park and turned the ignition off. Her annoyance began to steam up her frigid car windows as the vehicle cooled. She sat in foggy silence while she tried to gain some composure. She barely recalled backing out of the tight garage or the drive home. Why did she take her frustrations out on Bobby? He was her buddy, her advocate, her go-to guy; he didn't deserve to be treated like that. But neither did she. Ellen may be gone, but that didn't mean Julie had to have all the answers, especially about Michael. Michael was Ellen's problem, not hers; Ellen hired him, not Julie. Sure, she had given her two cents' worth about Ellen's final decision, but ultimately, it was Ellen's choice. It worked both ways. When Julie asked for Ellen's help, it was still Julie's decision. When together, they harnessed the power of both minds. But making both of their decisions without Ellen's input was an entirely different matter. Julie was tired of doing it alone.

Last night with Michael, she didn't feel alone. She appreciated having someone to help shoulder the responsibilities pushed onto her. Michael was hired to help ease their excessive workloads, and he was working hard to make progress by connecting with Ellen's clients. He told her that they had mentioned they were more than happy to have an attentive accountant handle their taxes this year. But when he suggested that Ellen neglected and took advantage of their clients' trust, she changed the subject. Michael hadn't earned the right to criticize Ellen. Yet she wondered, if she felt mistreated by Ellen's absence, did their clients feel the same way?

It was too soon to let Michael into her inner Ellen world, and wisely, he didn't push it. By their third beer, it was all forgotten, and Julie felt grateful to have a colleague and friend who could take care of himself without supervision. He was the solution to Ellen's overflowing workload and what both she and Ellen needed. Transitioning from a senior team of two to a team of three would require time and effort, but it would be worthwhile.

Julie suspected that her outburst with Bobby was linked to that night with Michael. She hadn't liked the weight of Michael's hand on her shoulder, how it slithered down her arm to open the door at J's. She felt like she was betraying Bobby, but that thought had seemed silly last night, and it still felt that way today. There was nothing between Bobby and her, except for a strange mix of friend, colleague, and co-conspirator. Their connection, developed over years of conversation and laughter, was older and deeper than this new one with Michael. Her relationship with Michael wasn't even close, and there was no reason to feel guilty. Or at least that's what she told herself.

Julie's memory of the other night was hazy. They drank more than they should have, and Julie turned down Michael's offer to drive her home. Instead, she called for an Uber and suggested he do the same. He dismissed her comment by comparing his towering stature to her tiny physique, bragging that he could handle twice as much booze as she could. Then, he kissed her on the cheek. At least, she hoped that's what happened. Her head turned mid-sentence, lips parted and open, as Michael aimed for her cheek for a friendly goodbye.

Julie's heart raced, and heat flushed her French-Canadian cheeks. She was not misremembering. She would not—no matter how drunk—allow her tongue to slip into his mouth to meet and tangle with his. No. That simply did not happen.

Stewing over her inner turmoil was not helping, and she opened the car door. An avalanche of icy air further frosted the windshield. Tomorrow morning, there would be hell to pay when she headed into the office. But tonight, she just wanted to go to bed and forget everything.

CHAPTER 70

KATIE

"HARTMANN AND ASSOCIATES, THIS IS KATIE. How may I help you?" She peered into the small mirror behind her telephone. Most people thought it was a vanity thing, but anyone who took the time to ask, learned that it was her reminder to smile. A smile on your face meant a smile in your voice. These days, she needed that reminder.

"Good morning, Katie. This is Anne V. It's that time of year again. I'm looking forward to seeing you. Once a year doesn't come soon enough." Katie recognized the tremulous voice of Ellen's favorite client with the unpronounceable last name. Everyone loved Anne's visits and her muffins.

"I hear you. We all do. Everyone's looking forward to the arrival of their favorite blueberry muffins," Katie teased. "And your smiling face, of course."

"You're too kind. Tell them soon. It depends on how soon you can get me in to see this new person, Michael Prescott. I think I'm supposed to meet with him this year."

Anne, a retired lawyer, understood that moving others up the professional hierarchy was standard procedure. She may be older, but she never missed a beat.

"Ellen would never forgive me if she didn't get to see you. I know how much she loves your annual visit." A little white lie never hurt, and Katie would plead innocence if anyone asked who Anne had requested.

"Whatever you think, we both know you're the real boss," Anne whispered. "Book me whenever and with whomever you think is best. My schedule is pretty light these days." Anne enjoyed staying busy with her extensive flower and vegetable gardens, but the end of summer meant her days became long and colorless. Katie suspected this was why Anne and other elderly clients loved visiting the office.

"How about the week after next? Ellen is out of town, and that'll give her plenty of time to get her head back into office things." Katie regretted the words as soon as they slipped out of her mouth. Involving clients in office politics was not stellar behavior. Her mirror reflected the frown she was feeling.

"Well, I hope she is off on some exotic vacation. Let's do two weeks from today to give her plenty of time to settle in. How about ten o'clock on that Wednesday? I'm afraid the days of early morning meetings are over. How did I ever feed and water four kids and get to the office by eight?" Anne's raucous laughter brought Katie's smile back.

"Ten it is. I'm looking forward to seeing you and your muffins." Katie's smile vanished. Michael was waiting at the desk, and her irritation with him drowned out Anne's goodbye. She hung up the phone and glared at him.

"Another appointment for me?" Michael's alabaster teeth made her want to scream.

"Nope, not for you. Just one more client demanding to meet with Ellen. Maybe next time." Katie loved twisting the knife into Michael's enormous ego, not that he noticed. She got up from her desk and walked into the kitchen. This time, Michael was smart enough not to follow.

CHAPTER 71

DAVID

DAVID STOOD ON THE BALCONY OF SAM'S COOKIE-cutter home. A lock of hair slipped free from its gel and flopped over his forehead as he leaned against the flimsy railing overlooking the downstairs foyer, his mother's last view, before plummeting down the stairs. Now, instead of her lifeless body filling the space, boxes like toddler building blocks were stacked everywhere. He blinked hard and wiped his eyes. It all happened too fast. With his mother's one misstep, he was shoved up the ladder of life. Now, he was part of the older generation, the one others looked up to for advice and guidance, the one asked to make life's difficult decisions. How did the death of a parent propel you into full adulthood, even when you thought you were already there? No one had warned him.

He didn't want to accept this next step of responsibility, but he had no other choice. It should've been Sam, or at least the two of them. But instead, he was all alone cleaning, clearing, and sorting through the remnants of his mother's life—and Sam's. To the left were keepsakes, things he would take home. The stack was insignificant compared to the one on the right that overflowed with items for the local thrift shop. His mother's clothes, other emotionless belongings, and Sam and Roxie's things were not worth saving. David had scheduled a pickup by Goodwill Industries of Middle Tennessee for Friday, two days from now. By then, furniture and kitchen items would be added to the heap for mass disposal.

That left the pile in the middle, the one the dogs were sniffing. He looked down from his second-story perch at the three dogs searching for their missing masters. The poor, abandoned creatures. Typical Sam; he never thought of others, not even canine others. In a rare moment of compassion, David headed down the stairs to find them a treat. By the time he got there, they had vanished.

He considered the middle stack of three small boxes filled with Sam's business records. Burn or save? He wasn't sure. From his quick review, it seemed that this time Sam had created a viable business. Brand & Broadcast was straightforward and above board, except for exaggerated claims of past clients, and the company appeared to be on the verge of genuine profits. Nevertheless, David's business acumen suggested that the company was dead in the water and couldn't be resuscitated or replicated without Sam's creative talents and vision. Even Sam would agree that burning the records was the right choice.

A week had passed since David arrived in Nashville to find his mother dead and his brother gone. Something big must have gone down. There was no other explanation for

Sam walking away from a legitimate company filled with the fame and fortune he craved. And what about their mother? Sam wouldn't have walked away from her either. They were enmeshed and equally devoted to each other, in a twisted sort of way. Sam would've stuck with Brand & Broadcast, and his mother, no matter what.

David closed his eyes, and one tear rolled down his cheek. He filled his chest with a deep sigh, puffed out his cheeks, and released it. One adventurous dog nudged his leg, and he bent down to scratch the spiky dog's head. The pooch responded by nuzzling his hand.

He scooped up the dog and buried his face in its black fur. The anguish from boxing up his mother's life erupted. "Mommy, what happened? Why did Sam leave you alone?" His sobs echoed through the emptying house. "Where is he, and why did you fall?"

CHAPTER 72

ELLEN

ELLEN PULLED ANOTHER FILE FOLDER FROM THE bottom drawer of Roxie's desk. It felt wrong to rifle through someone else's files without permission, but she had no choice. There must be a clue somewhere that would point her in the right direction. Who was Sam Davis, and where had he gone? Who was the man who had led him away? She and Henry had spent most of the week at Sam's office, answering phone calls from disgruntled clients and anxious employees. Their message was always the same: No, Sam was not there, and no, they didn't know when or if he'd return. And yes, it was a mess. Somehow, it helped that they were in the same boat: Henry, without a job, and Ellen, without a project.

Between calls, they sifted through the office files, searching for anything that might explain Sam's disappearance. All the project files they examined were intact, as if they had been tucked away for the night, not forever. However, the more Ellen explored the company's internal workings, the more confused she became about its owner. Larger-than-life Sam vanished in the details. And so did his wife.

Working with small businesses and being a small business owner herself, Ellen understood that an owner's finances were inextricably linked to their company. Obtaining bank loans or vendor credit without the owner's personal guarantee was virtually impossible. But that didn't seem to be the case for Sam Davis and Brand & Broadcast. Nothing connected them. No bank statements, no loan agreements, nothing, not even paid invoices. It was as if the company existed in a financial vacuum. But that was impossible. Without money, businesses could not survive.

She was missing something, something hidden in another file, another cabinet, another room. Something waiting to be found. Where was it? She rubbed her tired eyes and checked her Fitbit. Two in the afternoon. She and Henry had been at it since morning, and she needed a break.

"Henry?" Ellen wandered down the hallway, searching for him. She found him in the kitchen, helping himself to the office snack box.

"Want some peanut butter crackers?" Henry held out the familiar sleeve of orange crackers glued together with a smear of peanut butter. Her oldest son, Jack, had survived on them since he started packing his own lunch. Too many untouched lunches had convinced her that a sleeve of peanut butter crackers was slightly better than nothing.

"Perfect. I'm hungry, but I don't want to quit yet." Ellen ripped open the crackers and devoured the first one. She grabbed a glass and filled it with water from the cooler. The ice-cold liquid rinsed her mouth of the remnants of her morning coffee and washed down the dry crackers.

Ellen slumped into one of the chairs surrounding the small staff table. "Sometimes, a change of perspective helps me see what's right in front of me. I'm not finding anything useful. How about you?"

"More of the same." Henry sat down across from her and shook his head. "Nothing unusual, but I'm impressed with what I did find. Sam sent his concept ideas, movie trailers, and TV pilots to Netflix, Amazon, Hulu, all the big players. They all wanted to see more. On our drive to Atlanta, he said big things were about to happen, and for once, he seemed to be telling the truth. It doesn't make sense that he'd disappear." He popped another cracker into his mouth.

"I know. Nothing makes sense. Unless not making sense is the crux of it all." Ellen scratched her head, folded her arms on the table, and leaned forward. "What's really weird is that I can't find any financial records. Not a thing. A business without a money trail? How does that work? Sam wasn't independently wealthy, and even if he were, there would still be some records."

"Maybe they aren't here. I took a lot of things over to Diane to sign. Maybe they kept the records at home?"

"Diane signed papers?" Ellen was excited; the break had worked its magic. "What kind of papers? Did you look at them?"

"Nah, Sam sent them over in sealed manila envelopes, and she sent them back the same way. I did get a peek once or twice over her shoulder or across the table. I think they were legal documents or something. She never read them, but always signed where Roxie flagged, and I took them back as instructed." Henry's smile flashed his pride at being helpful. Ellen winced. Her sons did the same thing for her approval.

"I guess that makes sense. Pretty inconvenient, though. I like to have everything at my fingertips. And if they are there, David won't make it easy for us to look at them." Ellen's excitement began to fade. "Got any good ideas for why we need to see them?" She raised an eyebrow and sighed.

Henry dropped his gaze and fell silent for a moment. Then, with wide eyes, he asked, "What about the ten thousand?"

"Ten thousand? Ten thousand what? I'm not following." Ellen couldn't connect with Henry's train of thought.

"You know, the ten thousand Sam supposedly sent back to you. You never got it, did you?"

She shook her head. How could she have forgotten about that?

"Tell David you want to go through the records so you won't waste time tracking it down if it was never sent. If he's trying to hide Sam's disappearance, he won't want you involving any banks." Henry's face wore the same helpful, hopeful façade as her young sons.

"Henry, you're brilliant!"

Someone else would've gotten a hug and a kiss from her, but someone else wasn't Henry. She would not go there. Mo would not be pleased.

CHAPTER 73

HENRY

FINALLY, SINCE THEIR FIRST KISS, HENRY AND ELLEN had been scouring Brand & Broadcast's office for clues. The days were tedious and tiring, and they weren't any closer to discovering the truth. And their nights? Nothing. Ellen made up an excuse for a quick goodbye, claiming she was either checking in with her kids or too tired. Henry couldn't blame her; he was exhausted too, but he longed for an easy conversation at the end of a long day. Or any conversation. Things had shifted, and with all of Sam's crap, their relationship had taken a back seat until tonight. Tonight, as he pulled under the hotel's portico, Ellen suggested he park and join her for a nightcap. He didn't need to be asked twice.

"Thanks, I needed this." Henry leaned back in the cushy chair and grabbed his beer from the bartender covering both the bar and the tables. He took a long drink from the icy beer mug and set it on the table. The guy noticed he had drained half of it and raised his eyebrows. He nodded. Yes, he would have another. He and Ellen were work-free, and he was in no hurry.

Ellen tilted her wineglass to her lips for more than just a dainty sip. She peered over the rim of the glass. "I'm exhausted. I needed this, too." She took another drink and set it on the table.

Things felt awkward, and he missed the easy flow of other nights spent at this same table. Ellen's cheeks reddened. She must have noticed it too; perhaps her blush was from the sulfites in her wine. Some wines had that effect on her.

"It's happening, isn't it?" She patted her cheeks and giggled.

"That it is. We'll need to avoid this wine label in the future. But I've seen you look worse," Henry teased. "This one gives you a rosy disposition." Maybe if he reminded her of their other nights together, she wouldn't shut the door on him tonight.

"If you say so, but I feel anything but rosy. Is all our digging for nothing? Except for the missing financial stuff, everything is what you'd expect." She brushed the bangs off her forehead, combed her fingers through her hair, and settled back in her chair.

"Sure, just what you'd expect if you don't count the missing company executives." He laughed at his choice of words. "Sam would cringe if he heard me call him an executive. He's the creative soul behind the business; all the execution is left to Roxie."

"They were in this together, no doubt about it. Sam vanished, and so did Roxie. They must have planned it together; there's no other explanation, or David would be worried." Ellen tucked her hair behind her ears, and Henry knew he had lost her to her world of analysis.

"But how does it tie in with Diane's death? That can't be a coincidence, can it?" He might as well join her. It was better than nothing, and he abandoned his plan to take in the music scene tonight.

"You wouldn't think so," Ellen's voice trailed off as she considered it. "Weirder things happen, but then again, everything about this is weird, unless…" She paused. "You don't think they took money from the wrong people, do you?"

Henry waited for her to say it first.

"No. I refuse to go down the rabbit hole of foul play. Nothing even remotely suggests anything like that." Her voice, slow and emotionless, didn't invite discussion.

Henry slid his hand across the table to get her attention. He was here for her, someone to discuss things with, someone she could count on. She was staring into her glass of wine and didn't notice. He pulled it back, embarrassed that he tried.

Suddenly, her spine stiffened. She reached into her back pocket and slid her vibrating phone out of her jeans. "It's David. I'm going to take it. He's the one with the answers. We need to meet with him. This is getting ridiculous. We should be doing this together."

She pressed the answer button on her phone. "David, we were just talking about you. How are things going at the house?" Ellen sounded like she was chatting with a good friend, her way of encouraging people to open up. Hopefully, it would work with David.

"Right. Of course. I understand." It was a one-sided conversation, but Ellen appeared pleased. Her eyes sparkled as she smiled at Henry. "We'll be there tomorrow at eight o'clock. A little early for me in Nashville," she chit-chatted, and Henry envisioned David's sullen expression on the other end. "Sam never started until nine, but I'll make it happen. Thanks for calling. Sleep well." She flipped her phone upside down on the table.

"The universe delivers. He wants to meet at the house tomorrow before he goes home on Saturday. He's done packing things up and says everything will be gone by the end of the week, including the dogs." Ellen closed her eyes. "Those poor things. It looks like they're going back to the pound. I can't stand it."

Henry slid his hand back across the table, and this time she covered it with hers. Their eyes met, and he murmured, "Another casualty of this fiasco. It's all so unfair." He let her think he was talking about the dogs instead of them. He squeezed her hand.

"What a mess." She blinked, pulled her hand away, picked up her wine glass, and emptied it. "That's it for me. I need a good night's sleep to be ready tomorrow." She stood up and slid her phone back into her pocket. "In the words of Scarlett O'Hara, as God is my witness, we will get our answers. Or something like that." Then she bent over, kissed him on the cheek, and was gone.

Henry moved to the bar. "I'll have another." He grabbed his phone and started scrolling. Alone or not, he needed some music.

CHAPTER 74

LITTLE PUP

LITTLE PUP COWERED IN HIS BED. THERE WAS no comfort in its soft, sunshine-yellow cushion today. He stretched his neck to look over at Kramer. His friend's body trembled, and his nose was buried deep in the back corner of his herringbone-striped nest. Little Pup recognized the behavior; it was what Kramer did when the yelling lady was around or the man with threads for hair said Kramer was naughty. But those two humans were gone, and so was the lady with the auburn hair, gone for far too many days. Little Pup understood what Kramer was feeling.

Something was wrong, and it involved that other man, the one who came and stayed. He was grumpy, like the woman who yelled too much. Little Pup didn't like him and retreated to his bed whenever the other man was nearby. From there, he could watch him and knew when it was safe to venture into the kitchen for a sip of water. Archie and Kramer were slow to catch on, though. They whined for his attention, clambered at the man's feet, and begged for head scratches and belly rubs. The other man responded with well-placed kicks, never hard enough to hurt, but always the same. It didn't take long before they too, learned to retreat to their beds.

Little Pup looked over at Archie. He was sitting up on his bed, exuding defiance. His black, spiky-haired friend might have plenty of attitude, but he rarely strayed from his bed's macho theme of hunting dogs and guns. Archie was tough, but he wasn't foolish—unless a treat was involved. They all knew it was best to keep their distance, especially if the other man was carrying boxes down the stairs. He had been hauling them since early morning, and Little Pup hoped they would still be there to explore when the other man disappeared into the yelling lady's bedroom for the night. The sounds of TV meant it was safe to venture out from their respective beds.

Tonight, the three pups would do their research. Tonight, their noses wouldn't smell death, the scent that kept them frightened and cowering at a distance. Instead, their noses would investigate the boxes, just like they did when they snuffled garbage for goodies or whiffled their morning-breath diagnoses of the lady with auburn hair and the man with threads for hair. Nothing escaped their three snouts, even when the man with threads for hair told them to put their nose away. How could they put away the one thing that brought joy, warnings, and everything in between? Little Pup remembered the yelling lady at the bottom of the stairs and wrinkled his nose. It was a stench he'd never forget.

Tonight, he would find answers to his questions. What was happening? Why had the yelling lady stopped yelling?

Where was the man who had given them treats? Where was the lady who had rescued him from that dark, noisy place?

Little Pup's stomach quivered as he pondered other questions he was too afraid to ask. Who would take care of them if the other man left?

An involuntary shudder spread through his tiny body. Where would they go?

CHAPTER 75

ELLEN

ELLEN WATCHED THE EMERGING SUNRISE COLOR the sky over the tops of the adjacent suburban hotels. This area offered numerous options for weary travelers. Nashville's January typically overflowed with dreary clouds, but the sun, for once, didn't have to pierce through their gray heaviness. She smiled; it was going to be a good day. She was optimistic that today was the day she'd find some answers.

It was early, but not too early to make some calls. First and foremost, to her sons. They'd be awake because their dad was an early riser, and they loved to take advantage of alone time with him. One by one, sleepy-eyed, they'd wander down the expansive center staircase for morning snuggles. Or at least that's what they did before the divorce, and Ellen assumed it still happened whenever she was out of town and their father moved into the house. Keeping them in their own home with parents shuffling in and out helped ease her broken-home guilt.

"Mommy! Are you coming home?" Ethan's quiet question stirred a sick feeling in her stomach. She chalked it up to not eating breakfast.

"Soon, sweetie, just a few more days. I've missed you so much." Her youngest son's voice reminded her that she had a full life back in Portland. Here in Nashville, she had nothing except Henry. Sam's disappearance had taken away her dream of a lucrative online program. It was all gone, and no one seemed to care.

"Will you be here for my basketball game on Friday?" Ellen's stomach felt sicker. She'd missed last week's game too.

"Not this time, but I'll be your biggest fan next week, I promise. What else is going on?" She needed to change the subject, or her guilt would eat her up. "Having fun with your dad?"

Ethan chattered on about fun trips to second-hand stores, oversized pancakes, and unique things that made their dad special. When he ran out of steam, he handed the phone to Kevin, who, in turn, gave it to Jack. Her mind, jammed full of questions about her upcoming meeting with David, was happy to do nothing but listen. Her three sons deserved her quasi-undivided attention.

Thirty minutes slipped by, and Ellen felt more relaxed than she had in days. There was still plenty of time to shower and call the office before Henry picked her up. Tax season was starting, and she knew Katie would be in early. This time,

Ellen's stomach growled, not from guilt but from genuine hunger. She planned to grab a coffee and a muffin at the hotel buffet to eat in the car. Calling the office was more important than a leisurely breakfast, and she pressed number two on her phone to speed-dial the office.

Katie's standard Hartmann and Associates greeting reminded her that, besides her sons, she had a business in Portland with Julie and other devoted colleagues picking up her slack. Portland. With Diane's tragic death and Sam's disappearance this week, it was easy to forget.

"Ellen, you're a voice for sore ears! The phone's been ringing off the hook with clients wanting to see you. I put them off for a few days to give you breathing space on your return. Can we expect you on Monday?" In Katie's not-so-subtle way, she told Ellen to get her butt back now.

"I hear you loud and clear," Ellen laughed. "I'll be there bright-eyed and bushy-tailed Monday morning. I promise. There isn't much left for me to do here, and as much as I hate to admit it, I'm beginning to see that this is not my problem. I think it's time I learn to stay in my lane."

"Good luck with that. I have yet to see you refrain from helping someone who asks. Or from giving up on a lost cause, either," Katie laughed.

"But that's the thing, no one's asking for my help. In fact, except for Henry, no one thinks I have any reason to be here other than the fact that I happened to be here when Sam disappeared and Diane died," Ellen explained.

"Definitely in the wrong place at the wrong time. Maybe there's a lesson to be learned? Just because you can, doesn't mean you should, or something like that." Katie was an expert at guiding Ellen in the right direction.

"Or maybe it's time to stick to my original promise. This was to be my last trip to Nashville unless Sam came through. Obviously, that's not happening. It's time to walk away." She wished she could keep promises to herself like she did with her clients instead of always second-guessing herself.

"From here, it seems like the right thing to do," Katie kept her subtle nudge going. "What's happening with Sam's other clients? What about the movie and TV shows he was working on?"

"The clients behind those projects have been calling, but without Sam, there's not much we can do. Henry and I have told everyone they need to pivot, deep-six their project, or find someone else to finish them. Sam's IT guy is sending everyone their digital files." Ellen shoved her hair behind her ears.

"Wow, that's fast. It almost looks like everyone expects Sam to never return. Kinda weird, isn't it?" Katie nailed what Ellen was trying to ignore. Something had been off, yet, like her, everyone pretended not to see what was right in front of them. Maybe it wasn't her fault; maybe Sam was the king of deception.

"The whole thing is weird, and it's time for me to accept that my project is dead in the water." Ellen slid her hair out from behind her right ear and sighed. "Of course, some threaten to sue, but if there's no Sam, who do you sue? I'm hoping Sam's brother will have some answers for us this morning."

"Who's us? That Henry guy? Did I miss something?" Katie hinted. The office was in the dark about Henry, and if it were up to Ellen, it would stay that way.

"Like I said, we were together when we found Diane's body, and he's helping me with Sam's office. Henry's Sam's driver, but also an actor and musician."

"Hmmm, someone like you, in the wrong place at the wrong time?" Katie was fishing for details, and asked, "Anything more?"

Ellen was not about to bite. "Nothing to tell. He's a friend who's been a godsend during this mess."

"If you say so." Ellen heard the other phone lines buzzing in the background. "Do you want Julie? My other lines are ringing. Gotta go."

Katie didn't wait for an answer. Whether it was Ellen's intention or not, Julie was who she'd speak to next. Katie took care of everyone, not just Ellen.

CHAPTER 76

MICHAEL

MICHAEL HAD WAITED ALL DAY TO TALK TO JULIE, but she was never available. She kept her door slightly ajar, and her do-not-disturb message was clear. The door opened wide only when she went to the front desk to escort a client back for a meeting, but she avoided eye contact even when he conveniently passed her in the hallway. They had lost their momentum that night at J's. He had to regain it.

That night, Julie confided in him like a friend, and he was sure he'd won her trust when she opened up about how annoyed she was with Ellen. It wasn't like her, and Michael was surprised by the depth of her feelings. Maybe she and Ellen weren't as tight as they appeared, and as their rift grew, it confirmed his inclination to pull Julie away from Ellen and bring her closer to him.

Everything was falling into place. Julie would be an ideal second-in-command to his lead. She was a talented accountant, loved by her clients, and a veritable magnet for expanding a firm in the traditional way: client referrals. She was perfect because she had no desire to push herself up the ladder to the point of her incompetence. The Peter Principle would never apply, and Julie would forever be an overly competent workhorse at her boss's side. Ellen was no dummy, and neither was he.

Michael waited for Julie to return from taking her last client of the day back to the front desk. "So, the elusive Ellen is coming back?" He lowered his long, lean frame into one of Julie's client chairs. If she was surprised, she hid it well. He suspected she was not.

"Yup, she'll be back on Monday." She sat at her desk, flipped her hair over her shoulder, and their eyes connected. She looked away and began to shuffle the papers on her desk.

"I'll believe it when I see it. I'm starting to wonder if the woman who hired me exists." Michael tried a joke to lighten things up.

"Don't go there. It's been a long week, and I'm not in the mood." Her scowl said he had missed the mark. No biggie. He'd win her back.

"Gotcha. Just stopping in to see if there's any way I can help. I'm not that busy yet, so I'm all yours. Just ask." He had to let Julie find her way back.

"Thanks, but I'm fine." Julie's answer was short and emotionless.

"Well, you don't sound fine. You need a break. Are you up for J's? We both missed lunch today, and I'm starving. It'll be on me." He raked his fingers through his hair and raised his left eyebrow. "Come on, it's almost the weekend. Whadda ya say?"

"Sorry, I've got stuff to do at home." Julie slid open the center drawer of her desk and dropped in her pencil. Pleading would make things worse.

Michael rose from her chair and walked to the door. He glanced back over his shoulder to see her watching him with a puzzled expression. He fought against his instinct to smile.

"For the record, nothing happened. Too much to drink or something. We're all good." Michael didn't wait for her response.

CHAPTER 77

JULIE

JULIE BENT DOWN TO RETRIEVE HER HOUSE KEY from under the doormat. In the tiny northern Maine town where she grew up, no one locked their doors unless they were in bed or away. And even then, it wasn't necessary. Everything was everyone's business, and more people than not, noticed anything unusual. But here in the big city of Portland, no one bothered to know their neighbors, much less their daily routines. Locking your door was a necessary evil, if only for the sake of a police report or an insurance claim. Julie thought locking was foolish. If someone wanted to break in, they'd break in, locked door or not. She opened her door and put the key back where she found it. Whatever.

She flicked on the living room lights, revealing the remnants of her last uneventful weekend. Five days had passed, and somehow, she had never found the time to tidy up; now here it was, another boring weekend. A granny square afghan, a farewell gift from her mom, lay crumpled on the couch along with a pillow still holding the impression of her head. Coffee-stained cups, beer-drained bottles, pizza boxes, and Dunkin' Donuts bags littered the coffee table. Wrappers from unhealthy snacks filled any available space. Yuck! Why did she do that to herself? She needed the busyness of tax season to save her from herself.

Julie folded the throw and draped it over the back of the couch. After picking up the matching one off the floor, she fluffed both pillows. She carried the coffee cups to the sink to join the other unwashed remnants from the week. She dropped bottles into the returnable bin and crumpled up snack wrappers to add to the smelly, overflowing wastebasket under the sink. Her mother would be appalled to see how she lived. Using her right foot, she stomped down the garbage, lifted the bag from the trash can, cinched it closed, and set it by the back door to be tossed out tomorrow. Last week's garbage bag was proof that tomorrow never came. Best to take them both out now.

She didn't bother to throw on a coat since Portland's weather was usually moderated by its coastal proximity. But tonight was bitterly cold, and her deep inhalation burned her throat. The icy air froze her nostrils together, and the snow would have dry-crunched under her feet if the parking lot hadn't been plowed. The night was reminiscent of her frigid childhood. She lifted the grimy rubber lid of the association's shared dumpster and tossed in the evidence of her big-city-sorry life. Without thinking, she wiped her hands on her dress pants. Stale beer and donut crumbs left trails on both legs. Tonight was not her night. She headed back inside.

Julie untucked her blouse and unzipped her pants as she walked through the living room to her bedroom. The blinds were still up from the morning, and she glanced outside to see someone standing under the maple tree across the street. They would have been lost in its leafy branches had it been summer. With one hand hitching up her pants, she pulled down the blinds. Was the stranger looking in her window?

She continued to the bedroom and stood to the left of the window. The blinds were still closed after her morning shower, and she inched them forward to peer out. The person was gone, and no one was walking away to the right. She moved to the other side of the window and checked to the left.

A tall, trim man, coat collar up, face nuzzled down, was walking away. Julie widened the blind's opening for a better view. As if on cue, the stranger stopped in a puddle of light from the neighborhood's lone streetlight and looked back. A slash of white flashed through his parted lips. She shook her head, dislodged what she didn't want to see, and headed back to the kitchen for a beer.

CHAPTER 78

ELLEN

HENRY WAS SILENT THIS MORNING. HE WAS A MAN of few words, but today he had none. As usual, he waited under the hotel's portico when Ellen walked through the lobby. As usual, he opened her car door and helped her into Sam's massive SUV. But as they left the hotel's parking lot to meet David, there was no *how'd you sleep* or any other prompts to jump-start their conversation.

"You're awfully quiet." Ellen glanced at Henry. He stared straight ahead and didn't acknowledge her.

"Sorry, not feeling it this morning." Henry checked both ways, then eased the Escalade into traffic.

She tried again. "Late night?"

"You could say that," Henry mumbled.

"Hungover?"

"You could say that too." The corner of his lip smirked.

"And what adventure did you go on last night after I left you?" One way or another, she'd get him to talk.

"Some friends were performing downtown last night. I went to see them. I had hoped we could go together." Henry's voice faded.

"Wish you had told me. But I'm sure you had more fun without me." Ellen thought of the age of Henry's friends.

"I always have fun with you. It doesn't have to be all work, you know." Henry turned to look at her, and she saw a smile threatening to creep across his face.

"I know. David's phone call distracted me, and I was lost in thought about my ten thousand dollars." Her responding smile was a feeble attempt to broaden his. "We might get some real answers this morning." Henry's smile faded.

"Like it or not," Ellen continued, "my time here in Nashville is about to end." There, she said it. They had to face the truth. This was never going to work.

"All the more reason to make these final days as enjoyable as possible." Henry stared straight ahead but kept talking. "I know you'll be leaving soon to live your life back in Portland. And I know you think I'm too young. But it hurts that you'd write me off so easily. I deserve a say in this, don't I?"

"Ouch. You're right. You deserve more. You've been a good friend through all of this." She was sorry, but she had to stick to her plan. It was the only rational choice.

"Friend. Right. Just friends." He turned to face her, and his blue eyes searched hers. "But we're more than that. You feel it too. Can you deny it?"

"No, I can't. But that doesn't change things." She prayed he would understand; the last thing she wanted to do was hurt him. "Yes, I have a life in Portland. And you have one too, here in Nashville, with your music. And, yes, I can't get beyond the age difference, but even if we were the same age, it wouldn't change things. Like it or not, I'm an over-analyzer, and I look too far into the future, analyzing too many scenarios. But mostly, I can't step over my emotional boundaries." She sucked in a deep breath. This was harder than she expected.

"I know." Henry reached for her hand. She gave it to him willingly. "That's why I love you. But I need more than a brush-off or a quick goodbye. I need to hear that you feel it too, that I wasn't imagining it."

"You weren't imagining it. It's real." Her thumb massaged the back of his hand. "What's that quote from *Casablanca*, our favorite movie?"

Their words tumbled out together. "We'll always have Nashville." Henry picked up her hand and kissed it. Ellen's cheeks reddened.

They remained silent for the rest of the drive to Sam's house. Henry parked in the driveway, likely for the last time, and Ellen gathered her thoughts as Henry walked around the vehicle to help her down. His hand was warm in hers, and she looked up at his young, hopeful face.

"Let's get this over with and find some answers so we can enjoy our last two days together." It was all she could come up with. But she meant it. They deserved more than slogging through Sam's chaos. And, in a remote, sparkling corner of her being, she whispered, *I love you too.*

CHAPTER 79

DAVID

THE REMNANTS OF HIS MOTHER'S LIFE SURROUNDED him. After a night of tossing and turning, David gave up on sleep and got to work early. Not wanting to lose his momentum, he waited to make his morning coffee and loaded boxes into his rental car to drop off at FedEx for shipment home. Goodwill was scheduled to come this afternoon to take furniture and boxes of discarded belongings to their thrift store. That left Sam's business records. Destroy or not. He still wasn't sure what to do with those three boxes. His quick shuffling through Sam's records revealed nothing too private or incriminating, and David's business mind rebelled against destroying them, but there was no reason to keep them. Sam Davis and Brand & Broadcast were over and done.

He placed a K-cup into the coffee machine and pushed the button. He and his mother had the same taste in coffee, and he found quite a stash of their favorite brews. Oh, what he'd give to have her here sharing a cup with him. His exhale was deep and long as he carried the cup into the living room and settled into what he learned was Diane's favorite chair. By tonight, the rented house would be empty, and he would sleep at the Nashville Airport's Hilton to catch his early morning flight. This was his last chance to be close to his mother. The coffee tasted rich and robust but was laced with a hint of bitterness.

Sam and Roxie's little black dog left his bed and nudged David's leg at the sound of a car pulling into the driveway. David reached down to scratch the dog's head. Dammit, he was starting to like the ugly little thing. He thought about his youngest daughter back home. She'd been begging for a dog for years. Maybe he could be a hero for her; he'd been too late for his mother. He ruffled the dog's ears and answered the door.

"Come in, come in. Can I get you a cup of coffee?" After too many days alone with his memories and regrets, David was relieved to see Ellen and Henry.

"I'll finish this one first, but I'll be ready for another soon." Ellen hoisted her paper coffee cup, turned to Henry, and put her hand on his arm. "Do you need one?"

"Nah, I'm good." Henry touched her hand.

David thought they barely knew each other, but maybe there was more. Not that it mattered. After today, he'd never see either of them again.

"Let's sit in the living room and get caught up." There was no reason for David not to make this final meeting as friendly as possible. "It's been quite a week for me. For you too, I imagine. We have a lot of catching up to do."

Ellen sat at one end of the couch, while Henry occupied the other. The two remaining dogs left their beds to join their black companion. The smallest one leaped into Ellen's lap, and the fluffy white one settled into the space between them. The black dog whined at David's feet, and he gave in and picked him up.

"Looks like Archie has a new friend," Ellen teased. "He kind of grows on you, doesn't he?"

"Unfortunately, yes. He's ugly and cute at the same time." David scratched behind the dog's ears. "I can't believe I'm saying this, but I think my little girl would like him." He shook his head in disbelief. Was this why he hadn't made plans for the dogs yet?

"One down, two to go," Ellen laughed. "I've been worried about them. It would be so cruel to send them back to the pound." The little dog in her lap rolled over for a belly rub.

"I think that one's for you, Ellen." Henry put his arm on the back of the couch and tapped Ellen's shoulder. "He's buttering you up. Bet your three sons would love a puppy. Can we make that two down, one to go?"

"I've thought about it. They'd love a puppy, and our other dog, Random, is getting old. It might give her a new lease on life. I'll say yes, if you do. Kramer's a real sweetheart." The look Ellen gave Henry made David feel invisible, but if the problem of the dogs was being solved, he really didn't care.

"I'm not sure about that. Little dogs aren't my thing," Henry explained.

"Are you sure? He'd be your happy ending to this disaster." Ellen's voice was soft and tender. "He'll always have Nashville, you know."

Henry blushed and confirmed David's suspicions. Interesting, very interesting. Not that it mattered. He cleared his throat to remind them they were not alone.

CHAPTER 80

HENRY

HENRY STEERED THE CONVERSATION AWAY FROM the dogs and back to Sam's office. "Ellen and I've spent the last few days going through everything at Brand & Broadcast to find clues to Sam's disappearance. It's a shame that Sam's hard work is at a standstill. Good things were about to happen."

"Nice segue," Ellen chuckled. Kramer's dark eyes peeked out from his fluffy white face at Henry. The dog was a pro at looking forlorn.

"I agree with you," David said. "It looks like Sam had some great projects underway. I knew he had it in him. He was so talented as a kid, but he always missed the mark. This time, it looks like he could've made it." He patted the dog on his lap. "Oh well. It wasn't to be."

"Why do you say that?" Ellen cut in. "He's been gone a week. He can pick things up when he returns, can't he? I'm not trying to be callous, but he'll come back for your mother's funeral, won't he? After that, if I know Sam, it'll be business as usual." She was masterful at steering the conversation into uncomfortable waters. Henry was smart enough to keep silent and waited for David to respond.

David ran his fingers through his slicked hair and then through Archie's fur. Henry pictured the greasy fur of Archie's future and glanced at Ellen. Her serious expression said, *don't go there.* He stifled a laugh.

"First, there won't be a funeral. The coroner released her body to a crematorium, and her ashes will be sent to me. Even if there were a funeral, Sam wouldn't be there." David's voice was soft, almost sorrowful. Henry dropped his foolishness and leaned forward to listen.

David's face was a kaleidoscope of emotion. Anxiety, anguish, and indecision transformed into calmness, clarity, and resolution. Ellen's face filled with empathy. Henry was impatient for an explanation. He was sick of David side-stepping. He wanted the truth. Why didn't he want to tell the police that Sam had disappeared? Why did David accept Diane's death so easily?

"Sam is gone, and he won't be coming back." David's defiance was unmistakable. He was standing up to something or someone that Henry could neither see nor imagine.

CHAPTER 81

DAVID

DAVID LIFTED HIS DOG FROM HIS LAP AND SET it on the floor. He needed to move. As a boy, his constant movement drove his parents crazy, but it helped him cope with his anxiety. Ellen observed him and said nothing. She was perceptive enough to sense something big was coming. Henry followed her lead, although his hand nervously patted the back of the little white dog that had inched closer to him.

David rubbed the back of his neck and turned to face Ellen and Henry. It was time to unravel the secrets and lies that had held him hostage for far too long. His father and now his mother were dead. Sam was gone, and with him went David's allegiance. There was nothing left to protect. It was over. He sucked in a deep breath and began.

"None of this makes sense unless I start at the beginning." Ellen's kind eyes encouraged him to continue. He stuffed his hands in his pockets and began to pace.

"Sam was my half-brother. You know that. He was ten years old when Dad married Sam's mom. I came a year later, and Sam was still young enough to find a baby and toddler fascinating. I idolized him. Even though Mom saddled him with taking care of me, he never complained. He liked having me around. Before my dad and I came into the picture, it was just him and his mom. Sam was two when his dad left without looking back. Never sent money, left them to fend for themselves. They had no stability until my dad came on the scene, and little by little, Sam's life became less chaotic, more normal." David took a deep breath and continued.

"You see, Mom was an alcoholic. She hid it from my father. Sam and I hid it from him. It looks like she was still hiding it from us. I found her stash in the usual place, and the coroner said her blood alcohol was off the charts. Nothing had changed." David watched Ellen nod as if she understood.

"My dad was a hands-on father, honest and kind. He expected the best in people, and we became experts at looking good. But Sam never forgot those first ten years of his life. He had learned to expect the worst. And, as much as my dad rewarded Sam for the truth and never punished him for lies, Sam never changed. Neither did Mom. It's how they protected themselves and him. And I protected them all by keeping their lies secret."

David sat down in Diane's chair and took another deep breath. Archie jumped into his lap and, after circling three times, settled down to sleep. David's anxiety floated away as he scratched Archie's head and remembered his father's words: *The truth may hurt for a little while, but a lie hurts forever.*

CHAPTER 82

BOBBY

BOBBY SIGNALED FOR ANOTHER BEER. JULIE'S office lights were still on when he first arrived, so he headed down the pier to kill time at Portland's favorite waterfront bar. Given their disastrous last encounter, he wanted to give Julie plenty of time to leave before he cleaned 50 Portland Pier. Her behavior the other night was baffling, and he feared their relationship couldn't handle another episode like that. Julie never let stress get to her, and on the rare occasions she did, Ellen was there to calm her down. But not now. Until Ellen returned, Bobby would steer clear.

J's Oyster Bar was empty. January's frigid waters meant most of the bar's regulars were vacationing in Florida or crewing on a warm-weather boat far, far away. J, the bar's owner, slid Bobby's brew down the bar and returned to the pale-looking businessman at the opposite end that she was talking with. He must have wandered down from a nearby hotel in search of local color. Tonight, there wasn't much.

Bobby tipped his bottle back for another long slug of beer and felt a gentle touch on his shoulder. He shrugged it off, then pulled himself out of his head and spun around on his barstool. His scowl dissolved when he saw who it was.

"Shit, did I scare you?" Julie's husky laugh bounced off the bar's empty walls.

"After last time? Hell, yes." His smile broadened. "Just kidding. I was daydreaming and didn't hear the door open. That's what I get for sitting in your favorite spot. Wanna join me?"

"Why do you think I'm here?" Julie tossed her dark ringlets over her right shoulder. "I'm sorry for my behavior the other night. I didn't mean to take things out on you. Can you forgive me?"

"Consider it done." Bobby couldn't resist her sexy smile and beckoning eyes. He never could. Julie was back; he never doubted it. He remembered their night of sleuthing, her tight black jeans, and her even-tighter turtleneck. A familiar flush traveled up from his groin, and he pictured his mother. That'll stop it.

He signaled to J across the bar and pointed towards Julie. The dark brew's foam spilled over the edge of the icy mug, as J set it down on a white napkin in front of Julie.

"Put Bobby's on my tab, too," Julie said. "I owe him at least one or two for being a bitch the other night."

J nodded and walked back across the bar. Either the guy J was talking to wasn't as dull as he looked, or she was smart enough to know when to leave her patrons alone. The results were the same, and Bobby didn't care. Either way, he had Julie all to himself.

"You don't owe me a thing. You're under a lot of stress with Ellen gone." Bobby set his beer on the bar and turned to Julie. "If you wanna talk, I'm a good listener." Her dark eyes met his for a moment before looking away.

"Not really." She set her beer down, rested her left elbow on the bar, and twisted on her stool to face Bobby. "Ellen's back on Monday, and things'll be back to normal." Her sigh was deep and long. "It's the one time of year I count on Ellen being here, and I'm tired. There are too many things to do once tax returns start pouring in and all hell breaks loose. Dealing with Michael is just one too many."

For someone not wanting to talk, Julie was doing an excellent job. Bobby leaned his right elbow on the bar and twisted to meet her gaze. "What do you mean?" Julie was relaxing, so he'd keep her going. Gathering more information about Michael wouldn't hurt either. He trusted the guy about as far as he could throw him, and given their relative sizes, that wouldn't be too far.

"Don't get me wrong, he's a good accountant." Julie, never at a loss for words, hesitated. "That's what Ellen was looking for."

She spun away, looked across the bar, and took another swig of beer. "But he doesn't feel like one of us. I mean, what the fuck's up with those big white choppers?" Julie tossed her head back and burst out laughing.

Bobby sputtered his last gulp of beer into his right fist. "They're the biggest damn flashers I've ever seen. They're like a landing strip." He wiped his hand on his jeans, grabbed the bar's edge, and leaned back laughing, "You can see him coming a mile away."

Julie's face went blank, and she blinked hard as if recalling something unpleasant. Whatever it was vanished as quickly as it had appeared, and she slapped her right hand on his and giggled.

"I've tried. Believe me, I've tried to like him because Ellen wanted me to take care of him while she was gone. But he's too full of himself. We're a team at Hartmann, and we don't need anyone who thinks he's doing us a fucking favor by being there."

Bobby placed his left hand over hers and gave it a gentle squeeze. He looked up to see a playful smile illuminating her face. The corners of his eyes crinkled, and he held her gaze. "It's great to have you back. You were starting to worry me."

They tipped their bottles in silent solidarity. He was back in her good graces.

CHAPTER 83

JULIE

"ONE MORE?" JULIE TURNED TO BOBBY. THEIR moment of contention had passed, and the last hour was filled with playful banter and subtle flirting. Not that she had strayed too far. Bobby was, and always would be, a good friend. She couldn't imagine anything that would change that.

Bobby twisted his wrist to check his watch. "Sure, why not?" he laughed. "But you're a bad influence. I won't get home until well after midnight. You'll be on my shit list if I can't get out of bed tomorrow morning."

"Boo-hoo-hoo. No sympathy here." She tossed her hair over her shoulder. "You know how to say no, don't you?"

"I do, but have I ever said no to you?" Julie remembered one time, and that was the other night. Not one of her proudest moments. Best to leave it alone.

"Two more." Julie lifted her bottle to get J's attention. "We'll call it a night after these. But first, I need your advice."

"My advice? Be still my heart!" Bobby's reaction was not what she expected.

"Fuck, am I that bad? Tell me I'm not." Julie took pride in being open to others' viewpoints. Maybe she was just kidding herself.

"Don't get your undies in a bundle. I'm teasing." Bobby grabbed the two beers from J and handed one to Julie. "How can I help?"

"It won't be easy, but Ellen needs to take off her rose-colored lenses and see Michael-the-asshole instead of Michael-the-savior." Julie corralled her wild curls and wrapped them around her fist.

"We don't have time for her to wade through his bullshit. Michael needs to be gone—now." The more Julie thought about Michael, the angrier she became. Her initial admiration evaporated, replaced by something short of hatred.

"Well, I can tell you this." Bobby set down his beer. "Ellen doesn't like to be told anything, but she won't ignore the evidence. She may need some time to get there, but when she does, she'll be the first to admit she was wrong." Bobby sounded more certain of that than she was.

"Yeah, right. Time and patience, my strong suit. Not." Julie wiggled her butt on her stool to prove her point. "How do you propose I do that? I need him gone now!"

"Might I repeat myself? Don't get your undies in a bundle," Bobby was serious. "Michael will reveal his true self. It didn't take us long to figure it out, and it won't take Ellen long either."

"And what do I do in the meantime? Twiddle my fucking thumbs?"

"Exactly. But you'll be twiddling with the rest of us. We'll keep you on target."

"And who might this we be? You and your special little buddy?" Did she really say that? Shit, how could this work when her mouth had a mind of its own?

"You, me, and Katie. That's who. She's right there with us. You have your very own, very special ménage à trois." Bobby's twinkling eyes dared her to say more.

She tipped her bottle in surrender. Her mouth stayed shut.

CHAPTER 84

MICHAEL

DUMB MOVE. MICHAEL RUBBED HIS TEMPLES WITH both hands, then wiped the tension from his eyes. Despite his many attempts to get a few words from her, Julie ignored him all day. He finished his final phone call of the day, but she was gone. Did she see him outside her condo last night? What was he thinking, following her home? Dammit, he wasn't a stalker. Julie was entitled to say no to his invitation. What did he care if she lied that she had things to do? Who cared if it was just an excuse?

But the truth was, he did care. And he didn't like it. There was something about Julie that drove him crazy. His mission was more important than being sidetracked by a foolish romance. His first impression of her had undergone a drastic change. She was not an untalented bookkeeper parading as an accountant, too lazy to sit for the CPA exam. She was far from that. She had a curious, creative mind that sought out and found solutions to her clients' tax problems. She was every bit, if not more, talented than most of the CPAs he had worked with. If he was honest with himself, he was jealous of her talents.

He hated that Ellen hired her first, and that after last night's dumb move, it would be harder to lure Julie away. Before last night, he was certain he was gaining Julie's trust, and she would've been ripe for the picking. But now, he wasn't so sure. He needed to back off, to be part of Ellen's team, an equal to Julie, someone she could trust. If Julie doubted Michael, so would Ellen, and his plan would falter. But it would not fail. He had come too far, and the end was in sight. Ellen had been salivating for Michael to join the staff from the moment she met him, and he needed to keep playing her. It should be easy.

If he didn't make any more stupid moves, Julie would be his. And, with Julie at his side, Hartmann Associates would wither and die. Michael Prescott, CPA, would thrive in its place.

CHAPTER 85

ELLEN

ELLEN HAD A LOT OF QUESTIONS FOR DAVID, BUT now was not the time. David was a different man from that first day when Diane's body lay crumpled on the floor. Gone were his anger, superiority, and entitlement. The man from that day bore no resemblance to the man pacing across the room. Something had changed, and it showed in his face. The menacing demeanor, piercing eyes, and rigid posture had been replaced with a vulnerability that softened the image he struggled to present to the outside world. It was as if he had given in. But, to what?

The dog in David's lap was yet another sign that he had changed. They all had. Her hand rested on Little Pup, and Ellen glanced over at Henry. He was staring down at the white dog, which was inching closer to him. The three dogs provided a welcome distraction from the uncomfortable pause in David's story.

David cleared his throat, rubbed his chin with his left hand, and took a long, deep breath. His exhale was slow, almost painful. He began.

"My father said the truth hurts for a little while, but a lie hurts forever. I thought it only applied to the little lies of childhood, not the secrets I carried. I now know that's not the case." He dropped his head and stared at the floor.

Ellen's hand moved to her heart. What was it about Nashville and lies? First, Henry's omissions, and now David's? And the lies all revolved around Sam, the biggest liar of all. What else would David reveal? Ellen listened for more.

"Life was normal until Sam's last year of high school. I was just seven or eight, but old enough to know something was up. Sam stopped listening to my dad, pushed him away, talked back. Mom told Dad it was a teenage phase, that he'd come around. But it kept getting worse. Overnight, Sam became a different person. He stopped being my best friend. He stopped being my hero." David stood up, placed his little black dog in the chair, and resumed pacing.

"One night, after graduation, when Dad was out, there was a knock on the door. Sam ran to answer it, but Mom got there first. Sam pushed her aside, saying, 'Don't try to stop me. I'm going with my dad.'

"A man I didn't know, but it was obvious everyone else did, sneered at Mom and followed Sam upstairs. Two minutes later, they each carried a large box stuffed with everything Sam cared about. He didn't even say goodbye to me." Ellen watched David wipe away an escaping tear. Thirty years may have passed, but David's pain was as real as if it had happened today.

"Dad tried to find Sam, but to no avail. He didn't want to be found, and Mom had no idea where to start looking. She hadn't heard from his father for almost two decades, and Sam never let on that his birth father had contacted him. Mom and Dad were a mess, and so was I. But I pretended I was fine. Lying about Mom's drinking made me a pro."

David's pacing halted, and he looked down. "I sometimes think Dad's heart attack came from losing Sam. Mom's pain, on top of his own, was too much to bear." His words were nearly inaudible, as if his internal dialogue had become public.

"It was ten years before we heard from Sam again. He was in trouble and wanted Mom to send money to bail him out. I didn't want to talk to him, not that he even asked for me. I was so angry that he left us, angry that he didn't show up for Dad's funeral, and angry that he wanted our help now. I pleaded with Mom to let him go. Of course, she didn't. She sent him the money, and Sam disappeared again."

Ellen scratched her head. What was he suggesting? She appreciated that David needed to get this off his chest, but what did it have to do with her? She was getting impatient, tired of his games. She slid her hair behind her left ear and waited for more.

"A little later, we got the whole story. A family friend thought we'd like to know, and sent us a newspaper clipping. It's something you need to know too." David shooed Archie from Diane's chair and sat down. He looked across at Ellen. She returned his gaze and waited. Whatever was coming was arriving at eye level.

"You see, Sam Davis is not his real name. Or, at least, not his full name." David paused to let it sink in. "He was born Samuel Davis Hennessey."

"And Sam Hennessey has a criminal history."

CHAPTER 86

DAVID

THERE. IT WAS OVER. AND, JUST LIKE HIS FATHER promised, the pain was gone. Gone was the angst of carrying his family's secrets. Gone was having to choose his words wisely. He didn't have to worry about tripping over a carefully crafted story. He could live and speak his truth whenever, wherever, and with whomever he pleased. He was in command of his life, and protecting Sam Hennessey's double life was a thing of the past.

David lifted Archie into his lap and scratched the dog's ears. His body relaxed as he stroked Archie's coarse fur, and the need to pace disappeared. He looked at his audience. Henry was studying Ellen as if to gauge her reaction. But her face was an emotional blank slate, honed over hours and years of listening to clients' stories. It didn't give away anything.

"Interesting. Tell me more." Ellen's voice was calm and non-judgmental. She was a pro. Henry was not. He looked confused and dismayed by David's confession and Ellen's lack of expression.

Sam was born as Sam Hennessey Jr., but he took my dad's last name when they married. We were just Sam and David Garrett, my dad's two sons. Sam Hennessey didn't exist, nor did his birth father, as far as we were concerned. I think that's what hurt Dad the most. Sam was his son, not his stepson, not Diane's son, but his son. When Sam left without a word or any further contact, he had to accept that the Sam Garrett he loved and knew was gone.

Sam was eighteen, and it didn't take much for him to fall under his birth father's spell. I never asked for all the details, but they went to Nashville and became minor players in the growing entertainment scene. They came up with a get-rich-quick scheme and were indicted for selling illegal shares in a TV production company, claiming they held the rights to the life story of a major country star. That's when Sam called Mom for bail money.

David saw Henry's eyes light up. "Wow. I knew Sam was good at what he did; it showed in his work. His productions were amazing. Who was the star?" Henry was captivated by the prospect of rubbing elbows with a star, just like the duped investors had been.

"Doesn't matter. There was no star, no contracts, no production company. It was all bogus, a figment of their imaginations." David didn't stop for Henry's fandom. It was time to burst the bubble. "You may have noticed that Sam is slick. So was his dad. They were equally talented at convincing others to trust them."

David looked at Ellen. Her neutral facade shifted from ghostly pale to fiery red. He had hit a nerve. "Ultimately, they were convicted but never served time because the verdict was overturned on appeal due to a technicality; something about the statute of limitations."

"What? Wait. Did you say Nashville?" Ellen's anger interrupted his story. "Convicted here in Nashville, and he came back?" Ellen didn't like being duped. Who would?

"I know. The entertainment community is tight. I'm sure the scandal was in all the newspapers. Why would he risk it?" David rested his hand on Archie's back. The gentle rise and fall of the little dog's breathing calmed him.

"When Sam showed up asking Mom to move to Nashville, I couldn't understand why, but I never asked. Maybe he thought enough time had passed. Twenty years is a long time. Nashville has exploded, and people have short memories. It seemed like a huge gamble to me, but Sam convinced Mom that he wanted her back in his life, and I couldn't talk Mom out of going. She missed her Sammy, and as far as she was concerned, he could do no wrong." David expected his stomach to lurch, as it always did when he thought of his mom and Sam and the secrets they carried. Today, it didn't. His father was right.

"And that brings us to now. I didn't report Sam missing because he's done it before, and he'll do it again. Like it or not, that's who Sam Davis Hennessey is. He's gone, and as far as I'm concerned, he's not worth looking for. Trust me, it's time to forget about him and go on with your lives."

CHAPTER 87

HENRY

HENRY WASN'T SURPRISED BY DAVID'S STORY; HE had expected at least some version of it. But expecting it didn't make the truth more palatable. He had stowed away his negative expectations to make room for comforting hope. Hope that his assumptions were wrong. Hope that muted his misgivings and amplified his desire for a fairy-tale ending. But David's truths stripped away hope's cover and revealed Henry's misguided view of things. No wonder Ellen didn't take him seriously. He was still such a child.

His hand reached for Kramer. The fluffy white dog snuggled closer as the conversation grew tense, and he interpreted Henry's hand on his back as a signal to burrow into his lap. Henry didn't push him away. Somehow, the dog made him feel less ashamed about keeping Sam's secrets and gave him the courage to look at Ellen. Maybe a loyal companion wasn't such a bad idea.

She, too, was focused on the sleeping dog in her lap. Henry watched the gentle up-and-down movement of Ellen's hand as it rested on Little Pup's belly, and his runaway breathing slowed to match its rhythm. His guilt and shame dissolved. There was nothing to be ashamed of. Expectations, whether good or bad, were a natural extension of hope. He'd rather be at fault for being too optimistic than too pessimistic.

Ellen's smile sagged. "I'm so sorry, Henry. I know how important your job with Sam is to you, and now it's gone. Sam was your mentor, and his projects allowed you to showcase your talents. It's a big loss. For everyone, including you."

Leave it to Ellen to think of him first. "The same could be true for you," he said. "Sam strung you along because you were so passionate about *The Money Dynamic*. I was too with my career. We were easy flies to catch in his web of deception."

"You could interpret it that way. But I see it another way." Ellen tucked her hair behind her ear; things were about to get serious. "Yes, we were both passionate, but so was Sam. He wouldn't have wasted time on us if he didn't see something he liked. The same goes for all the other projects he was working on. Even if you can't see it today, it's reflected in what he produced. It's pretty damned impressive. And so are you. This is not the end."

Henry was smart enough to listen to Ellen's experience. Working for Sam was his first real job. And even though it was gone, the breadth and depth of everything he learned wouldn't go with it. All the good, the bad, and the ugly would be with Henry forever. And part of the good was Ellen. He reached across Kramer to take her hand. Little Pup rustled when she accepted it.

"Thanks, I needed that. You always say what I need to hear." Henry squeezed her hand. "What will I do without you?"

David cleared his throat, and Henry's face flushed in response. Ellen's did not. Henry squeezed her hand for reassurance.

CHAPTER 88

ELLEN

ELLEN WAS GRATEFUL FOR DAVID'S REMINDER that they were not alone. Henry's questions and concerns could wait. They had tonight and all day tomorrow, but this was their last time with David, and she had questions that only he could answer. They needed to move on.

"Thanks for your honesty, David. I wish I were surprised by everything you've told us. I had so many chances to see the truth, but I was blind to what I didn't want to see. Even though I was prepared to make this my last trip, I still hoped Sam had good intentions and would come through in the end." She rested her elbow on the arm of the sofa, leaned her chin on her hand, and asked David, "Is it possible to be a liar and have good intentions? Or am I just being naïve?"

"Good intentions." David's voice dropped almost to a whisper. "Sam always had good intentions. But you know what they say: *good intentions with a bad approach often leads to a poor result*. It's what Dad said. Guess Sam wasn't listening."

"But that's the thing. I believe he had all three: great approach, great results, and good intentions." She turned to Henry. "You worked with him. Am I being an idiot?"

"Of course you aren't," Henry said. "He might've had all three, but it wasn't enough. Something went wrong. Maybe he owed money to the wrong people. More and more, he started avoiding calls and was more hyper than usual."

"Hyper, right," David agreed. "That's how I could always tell something was wrong. He talked faster, hopped from one foot to the other, and wouldn't look you in the eye. It was a dead giveaway."

"I never saw that side of him, but I should've known the moment his excuses started rolling in. But then again, most of his lies came over the phone, and when I was here, he was in full control. I'm sorry, I missed it. If I hadn't, I might not have sent that last ten grand." Ellen hated to make it about money, but there it was, raising its ugly head. "I believed that he was really sending it back to me. I'm such a fool."

"Ten grand! A lot to lose for anyone," David commiserated. "If you don't mind me asking, how much did you invest with Sam?"

"Invest? Maybe, but I'm not sure it was a wise investment. He earned a lot of it for sure, but with him gone, it was probably for nothing." Once again, she was making excuses for someone who didn't care. Would she ever stop being such a Pollyanna?

"Total between Sterling and me? About sixty grand." She shook her head, and her dimples disappeared.

"That much? I had no idea," Henry said, squeezing her hand again. "Can you forgive me for not telling you sooner?"

David leaned forward, and Archie jumped off his lap. "Wait, you've lost me. Tell you what, sooner? And who is Sterling?"

Ellen let Henry answer. "I overheard Sam's little white lies but didn't tell Ellen. It's something I'll regret forever."

"Believe me, I get it," David said. "Been there, done that. But who's Sterling?"

"Sterling and I started *The Money Dynamic* together," Ellen continued. "Sam's sales pitch, obvious talents, and excitement for a money program written by a psychologist and an accountant blinded us. We jumped in with both feet. At first, Sam came through, but weeks, months, and more than a year went by with nothing but excuses, and Sterling cut his losses and dropped out. If I had followed his lead, I could've saved my last ten grand. Talk about throwing good money after bad." Ellen was disgusted by her inability to let go.

"Stop beating yourself up, Ellen. It won't do any good." Henry reached for Ellen's hand. "Maybe David can help find that ten grand?"

Henry had placed Ellen's cards on the table. It was time to move past her pity party and move on.

CHAPTER 89

DAVID

"WHAT CAN I DO TO HELP?" RECOVERING ELLEN'S ten grand was a long shot, but David was willing to listen. "I'll do what I can. But first, don't second-guess yourself. Sam is easy to like, be dazzled by, and find excuses for. Until he's not. Then you're left with egg on your face. I've been there too many times. It took time and therapy to see that it was never my fault. It's not your fault, either. Sam's a slippery character; he's tough to grab hold of."

"You can say that again! Whenever I confronted him, he slithered from my agenda to his and convinced me I was being unreasonable. He knew all my buttons and wasn't afraid to push them." Ellen raked her fingers through her hair and rubbed the back of her neck. Henry stared at his dog.

"He was uncanny at reading people," David continued. "If only he had used it for good. So much talent; so much wasted." Even with Sam lost and probably gone forever, the pull of his brother tugged at him. Would he ever be free?

"So again, how can I help?" It was time for David to release Sam and his problems and assist everyone in moving forward.

"Henry and I spent this week combing through the files at Brand & Broadcast to find some clue as to what went wrong and why Sam disappeared. Being an accountant, I wanted to follow the money. There's always a story to be told." Ellen was true to her profession; everything revolved around money.

"Makes sense. What did you find?"

"Nothing. Not a thing. And that's the problem. What business doesn't have financial records, especially with multiple projects underway? We couldn't find anything. It's as if the company and Sam were running on fumes." Frustration and fatigue seeped into Ellen's voice.

"Okay, I can help with that, although I'm not sure how much help it'll be. I found three boxes of company files and couldn't decide what to do with them. My gut reaction was to destroy them."

"Don't do that!" Ellen's reaction was swift and decisive. "You can't ask a CPA to be a party to financial destruction." Her laugh softened her initial response.

"Settle down," David chuckled. "You've made my decision for me. They're all yours. There's nothing more to hide, and if you can find a trail back to Sam, have at it! He's all yours, and so are those boxes."

He pointed at the last three boxes sitting in the foyer. He was done. Done with Sam and done cleaning up his messes. David was free.

CHAPTER 90

HENRY

HENRY LOADED THE LAST OF THE THREE BOXES into the back of the Escalade and cringed. Three more boxes to distract Ellen. He didn't want to complain, but he wasn't ready to spend another day pawing through papers. And yet, like it or not, he was here to support Ellen in whatever way it played out. He wasn't stopping now.

"What's your plan for these?" An innocent question whose answer Henry guessed.

"Don't look so glum." Ellen placed her hand on his shoulder, and his tension began to ease. "I promise we won't spend the whole day on this."

"But…" Henry hesitated.

"But? I don't understand." Ellen slid her hand down his back. Henry tried not to melt.

"There's always a *but*." Damn it; he was starting to whine. "I know you well enough. Not spending the whole day doesn't mean we won't spend *most* of the day on this. Am I right?" Henry made light of his whining by adding a broad smile.

"You are. But my curiosity is killing me. I gotta see what's in those boxes. Let's go back to the office and at least sort through them. I promise we'll be done in plenty of time to do whatever you want on a Friday night in Nashville."

"I'm going to hold you to that," Henry teased. "I'll be a bear if you don't."

"I promise I won't. We'll sort through the contents, toss what's worthless, and ship the rest to Portland. It's very doable for today, and that'll give us tonight and all day Saturday to enjoy Nashville and each other."

Henry wrapped Ellen in his arms and kissed the top of her head. "Let's get started."

CHAPTER 91

ELLEN

SUNDAY MORNING. ELLEN BOARDED HER FINAL flight from Nashville with mixed emotions. The excitement of reuniting with her sons contrasted with the melancholy from Henry's final goodbye. The previous two days had been more than she hoped for. Music, laughter, and love reminded her of what she had missed over the last five years. It was too easy for a single mother of three boys to forget her own needs. Henry had reminded her.

She buckled her seatbelt, closed her eyes, and waited for the gentle swaying of the plane's taxiing to lull her to sleep. She had no energy to talk to her fellow seatmates or open a book, but her mind didn't get the memo. It was a jumble of sounds, sights, and smells from her final days with Henry.

Friday night, after being cooped up in Brand & Broadcast's offices all day, they were ready for some action. Ellen followed Henry as they bounced from one music venue to another. They listened to bluegrass, gospel, jazz, and blues before joining his friends at The Listening Room Café for late-night country rock. They shared the best of Nashville's greasy burgers, crispy fries, unhealthy bar food, and beer — lots and lots of beer. She fit in easily with Henry's friends and, for a moment, their age difference disappeared.

Henry picked her up at the hotel on Saturday morning at ten to kick off his perfectly planned day. He skipped their usual mediocre hotel breakfast. Instead, he took her downtown to 417 Union for classic American fare. The aroma of good home cooking wafted through the upscale diner and stirred Ellen's growling stomach. They lingered over coffee, buttermilk biscuits, and candied bacon, then shared an order of lemon blueberry pancakes. They finished well past noon, and afterward, they strolled through the Victory and Bicentennial Mall Parks surrounding the nearby Tennessee State Capitol. The weather was a balmy sixty-five, unusual for Nashville in January, unheard of for Maine. They meandered from one park bench to another, enjoying the beautiful day and each other's company. Fresh air and sunshine were exactly what she needed. Best of all, she left Sam and his problems far behind.

The plane gently rocked as it approached the runway, and Ellen began to feel drowsy. A Mona Lisa smile played on her lips as she remembered their last dinner together. Henry's quest for the perfect, intimate restaurant mirrored what she would have chosen. Tables draped in white were discreetly set apart to muffle the soft conversations of other diners. Classical music whispered in the background, and exquisite lighting was bright enough to gaze into Henry's eyes, yet dim enough to create a sense of privacy. The menu complemented the elegant setting and offered at least one perfect choice for even the most eclectic diner. Everything was orchestrated for pure romance, and if nothing else, Ellen was a romantic at heart. Henry understood her well.

Ellen's enigmatic smile shifted into one of pure contentment. *A jug of wine, a loaf of bread, and thou* echoed through her being. As the plane climbed into the sky, she drifted off to dream. Yes, their time together was over, but they would always have Nashville.

CHAPTER 92

MICHAEL

AS MICHAEL EXPECTED, HARTMANN AND ASSOCIATES was empty on a Sunday morning. In a few weeks, this would change as the staff's overtime hours began to increase. The one good thing about the long hours of tax season was that Ellen's firm had no rules, either spoken or unspoken, about when to work those extra hours. Each person could decide for themselves. Some worked late every weeknight and took the weekend off; others worked eight to five on weekdays and added a day or two on the weekend. Unlike today, the office was never vacant once overtime began.

He laid the floral bouquet he carried on the reception counter, stripped off his down jacket, and opened the coat closet. It was filled with abandoned coats, umbrellas, and other belongings left behind from the summer. Soon, forgetful clients would come in for tax meetings and reclaim them. Today, his coat was the sole reflection of the day's frigid temperature. He straightened his jacket's shoulders on a hanger and closed the closet door.

He cranked up the office thermostat, grabbed the flowers, and headed to the kitchen. If he remembered right, there were vases under the sink from past arrangements delivered to die in some accountant's office. He chose a red vase, filled it with water, and swirled in the prepackaged plant food. He angle-cut the ends of the stems and dropped the entire bunch in the vase. Red roses laced with baby's breath unfurled into a good enough arrangement. If he had thought of this sooner, he would've bought a more impressive one at a flower shop yesterday instead of having to choose from the grocery store's early Valentine's Day stock.

Michael carried the arrangement to Ellen's office and placed it on a coaster. Damn, he forgot a gift card. He ripped the top sheet from a Hartmann and Associates sticky note pad and wrote, *Welcome back!* He paused. Should he sign it? Should it be *All of us? Senior Staff? Michael?* The decision was easy. He signed his name and stuck the note to the side of the vase facing the door. Why should he give anyone else the credit? It was his idea, not theirs, and by signing his name, Ellen would speak to him before anyone else. He'd be in control of any narrative buzzing around the office.

Most of the staff at Hartmann and Associates accepted him as the newest hire, but he considered himself above them, not one of them, and he didn't engage much. He was superficially friendly but didn't encourage anything deeper. The two CPAs at his level were too busy managing their own client work or supervising their assigned staff. They weren't worth getting close to, either. If they had done their jobs better, Ellen wouldn't have felt the need to hire him.

That left Julie, and as much as he hated to admit it, Katie. Michael couldn't understand the influence Katie had at

Hartmann and Associates. She was just a receptionist; why did her opinion matter? But somehow, it did, and Katie was very clear about her dislike for him. Everyone else liked him. What was her problem? He ran his tongue over his perfect teeth.

Which brought him to Julie. Julie was putty in his hands at first, and now she was drifting away. Sure, following Julie home was a misstep, but there was more to it. Katie must be feeding her crap. What else could it be? He had to win Katie over and Julie back for his plan to succeed. Using Ellen was the fastest solution for both problems.

He sat in Ellen's chair and put his feet on the desk. A peevish seagull pecked at the sliding glass door. Ellen's favorite pen hit the glass, and the pest flew off. *Bullseye!* He repositioned the red vase on the desk, retrieved the pen, and slipped it into his pocket. His work was done.

CHAPTER 93

ELLEN

ELLEN STEPPED GINGERLY ONTO PORTLAND Jetport's escalator for the ride down to baggage claim. She felt groggy from a much-needed nap after yesterday's too-full and too-late night and slept through the flight's beverage cart and credit card hawking. The landing at LaGuardia had jolted her awake, and she used the brief layover to stretch her legs and find a pet relief area for Little Pup. The dog crate she bought for the trip fit under the seat in front of her, and Little Pup didn't make a sound on their initial flight to New York. She hoped her good fortune would continue. By the time the plane took off for the second leg of their trip, they were both fast asleep. She needed the four-and-a-half-hour journey to transition back to her role as a mother. Little Pup would be well-rested when he met his new family.

It was the weekend, and she hoped her boys' father had brought them to the airport to meet her. She hadn't asked, but it's what he did when they were married, and they had worked hard together to maintain civility during their divorce. The boys didn't need to suffer for their mistakes. She searched the crowd and came up empty. She should have told him how much she needed her sons right now. But communication was never their strong suit, and she could get an Uber for the short ride home. She stepped off the escalator and headed to the baggage carousel.

"You're back!" Ellen heard Jack's voice first. Six arms embraced her from behind amid Ethan's squeals of Mommy and Kevin's sober Momther, his special name for her after a clever misspelling on his Cub Scout's wood-burning project.

"My sweet boys, you're here!" She mouthed a thank you to their father standing in the background. "Oh, how I've missed you!" She dropped three kisses on three heads.

They indulged her hugs and kisses until Little Pup began whimpering. She set the carrier on the floor, opened the door, and lifted him out.

"Kevin, dig around in my carry-on until you find his leash. It should be near the top." Ellen hugged the little dog, attached the leash, and set him on the ground.

The three boys plopped down and formed a safe circle around Little Pup. The dog's sniffer went into full gear as he investigated each boy. Ellen's rambunctious threesome became quiet and calm as they let the little dog greet them. After three rounds of getting acquainted, Little Pup was done and settled down for a nap.

"I think he likes you," Ellen laughed. "Should we keep him?"

"Mommy, is he ours? What about Random?" Ethan's eyes sparkled with wonder as he reached for her hand.

She scooched down, joined their circle of love, and thought about their curly-coated Wheaten terrier. "He's here to stay. Don't worry about Random; she's getting lazy in her old age. He'll keep her young." She scratched the dog's ears. "He's called Little Pup."

"Weird name," Jack piped up. "But he's kind of cute anyway." He grabbed the dog's leash and walked toward the baggage carousel. "He can sleep in my room."

"We'll see," Ellen said. The other two boys grinned wickedly at their oldest brother. They relied on their mother to keep things fair.

Bringing Little Pup home had been the right decision. Ellen envisioned Henry snuggling with Kramer, and David's daughter squealing with delight at the sight of Archie's spiky black hair. The dogs had found their happy ending. Would she?

CHAPTER 94

KATIE

KATIE PUSHED THE RED BUTTON ON THE COFFEE maker. Most mornings, especially Monday mornings, called for a good cup of black coffee. She tried to be the first one in the office to make that first pot the way she liked it: robust with a spicy sprinkle of cinnamon. Others might complain, but they had plenty of opportunities throughout the day to brew whatever and whenever they wanted it. For now, the early bird got the worm.

While the coffee brewed, she quickly made her rounds of the office to ensure that everything was in order for the upcoming week. Bobby was skilled at his job, but with instructions to never touch anything on anyone's desk, it meant there would be the previous week's used coffee cups or water glasses to collect. It wasn't her responsibility to clean up after others, but she enjoyed doing it. Making everyone else's day run smoothly was her main priority.

The overpowering smell of cheap roses accosted her as she headed down the hall. She followed her nose to Ellen's office, where the offending roses sat on the desk in Katie's red vase. A not-to-be-missed sticky note with handwriting she recognized was stuck to the front. What a snake! She wanted to rip it up and throw the whole thing away, but she didn't. Ellen was a big girl; she could read between the lines as well as Katie could.

Katie juggled five dirty cups from Julie's office, remnants of a day overflowing with clients, and returned to the kitchen. After loading the dishwasher, she filled a clean mug with her aromatic brew. She breathed in its energizing scent and carried it to her favorite window. The first sip calmed her nerves, still jangling from those stinking roses. The hot coffee and the peaceful scene worked their magic, and she relaxed. Everything would fall into place. She and Ellen had agreed on the perfect cup of black coffee, and they'd agree about Michael too. She was sure of it.

Her reverie was interrupted by the sound of the elevator doors opening, and her automatic receptionist smile spread across her face. Was it Ellen? No one seemed to know when she would return, but they all hoped it would be soon. She turned away from the windows to see who was arriving this early.

Julie's curls, damp from her morning shower, were stiff and frozen as she stripped off her coat. "Didn't your mother tell you to never go out with a wet head? You'll catch a raging cold!" Katie scolded.

"Waste of time. With a mop like mine, I'd have to get up an hour earlier to dry it. I'll take my chances." She tossed the icy ringlets over her shoulder. "Coffee ready? Didn't have time to stop at Dunkin' on my way."

"You'll have to suffer through a cup of mine. Cream and sugar should make it palatable for you," Katie teased.

"Your coffee would put hair on anyone's chest. It could add to this wild mane if I don't dilute it with some sweetness." She lifted the damp, dark curtain from her shoulders and turned toward the kitchen.

"You'll need a stiff cup when I tell you about Michael's latest trick." Katie decided to test her latest theory, believing that Julie's infatuation with Michael was dwindling.

"What? What's he up to now?" Julie stopped and turned around.

"He bought Ellen a bunch of cheap roses to welcome her back. Can you believe it?" Katie giggled.

"What the fuck! Someone should tell him how *not* to impress Ellen. You better prepare her so that she can fake her response. This is going to be epic!"

The elevator dinged, and not knowing who had arrived, they tried to control their laughter. Michael stepped off.

"You're having way too much fun on a Monday morning. What's so funny? You must've had a great weekend. I know I did." Michael flashed his signature Chiclet's grin. They both ignored it.

Katie moved to her desk, slid a coaster under her coffee cup, and turned on her monitor. "Anyway, Julie, I'll keep you informed." Julie walked into the kitchen, leaving Michael speechless for a change.

CHAPTER 95

JULIE

IT WAS LATE AFTERNOON BY THE TIME ELLEN made it over to Julie's office. After ten years of working together, Julie knew better than to crowd her on her first day back. Nothing was so urgent that it couldn't wait until Ellen had settled in, and that required uninterrupted time. Tasks multiplied whenever you were away, and answering emails, sorting through snail mail, and returning phone calls could be overwhelming. Sometimes, it didn't seem worth it to take a vacation, and even though Julie tried to fill in the gaps during Ellen's lengthy absence, there were still tasks that Ellen had to handle on her own.

Ellen slid into Julie's client chair. The dark circles under her eyes said she was beyond tired. A weary exhalation escaped as Ellen leaned back and folded her arms behind her head.

"You look exhausted," Julie called it as she saw it. "Time to put your feet up and call it a day. Go home."

"I am, and I will. I was so tired when I got home yesterday, but I had been away for so long that the boys' wishes were my command. Thank God they go to bed early. Another late night would've been too much. I turned off their lights and went straight to bed. Tomorrow will be easier." Julie would ask about those other late nights another time.

Ellen leaned forward on the desk. "I want to apologize for forcing you to hold the bag while I was gone. I knew you could handle it, but I didn't think it would be that long," she said. "I left you with too much to do preparing for tax season. But at least you had Michael. He said he helped with a lot of the stuff. I'm glad I hired him." Ellen's tired eyes told Julie to let go of Michael's exaggeration for now, but not for too much longer.

"What'd you think of his flowers?" Julie changed the subject. She wouldn't let that go.

"His heart was in the right place; you can't fault him for that. He doesn't know about my aversion to flowers in the office. At least they weren't those damn stinky stargazer lilies. They make me gag every time." Ellen rubbed her left eye and sighed. "It was kind of sweet."

"Sweet? Is this the same Ellen I know and love? Sweet is not something that impresses Ellen Hartmann. What happened in Nashville?" Julie teased.

"Ok, maybe it is a bit of brown-nosing, but soon, he'll learn that teamwork is what counts most at Hartmann and Associates. Until then, let's cut him some slack." Ellen rubbed her eyes and blinked hard.

Julie heard her father's whisper from deep inside, *stick a fork in her; she's done,* his favorite words whenever her mother was overtired or overwhelmed. "Go home. You're exhausted. We can catch up tomorrow. All routine stuff anyway."

Tomorrow, Julie would begin to trickle the truth to Ellen about who Michael really was. He and his pearly whites weren't going anywhere—yet. Hopefully, it wouldn't take too long. Julie was so over him.

CHAPTER 96

LITTLE PUP

LITTLE PUP STUDIED THE CAGE IN THE CORNER OF the large room in his new home. The lady with kind eyes wanted it to be his safe space, but it reminded him of that other place, with its cold, hard floors filled with terrified dogs and too much noise. It was too soon to forget. He thought he'd never have to return to a cage after leaving that terrible place. He liked his other new home with the man with threads for hair and the lady with the auburn hair, even with the yelling lady there. And then life changed. The man and lady were gone, and the yelling lady stopped making noise.

When the home was emptied of everything except Little Pup's belongings, the lady with kind eyes showed him the cage in the corner that she had brought with her. He fled to his bed and closed his eyes. If he couldn't see it, maybe it would disappear too. The soft cadence of her words soothed his distrustful soul, and the tasty treat she laid on the soft cushion inside the cage called to his hungry stomach. She was patient while he gathered his courage and sniffed the cage's perimeter. His hungry stomach couldn't wait any longer; he ventured in, snatched a favorite Snausage, and scurried out. After the third time, he stayed to enjoy his snack. She kept the door open and let him be.

The next day, she murmured sweet sounds in his ears, placed him inside, and closed the door. The latched door frightened him, but he trusted her kind eyes and soothing voice. She carried him inside the cage to the big black moving machine. Little Pup worked hard to stay calm because that was what she wanted.

Eventually, the two of them set off in the big moving machine, and when it finally stopped, the lady with the kind eyes lifted the carrier with Little Pup out. She swung the cage with him inside next to her as she walked through a noisy place filled with many people but no other cages. His eyes grew heavy from the movement, and he fell asleep. He awoke as she navigated through a cramped space packed with too many people. She murmured to him as she slid his cage under the seat in front of hers. He calmed himself by picturing her kind eyes and fell back asleep.

And now he was here, in his new home, with the lady with kind eyes and her three little men. Sometimes, the three played, and sometimes they fought, but mostly they liked each other. The three were like his pack with Archie and Kramer. He sighed. It would take time, but maybe, if Little Pup was lucky, this new pack of three would take him in too.

CHAPTER 97

MICHAEL

MICHAEL WAITED AT THE FRONT DESK FOR KATIE to be free. He didn't need to be there, but he wanted to get on Katie's good side. Her feelings for Michael were anything but subtle, and a little schmoozing couldn't hurt. Since Ellen's return, he tried to keep himself busy, but Julie kept her distance, making it hard for him to ask her for work. Administrative tasks might be beneath him, but pretending to be a team player could help him gain an ally. Michael braced himself, ready to overlook Katie's attitude.

"Can I help you with something, Michael?" Her voice was cold and unforgiving.

"Thought I'd see if there's anything I can do for you. I have some time, and I know how busy you are answering the phone." He leaned his left elbow on the counter and struck his you-gotta-friend pose.

"Well, aren't you being Mister Nice Guy." The smirk on her face told him she didn't mean it. He ignored it.

"Well, why are we here if not to help each other? We're all part of the same team." He recalled Ellen's teamwork speech from his interview. Now that she was back, it was time for him to put it into practice.

"Right."

He waited for Katie to say more, but she was not forthcoming. The silence between them was loud and painful.

"So anyway, just ask," he began. The elevator's ding interrupted any further discussion.

A hand truck, pushed by a UPS brown-uniformed employee and loaded with two boxes, rolled out of the elevator. "Hey Katie, how've you been? It's been a while, but I promise, it won't be long before you'll be sick of me. I don't have reams of paper for you this time, just these boxes for Ellen. Where do you want them?"

"Over by the closet is good. Nice to have you back, Sally. You're right; soon you won't bring the paper fast enough. So much for electronic files; clients still want their paper returns. Maybe someday," Katie said.

"That's what all you professionals say, but I don't see it happening any day soon. Job security, as far as I'm concerned," Sally laughed.

Michael waited for an introduction. It didn't happen. Instead, Sally slid the boxes off the hand truck, headed to the elevator, and left with a wave of her hand.

"If you want to be useful, carry those back to Ellen's office," Katie sneered. "You should be good for that." He let it pass. Teamwork was his new agenda.

"No problem. If there's anything else, let me know. I'm available." Michael spread his lips in his best smile and winked.

This time, Katie did the ignoring.

CHAPTER 98

ELLEN

MICHAEL'S FACE WAS RED AND SWEATY FROM hauling the two Nashville boxes into Ellen's office. They were heavy, and only a fool would carry both at once. She reminded herself that he was new and trying to impress, and dropped her judgment. You couldn't fault a guy for overextending his abilities. We're all imperfect humans who try too hard in untested territory.

"Leave them over there by the sliders," she said. Michael dropped the boxes with a thud, startling her friendly seagull pecking at the window. It flew off, wings flapping and voice squawking.

"Looks like boxes straight from Nashville. More work for you?" He wiped his dripping forehead on the sleeve of his white shirt. Although Hartmann and Associates dressed in business casual attire, Michael preferred a crisp white shirt. At least he didn't wear a tie. "Anything I can help with?"

"Thanks for offering, but I need to deal with those myself." Ellen didn't have time to explain in depth, but Michael needed some attention from her. "Are you looking for work? It's tough to hit your stride when you start a new job." She rummaged around her desk, looking for something to give him.

"I am a little light right now," he replied. "I'm waiting for Julie to be free to see how I can help her today."

"Here. Help me with this." Ellen picked up the long list she had been avoiding. Perfect. "It's a list of clients that need to be called for appointments. I'd give them to Katie, but this time of year, she's too busy with incoming calls, and everyone ends up on hold. Clients hate that. Do you mind?" It wasn't meaningful work for an accomplished accountant, but it would keep him busy until tax returns started flowing in.

"No problem," Michael smiled. He had a spectacular smile that the clients would love. "It'll give me a chance to connect with them. I know you want me as your right-hand guy."

Not exactly, Ellen thought. Julie held that position, but Michael would eventually learn that no one could replace Julie. But now was not the time to squash his enthusiasm.

"Here you go." Ellen handed Michael a spreadsheet with names and phone numbers. "They all expect a personal call from me to set up their annual one-hour tax appointment. It was a nice idea at first, but now, not so much, and I haven't been able to break their habit. I'm sure they're wondering what's taking me so long. God forbid they pick up the phone and do it themselves," she laughed.

Michael studied the list but didn't respond. Ellen attempted to explain further.

"Tell them you're helping me with the calls but that they're meeting with me, not you. You can access my shared calendar from your computer. Leave a little space between appointments so I get a break." That should keep him busy until the real work started to pour in.

"You got it, boss. Happy to help." Michael's grin was odd. She wasn't sure what it meant, but she was impressed by his willingness to take on this mundane task. Others might hesitate to do admin work, but not Michael. She had made the right choice; he would fit in well with the rest of her team.

CHAPTER 99

STERLING

STERLING SLID HIS GLASSES ONTO HIS BALD HEAD and rubbed his eyes as he walked to the window to gaze at the waterfront. After that last session, he needed to clear his mind. It wasn't the previous client's emotional issues that had him reeling; it was the information embedded in the client's lengthy list of grievances with the world. After that, focusing on the remainder of the session was brutal.

What should he do with the information? As a therapist, everything about a client was confidential, and sharing any of it could put him in a precarious position with his profession's rules and regulations. But what if it hurt his friend and colleague? Maybe it was true, and Sterling was out of the loop. If so, it would be best to say nothing. However, if it were false, the damage would be significant. He leaned toward subtle disclosure. He hated being caught between his professional and personal values. It wasn't easy to find a clear path forward, but that didn't mean one didn't exist.

He turned from the window and glanced at the clock hanging on the wall behind his clients' heads so that he could keep an eye on the time. Fifteen minutes until the next unburdening. Time enough for Starbucks, his secret indulgence. He shuffled the quarters in his pocket from the laundry machines in his rental property. His wife would never know.

By the time he returned with his tall cappuccino, he had a plan. Waiting in line had given him the time and the discipline to reflect on his dilemma, something he encouraged his clients to do when searching for a solution. It was too easy for people to either run from the problem or rush into a solution. Taking the time to discover the right answer was time well spent.

He took another long drink of his cappuccino, set it on the side table, and pulled his phone from his back pocket. He scrolled through his contacts and located the number.

"Ellen, it's Sterling. But I guess you know that," he laughed. It felt like years since they had last talked a month ago. He missed their time together when their creativity flowed and their excitement for launching *The Money Dynamic* was at its peak. Creating, debating, and fine-tuning their program was what they did best. Taking it to market was not their forte, and their decision to work with Sam had been easy, but it turned out to be one of their less successful choices.

"Hey, Sterling. Good to hear your voice." Ellen sounded in a good mood. Great. Let's hope she stayed that way after they met.

"Can we get together? I have something to go over with you," he said. "Maybe Friday, my day off?" Sterling tried to keep his request casual and light; there was no need to raise any alarms.

"Sure thing. Friday's supposed to be sunny and mild. Let's go for a walk and talk. I was just about to call you about my last trip to Nashville, but it can wait until Friday. I want to share it in person." Ellen was equally mysterious about her news.

"Did you say *last*, as in the most recent, or as in the *last* ever?" Sterling's curiosity was piqued.

"If I have to wait," she teased, "you'll have to wait. It's too crazy a story to tell over the phone. See you on Friday—usual time and place?"

"Let's make it ten. It's my morning with the girls, and by ten, it'll be a little warmer. I'll be waiting for you here." He hung up, double-checked that his phone was set to vibrate, and slid it into his back pocket. Friday at ten would give him plenty of time to plan how to tell Ellen.

He glanced at the clock: 11:58. Perfect, still on time. He stood up, stretched his arms overhead, then touched his toes. His decision was made, his mind was clear, and he was ready to face his next client's problem. He walked across the hall to the waiting room to retrieve them. Eight more to go. He had a long day and night ahead of him. Again. He hoped Ellen's news would revive *The Money Dynamic* and that somehow, he'd be rescued from these interminable days.

CHAPTER 100

MICHAEL

MICHAEL COULDN'T BELIEVE HIS LUCK. ELLEN played right into his plan. No more sneaking around or waiting for Katie to pass on calls; Ellen's spreadsheet filled with clients' names and numbers was all he needed. His decision to move forward now, instead of waiting until after April 15, had been the right one. Clients wouldn't have time to second-guess their choices. They were already anxious with the filing deadline approaching, and searching for a replacement accountant would only add to that stress. Michael would end their search before they even realized they needed one.

He scanned the list for a good place to start. There it was: Jim Trask. Years ago, he had played tennis with the old guy when their usual partners hadn't shown up. Maybe Jim would remember him. After making sure his office door was closed tight, he punched Jim's number into his phone. For the first time, Michael appreciated the subtle rules of the office. Everyone at Hartmann and Associates respected a closed door, and Michael needed privacy to work his way down Ellen's list.

"Jim, it's Michael Prescott. I'm not sure if you remember me from our tennis match years ago. Are you still as good as you were back then? If I recall correctly, you beat my as—soundly." Michael caught himself at the last minute; Jim hadn't reacted well to his choice of words on the court.

"I wouldn't say soundly. Let's just say it was a good match," Jim laughed. "I'm not playing much these days. Arthritis. It's doing a number on my knees. These days, pickleball is more my style."

"Staying active is all that counts." Michael had nothing more to say about pickleball, a pathetic sport for old-timers. Damn if he'd ever give in to that.

"I guess you're wondering why I'm calling." Michael got straight to the point.

"You're right about that. I can't imagine what's on your mind. Or are you selling me something?" Jim's response hinted that he wouldn't give him much time.

"Nothing like that, I promise. Let me cut to the chase. Ellen Hartmann is retiring, not because she's old." Michael regretted his choice of words but continued. "Because she's moving on to other things. She's asked me to take over her tax business. With her blessing, I'm calling to schedule a time for us to meet and review your tax information. Ellen wouldn't have chosen me to succeed her if she didn't trust my abilities." Michael made his pitch easy to agree with.

Jim said nothing, and Michael was clever enough to stay quiet. He waited.

"Goodness, I wasn't expecting that. Came out of the blue, didn't it? I've been with Ellen for decades." Jim sounded shaken by the news.

"Not really. She's been at the office less and less, working on her other projects. I'm sure you've noticed that it's tougher and tougher to get hold of her. She agreed to let go of taxes and turn things over to me. Most of her existing staff will join me at our new offices out by the mall. I promise you, parking will be a whole lot easier." Michael tossed him a bone.

"I'm sure it will. I didn't particularly appreciate driving down that pier and parking on that dock. Too dangerous as far as I'm concerned. Staying on terra firma will be a good thing." Jim chased the bone.

"How does Thursday at nine work? I'll come to your home and make it even easier. I know arthritis can be tricky in the cold." Michael threw out his best suck-up lines. "You can fill me in about pickleball. I've never tried it, but I'd like to."

"Perfect. Beth will have coffee ready and waiting, and if we're lucky, she'll make her famous sour cream coffee cake. Thanks for making this so easy. See you Thursday at nine." Jim signed off.

Thank you, Ellen Hartmann, Michael beamed to himself. It was the perfect start to Ellen's perfect ending.

Michael punched another number into his phone. "Ok, let's do it. Send me that lease." There was no need for niceties or special treatment anymore. "I told you it wouldn't be long. A February first start date will be perfect." He hung up.

Time to get busy. Michael's white-toothed dishonesty faded into tight-lipped duplicity. Ellen would never see what hit her before the office of Michael Prescott, CPA, overflowed with her clients.

CHAPTER 101

ELLEN

ELLEN EASED HERSELF ONTO THE FLOOR, HER back screaming in protest. Too much sitting and not enough walking had done this to her. It was one of the reasons she had started her morning walks, along with the mistake of getting a puppy in the middle of winter. Now, it had been almost two weeks since her last walk. The drama in Nashville had gotten in the way, and she still hadn't figured out how to walk two dogs with noses pulling in opposite directions. This morning, it was enough that the two canines were willing to coexist.

She had hoped to ease her aching back with a lunchtime walk and had checked the weather by looking outside her sliding glass doors. The seagulls were lined up on the roof of the building on the next pier, clinging on for dear life, and a lone seagull struggled to land on her deck. Blustery winds meant it was not ideal for any of them. She scrapped the plan and decided to try again tomorrow.

She unpacked the two boxes from Nashville, spread the folders around her, and sorted their contents into three piles:

Projects: Inter-office notes to and from staff about Sam's many projects were probably meaningless. She had debated shipping these to Portland, but erred on the side of sending them. Sometimes, innocuous notations were the key to unraveling more.

Miscellaneous: Scraps of paper were just that, but Sam's cryptic notations intrigued Ellen. They hinted at Sam's motives and state of mind. Here in Portland, she could take the time to decipher what they meant.

Finance: This is the one she was most interested in. Sorting through the boxes last Friday with Henry, loan documents with Diane's signatures, and Roxie's spreadsheets tracking the flow of money in and out of the office enticed her and had made it challenging to live up to her promise to Henry to wait until she got back to Portland. But she did, and now she couldn't wait to dig into the details.

She finished unpacking and sorting the two boxes. After another quick review, she gathered the project files and placed them at the bottom of the first box. It was unlikely she'd need them. She performed a similar cursory review of the miscellaneous pile and transferred a few cryptic notes to the finance pile. Then she laid a sheet of red paper over the project files at the bottom of the box and filled it with the remaining miscellaneous papers.

That left the financial pile, now almost an entire boxful. Her task was to unravel the mystery of Sam's disappearance, but whenever something referred to *The Money Dynamic* or herself, she struggled to maintain her focus. It wasn't just about finding her lost ten thousand dollars; it was bigger than that. At least, that's what she tried to convince herself of. But her credit card debt and its rising interest rate made it hard to believe. Why had she burdened her finances with extra debt? Why had she fallen for Sam's promises? Why had she ignored her better judgment? She didn't like what the answer could be.

"Stuff from Nashville?" Julie dropped to the floor next to Ellen. Being ten years younger was not lost on Ellen. Her mind drifted to Henry.

"I can't seem to let this go." Ellen slid her hair behind her right ear and turned to Julie.

"Fuck that," Julie's reply was unexpected. "Sam's stolen enough of your time. Let it go. We need you here."

"I know, I know. I've pushed too much on you over these last few months." Ellen slid her hair behind her other ear and cradled her cheeks. Would this never end? Why couldn't she drop Sam and her ill-fated project? The firm needed her attention, not her neglect.

"And now I'm dropping too much on Michael," Ellen shook her head in disgust.

"Michael? What the hell are you doing with him?" Julie's attitude was off-base, out of left field. What had she missed?

"He said he had free time, so I asked him to make some calls for me. I think we're lucky to have found him. He's ready and willing to do anything."

"Too ready and willing, if you ask me," Julie muttered.

"Okay, I'm lost," Ellen said, unable to ignore Julie's attitude. "What's going on?"

"Ignore me. Your head is still in Nashville. I need it here in Portland first." Julie tossed her long hair over her shoulder and picked up twenty or thirty papers from the financial stack. "How can I move this along? I'll never have your attention until that asshole Sam Davis is put to rest."

Julie's comment confused her, but she was right. Ellen needed to move beyond the chaos of Nashville now. She could ask Julie about her thoughts later. It was time to move on.

Ellen picked up the next papers in the stack. "I need to put this whole thing behind me, but first I have to organize these papers to examine them in more detail."

"And I'll do the opposite. How you organize without knowing the details makes no fucking sense to me." Julie buried her nose in the first document.

"A match made in heaven," Ellen laughed. "We'll be through this in no time."

CHAPTER 102

BOBBY

BOBBY PUSHED HIS TRASH BARREL DOWN THE dark hallway. The office had seemed empty and locked for the night, but now he noticed a dim light from Ellen's office spilling into the darkness. It was unusual for Ellen to work late at this time of year, even when she had been out of the office. Her overtime would begin next month, once staff inundated her desk with tax returns for her to review and sign.

Bobby's suspicions were aroused. He didn't like his new cynical side, but his doubts raced toward Michael. They didn't slow down, didn't pass go; they went straight to the man he didn't trust. He wasn't alone in feeling this way; Katie had sensed it from the beginning, just like he did. Something about the man's smarmy grin and overly exuberant attitude put them both on high alert. Julie had been duped and, for a time, fell under the spell of the manipulative, ego-stroking jerk. Then, all of a sudden, she was on their side. Bobby might never know what made Julie see the light, but now there were three of them, and their new triumvirate was tasked with helping Ellen grasp the truth about Michael.

Bobby left his barrel behind and crept down the hall toward the light. If Michael was invading Ellen's space, he didn't want his squeaky wheel to give him away. He had to catch him red-handed. He peered into the office as he approached. Ellen was not at her desk, nor was anyone else. He breathed a sigh of relief; she must have forgotten to turn off her light. As much as he wanted to find Michael doing something nefarious, he wasn't ready to confront him alone. The man was younger, taller, and ridiculously more fit, and Bobby wasn't sure what he might be capable of. An empty office was a good thing. He strode into the office to retrieve Ellen's wastebasket.

"Holy shit! Can't you give a girl some warning? Where's your squeaky trash barrel?" Bobby whipped around to find Julie sitting on the floor in the corner of Ellen's office, her hand over her voluptuous chest. His smile broadened, and they both laughed.

"I could say the same for you. What're you doing hiding in the corner? Bad girl today?" He offered his right hand to help her to her feet. He didn't want to embarrass himself if he joined her on the floor and couldn't get up gracefully.

"Thanks for the hand up; another few hours and I would've had to crawl out of here. Not a pretty sight to behold." She twisted from left to right and stretched to touch her toes. Bobby tried not to stare or ask her to repeat.

"I doubt that," Bobby teased. "You're always a pretty sight."

"Yeah, yeah, tell that to someone who falls for your bullshit. After training with Michael, I'm the proverbial MBD, Master Bullshit Detector," she explained. "Watch out. I can smell you a mile away. You're in trouble now." Julie's laugh was deep and hearty. It usually buoyed his outlook, but not tonight.

"I was sure I'd find Michael in here up to no good," Bobby said, ending their usual flirty banter. "I don't know what I thought I'd catch him doing, but I'm sure he's up to something. It's time to find out what it is. We need a plan." He sat down in one of Ellen's client chairs. Julie sat in the other.

"I'm with you, and we need to execute it sooner rather than later. Michael's already influencing Ellen, and she's trusting him way too much. Her head is still stuck in Nashville," Julie sighed. She gathered her wayward curls into a ponytail and slid an elastic off her wrist to hold it in place. Bobby waited.

"That's why I'm still here, sorting her Nashville boxes. Not because I'm a great employee, which I am by the way, but because Ellen needs to finish this so she can focus on what's happening here in the office. Hopefully it's not too late."

Julie's smile faded, and Bobby reacted to its absence. It was time to get to work. The siege of Michael Prescott was about to begin.

CHAPTER 103

ELLEN

ELLEN STOOD ABOVE THE MISHMASH OF PAPERS in the corner of her office. Julie had worked late, and Ellen didn't dare disturb the unorganized mess she left behind. Julie could decipher what the scattered, unruly piles meant, but no one else could. From experience, Ellen accepted that there was a rhyme and reason for their disorder, and she waited to restore her office until after Julie deciphered her cryptic collage of records.

Ellen's resident seagull tapped on her sliding glass door, and she gave it a quick nod while trying to avoid looking in that direction. Her preference for a place for everything and everything in its place clashed with Julie's disorganization. Ellen's seagull, intrigued by the chaos, started to peck frantically.

"Is he bothering you?" Michael appeared out of nowhere and rapped on the glass. The seagull flew off with a squawking tirade.

"Never!" Ellen shouted in surprise. "He's my friend, and now you've scared him off. He greets me most mornings." She stopped herself from saying more. Michael was new; how would he know?

"My bad," Michael mumbled. "Didn't know you were a seagull lover." This time, his broad smile failed to ease Ellen's annoyance. She'd never understand how anyone could be rude to a harmless bird.

Ellen tried to steer Michael's interruption toward a conclusion. "What can I help you with this morning?"

"Just checking in," Michael's perfect teeth shone. "I'm almost done setting up those appointments for you. Your clients are wonderful people. I enjoyed getting to know them." He took the liberty of lowering himself into one of the client chairs.

"Really? I didn't notice any appointments on my calendar. Maybe you didn't hear me ask you to add them?" Ellen wasn't sure why she was so grumpy, but it showed up unbidden.

"So sorry. I was saving them to enter all at once. I'll take care of that next. I didn't mean to cause a problem." Michael leaned back as if he were planning to stay for a while. His grin didn't fade, and he stared at Ellen.

"Not a problem, just need to know what times are free for me to book. That said, I have a lot to do this morning, so unless you need me for something else?" She hoped he would take the hint and move on. This was not the time of year for idle chitchat. He'd learn that soon enough, or she hoped he would. Was this what Julie was hinting at? At Hartmann and Associates, they were in the office for one reason—to work.

If they weren't working, they had personal lives calling them. None of them needed the office to fill their social calendar, and small talk just took them away from their real lives.

Ellen turned on her monitor as a further hint for Michael to move on. She opened her pencil drawer and took out a pen. He didn't leave, so she grabbed her yellow pad and began writing. She dared not look at him, fearing he would initiate another conversation.

"Oops, sorry." Julie's voice broke the silence. "Didn't know you were busy." She began to walk away.

"No, no, stay. Michael was leaving." She turned to Michael and mirrored his flashy smile. "Can you close the door on your way out?"

CHAPTER 104

JULIE

THE DOOR CLOSED, ALMOST SLAMMED, AND JULIE couldn't resist commenting. "What a jerk! He can't stand it if it's not all about him." She slumped into the other client chair, the one Michael hadn't warmed with his patronizing butt.

"He's trying to figure out where he fits in. It'll come; give him some time." Ellen was being nice, not realizing that Julie had long since moved past that stage. She'd remain quiet for now; Ellen would discover the truth for herself soon enough.

"Sorry about the mess I left." Julie shifted the conversation. "Some interesting stuff in there. Doesn't surprise me that Sam disappeared." She leaned forward on Ellen's desk. Ellen leaned back as if bracing for bad news.

"What'd you find?" Ellen tucked her hair behind her right ear.

"I found a bunch of loan documents made out to and signed by someone named Susan D. Garrett? Do you know who that is?" Julie was shocked that this woman had borrowed such enormous sums, and she was itching to find her connection to Sam.

"That's Sam's mother. She went by Diane." Ellen didn't offer anything else.

"The one who died, right? She certainly picked the right time to go." Julie regretted her flippancy. This was a real woman to Ellen, not the stranger she was to Julie.

Ellen skipped past Julie's faux pas. "What do you mean?"

"If everything is in these boxes, she signed for almost a million dollars. Let me tell you, Brand & Broadcast, or rather Sam's mother, was on the hook for some major payback. I can't imagine how they thought they'd be able to pay it back. It was all demand notes, so they were at the mercy of the lender whenever repayment was demanded. And the interest rate was ridiculous. Almost as bad as the greedy credit card companies. I hope they were good guys." Ellen scowled, and Julie was puzzled at her reaction.

"Who was the lender? A bank or venture capitalist?" Ellen's questions mirrored Julie's. She wished she knew the answer.

"Can't tell you for sure. Not a bank or other ordinary lending organization. I thought it might be a venture mafia or something like it. You know, one of those groups that pool their money to help startups, but I can't find the name anywhere. Google was worthless. *Redoubtable* doesn't seem to exist." Julie leaned back in her chair, giving Ellen time to absorb what she had said.

"Redoubtable." Ellen rubbed her eyes and slid her hand under her chin. "Never heard of them, either from Sam or anyone else. But at this stage, nothing surprises me. Looks like Sam's dragging me down another rabbit hole." Ellen's frustration was clear.

"Well, here's the thing." Julie pulled Ellen back to the here and now. She'd had enough of the Sam Davis saga. "I know you want answers, but sometimes there isn't an answer, or at least not one that can be easily found. Sam Davis has disrupted your life long enough, and we need you here. Now." She was coming across strong, but a nudge wouldn't catch Ellen's attention.

"I hear you, I really do. I know you need my attention here. But I hoped I'd find more. I had ulterior motives." Ellen's face flushed. Was it from embarrassment or anger?

"Ok. I'm listening," Julie soft-pedaled. "Tell me more. No judgment, I promise."

"I know it was stupid, but I sent Sam another ten thousand dollars a few weeks ago. I never mentioned it because I was embarrassed that I fell for his shit again. It didn't take long to figure out that what he promised to do with it wasn't coming through, so I asked for it back. He said it was on its way numerous times. I hoped he hadn't lied and that it was still coming." Ellen's face went pale. "I borrowed the money on a credit card. Stupid move, I know."

"Okay, let that go right now." Piling on guilt and shame never helped. Ellen was good at doing it herself. "Hoping won't make it happen. It's over. If he sent it, it would be here. And if he didn't, his money, or his mother's, is long gone. Even if it was still there, there's a shitload of creditors ahead of you, not to mention the shady Redoubtable. The probability of getting it back is zero." There, she said what

Ellen needed to hear. Retrieving Ellen's money was a lost cause and a lot to digest, but Julie wasn't leaving until Sam Davis was out of the picture forever.

Ellen dropped her head in her hands. "You're right; I know you're right."

Julie said nothing and waited for Ellen to collect herself. It wouldn't take long.

Ellen took a deep breath and tucked her hair behind her ears.

"You know me, I hate unanswered questions. Living in ambiguity is not my style." Ellen's pursed lips gave away her self-disapproval.

"Look at it as another *AFGO*: another fucking growth opportunity." Julie tried to lift Ellen's spirits with some twelve-step jargon. As former Al-Anon patrons, Ellen for her boy's father and Julie for her own, they often groaned over AA's many acronyms.

"Jeezus, I've had enough of those. Give me a break!" Ellen laughed. "I hear you loud and clear. Consider it over and done. Time to make the donuts. Tax season is waiting."

Julie glanced at the mess in the corner but didn't offer to pick anything up. Ellen would sort through it one more time. The records wouldn't be destroyed; instead, they'd be stowed for safekeeping. Just in case. That was Ellen's style.

CHAPTER 105

MICHAEL

MICHAEL DEBATED WHETHER TO ENTER FAKE appointments into Ellen's calendar. If he included his appointments with Ellen's clients, it would seem he had done what she asked. But if she needed to change something, she'd call the client and discover that the client was no longer hers. He hoped she was too busy with other matters to notice, but the more he learned about Ellen, the more he realized that nothing slipped by her.

But if he stalled, it bought him time to harvest more clients without interference. Everything was moving at the right pace, and he didn't want anything to disrupt it. Another week, and it would be a done deal. He'd be out of here, welcoming Ellen's former clients to his new digs. He combed his fingers through his thickening hair. It was time for a haircut; he needed to impress his new clients. A slow grin opened his lips, revealing his newly whitened teeth. With a fresh haircut, he'd be hard to resist.

Stalling was his best option. If Ellen wanted him to explain, he could come up with a lot of excuses. He could say he planned to do it when all the clients were called, that he wanted Katie to do it right, or that it was next on his to-do list. She couldn't argue with any of those, except maybe the first. If she pressed him on that one, he'd say he misunderstood their previous conversation and skirt around it. Gaslighting was his specialty.

He gazed from his desk across the office at Ellen's closed door. His desk was well-placed, something he had taken care of on the first day. The repositioned desk allowed him to monitor everyone's comings and goings, especially Julie's. Hartmann and Associates' open-door policy was perfect for using his eagle eye to plan his next move. There was no doubt that Julie was his most important prey to watch. She was his trophy victory. He had to win her back.

Michael watched as Ellen's door opened. Julie was smiling when she stepped out. Whatever they had been discussing must have turned out in Julie's favor, and he worried that she was pulling Ellen back into the daily grind of the office. He needed to keep Ellen distracted a bit longer to piss Julie off. He'd use Julie's anger to make his move.

"Julie, do you have a minute?" Michael called out as she walked by. Having her sit across from him at the desk would help her get used to her future boss. He resisted the urge to lean back with his hands behind his head. It was too much of a power move, and he'd save it for later. Today, he was a colleague, not a boss.

"Sure, whadda you need?" Julie sat down. At other times, when he tried to talk to her, she would always stand, looking annoyed and impatient. Her sitting down across from him was a significant change. She was coming around. He kept his gloating smile to himself.

CHAPTER 106

JULIE

JULIE LEANED BACK INTO MICHAEL'S CLIENT CHAIR and crossed her legs. His timing couldn't have been any more perfect. She flipped her riotous waves over her shoulder and waited for him to continue.

"I'm finishing the calls to Ellen's clients and wondered if I could do the same for you. I know your client list is as extensive as Ellen's, and I want to help you however I can." His whiter-than-usual teeth were blinding.

"Thanks, that would be great, but let me get organized first." She leveraged her reputation for disorganization to buy herself some time. "I'll have it ready for you tomorrow, Monday at the latest."

She leaned forward on the desk, placed her elbows on it, and rested her chin in her clasped hands. She opened and closed her eyes seductively. She knew his weak spot.

"Michael, I need to apologize," Julie gulped in fake distress. "I've been a bitch."

"Whoa, whoa, whoa. Don't call yourself that! I won't allow it."

"Whatever." Michael's attempt at angst gagged her, and irritation crept into Julie's voice. He didn't seem to notice. She paused to refine her delivery.

"All this bullshit with Ellen in Nashville got to me. It was wrong to take it out on you." She brushed her dark curls over her shoulder and shook her head. A little drama wouldn't hurt.

"I understand. No harm, no foul," he said.

"Huh?" Julie acted confused, although she understood her brother's favorite saying. Men loved knowing more than women.

"Sorry, athletic saying from my glory days," Michael rushed to her rescue. "Did I tell you I went to college on a baseball scholarship?"

"I didn't," Julie stretched her arms overhead and twisted from side to side. "Sorry, still sore from last night's workout."

Michael blinked hard as her sweater rose to reveal her toned abs. It was his turn to gulp.

"Anyway, can I make up for my bitchiness and buy you a drink at J's sometime? Like old times?" She pulled down her sweater and flicked her long eyelashes.

"Yes, please," he enthused. Had she laid it on too thick?

"How about tonight?" She didn't wait for him to overthink it.

"Works for me. I need a night off from the gym anyway."

She rubbed her right hip. "Those squats last night are biting me in the ass today. Let's go right at five. Soon, leaving early will be a luxury."

Julie stood up from the chair, rubbed both hips, and called over her shoulder, "See you soon!" She sauntered out of Michael's office and across the bullpen. She hoped her supreme sacrifice would come through.

CHAPTER 107

KATIE

"I'M SORRY. MAY I PUT YOU ON HOLD?" KATIE HATED to lie and hated doing it even more to a client who never demanded anything. The poor woman had probably been taken advantage of her entire life, and now Katie was doing it. "Busy time of year," she apologized, "I'll be back as soon as possible."

She set down the receiver, followed Julie into the bathroom, and locked the door. "It's Katie, don't panic," she whispered to the stall. "I probably didn't need to lock the door, but you know, better safe than sorry."

The toilet flushed, and Julie emerged, zipping up her pants. "Damn, these are tight. Worth wearing today, though. Michael swallowed it hook, line, and sinker." She spoke to Katie's reflection in the mirror.

"Tonight?" Katie asked.

"Tonight. Michael and I will head to J's at five o'clock for a drink. I'll hold my nose and keep him busy for at least an hour." Julie finished drying her hands and turned to Katie. "I texted Bobby to let him know. He said he'd be here shortly thereafter."

"We'll move as fast as possible," Katie explained. "It shouldn't take long to go through Michael's office. I told him he had to give me his passwords to comply with our WISP plan. I'll go through his computer while Bobby goes through everything else. We'll text you when we're finished so you can make up an excuse to leave."

She heard multiple lines start ringing. "Gotta go, they're calling me—literally."

She hurried back to the reception desk, but not before hearing Julie's final words, "What the hell is a WISP plan?" Katie shook her head and laughed. Julie, perpetually lost in her clients' problems, wouldn't have a clue about their security policies, procedures, and controls. Soon, all the plan's annoyances would pay off.

CHAPTER 108

JULIE

JULIE STOOD ON THE WOODEN DECKING OUTSIDE Fifty Portland Pier, gazing up at the sky. It was just after five, and although sunset was officially over, the lingering glow from the disappearing sun enveloped the pier in its murky remains. A breath of fresh air while she waited for Michael to gather his things and join her would do her good. It had been a painfully blue, cloudless day, and the dry, crisp air promised a spectacular evening overflowing with stars. The beauty of it all shored up her stamina for the task ahead.

As Michael opened the door, two headlights turned from busy Commercial Street and headed down the pier. The streetlight glinted off the silver truck rumbling over the pier's ancient timbers. It was Bobby, and she turned away. She didn't want any unconscious reaction to give away tonight's ulterior motive.

"I'm glad we're doing this again. It was fun last time." Julie placed her hand on Michael's forearm and gave him her best come-hither look. "Sorry for my temporary grumpiness. I mean it."

"Please stop that. There's nothing to apologize for." Michael moved closer, held her hand in his, and for a moment, she thought he might kiss her.

She slipped her hand away. "I don't know about you, but I'm looking forward to a beer. It's been a long day." She stepped off the wooden sidewalk and into the middle of the street. At this time of evening, Bobby's truck was most likely the last vehicle they'd encounter, and in the dim light, she was safer staying off the creaky and shadowed planks.

"Scotch will do it for me," he said. "I hope they have a better selection since the last time we were there." She remembered that night and how uncomfortable she had felt with Michael's critique of her favorite bar. Julie continued walking and kept her mouth shut. She needed to stay in Michael's good graces if their plan was to work.

Michael laid his hand on her shoulder and guided her through the bar's door. She resisted the urge to shrug it off. She was not anyone's woman, and certainly not his, but with any luck, tonight would be the end of their relationship. Tonight, she could tolerate anything.

Julie stepped over the high threshold, tossed her coat on top of the hangerless coat rack, abandoned her usual seat near the door, and moved to the other side of the bar where the local fishermen sat. From there, she could see Bobby's truck leave the pier if Katie forgot to text when the coast was clear.

"The usual?" J raised an eyebrow, code for not him again. She cringed. J must remember his previous disruption and disapprove of Julie bringing him back.

"But of course," Julie replied. "He'll have a scotch, neat."

"Do you have anything better than the last time I was here?" Michael laughed. "That stuff was rotgut." His humor hit J's brick wall with a thud.

"Same bottle, same brand. Not much call for scotch here. Ya still want it?" J left to get Julie's beer.

"Make it two doubles and put it on the rocks. Ice might make it tolerable," Michael called to J's back, then said loud enough for the entire bar to hear, "She's got an attitude tonight."

"Nah, that's J. Ignore her, and you'll be fine." Michael needed to sit down and shut up for at least an hour. It didn't take much for J to give you a piece of her mind or to ask you to leave, and Julie couldn't risk either.

J slid a frosty glass of Shipyard's Prelude in front of Julie. "Thanks for remembering," Julie lifted her glass and toasted J. For most of the year, Julie's usual was Blue Fin Stout, but during the holiday season and its surrounding months, she relished her favorite winter warmer.

J dropped Michael's drink in front of him. In classic J fashion, she had turned it into an unappetizing highball. "If you educated yourself about a man's scotch," Michael poked. "You might have better clientele."

Julie cringed and waited for J's reaction. This time, there was none. It was going to be a long, painful night, and she prayed that there would be more length than pain. Bobbie and Katie needed an hour. She signaled for another beer. She deserved it.

CHAPTER 109

KATIE

KATIE'S HEARTBEAT HASTENED, AND HER ADRENALINE flowed as her body's flight or fight response kicked in while waiting for Bobby. Tonight, they would fight for Hartmann and Associates. *What* they were fighting was still unknown, but *who* and *why* they were fighting was another thing. The three of them understood that the lifeblood of their accounting firm depended on proving the truth of their convictions: Michael Prescott was the enemy.

Katie had been planning tonight's tactics since Julie confirmed it was a go. They had to search Michael's office without leaving a trace. She would take the computer, and Bobby would do the rest. There were three physical areas for him to search: the desk, the bookcase, and the file cabinet. Although the details were still shrouded in secrecy, once before he had helped Julie solve a mystery, and Katie trusted him. Bobby was their right-hand man in more ways than one. Whenever and whatever you needed, he was there.

Katie heard the elevator cables creak as they lifted someone from below. Her physical responses rose accordingly: her breath quickened, her mouth was dry, and her heart thumped. She heard the doors open and held her breath. Michael had left to join Julie outside, but she was still wary. Tonight, there could be no glitches.

Bobby's trash barrel preceded the man himself, and Katie breathed a sigh of relief. "You ready for this?" she called out to him.

"You better believe it. I was born ready." His infectious smile and confident response eased Katie's tension.

"Okay, here's the plan. You go through the physical things, file cabinet, bookcase, desk drawers, and I'll dig around his computer." Katie looked up to confirm his understanding. He nodded in agreement.

"How much time do we have?" he asked. "Is this a rush job, or can we take our time?" Accustomed to Bobby's slow speed, Katie was pleased to hear he could step it up if needed.

"Julie's giving us an hour—it's all she can stand," Katie laughed. "The way she sees it, she deserves a medal for drinking with him. I've never seen her whine so much."

"Glad to hear he's lost his sparkle," Bobby's voice dropped, and Katie sensed some emotions hiding in Bobby's comment. Now was not the time to delve further.

"Let's get to it then. If we string this out too long, I'm afraid Michael won't survive," Katie snickered as she led Bobby down the hall.

"Or Julie will be so drunk we'll have to escort her home." Bobby's voice was soft and tender. Katie blinked. A strange comment made even stranger by its delivery.

CHAPTER 110

JULIE

THINGS WERE GETTING MORE UNCOMFORTABLE by the minute. She couldn't believe what a major asshole Michael was being, and sitting on the fishermen's side of the bar only made it worse. The last time they were here, or at least what she could remember from that night, Michael was annoying but not insulting. Sitting across from them that night, the regulars could guess his insulting words, but tonight, there was no guessing. Michael was loud and clear that he found them, and others like them, a sorry lot.

Julie elbowed Michael. "Hey Michael, tone it down a bit. The natives are getting restless." A little humor might get his attention. She flipped her long curls over her shoulder.

"Screw them if they can't take a joke. I have as much right to be here as they do." His voice was rowdy and menacing. He slammed his drink on the bar and glared in the locals' direction.

"I wouldn't be so sure of that." J intervened. "Tone it down, or I'll ask you to leave."

"He's fine, J. I'll handle this. I'm afraid your 'rotgut' is getting to him." Julie used air quotes to let J know she was on her side, not Michael's. "One more for the road, and we'll be out of here."

"If you say so, but this is on you, Julie. If things go south, it's all your fault. I warned you." Julie knew this scary side of J, but it had never been directed at her. It terrified her.

"Michael, can you behave while I run to the ladies' room?" She placed her hand over his, squeezed it, and gave him her sexiest smile. "I mean it. I don't want to come back to a bar fight. Trust me, you don't want to mess with these guys." She left for the bathroom.

After locking the door, she pulled out her phone. She couldn't stand being with Michael much longer. His condescension and disregard for others' feelings choked off any speck of respect she once had for him. How had she missed it? She shuddered, remembering how she had fallen under his spell when he first arrived and how his words had an uncanny knack for turning off her asshole radar and dismantling her defenses. Never again.

She held her phone in both hands and tapped out a message. *Done? I can't do this much longer.* Katie's reply needed to be quick. It was only a matter of time before she'd have to push Michael out to preserve the peace. She'd be on the hook for a lot of free drinks in the future to make it up to her fellow patrons.

Not yet. 15 more? Katie replied.

Julie had no choice. *OK.*

Tonight, fifteen minutes was an eternity. There was one way to keep Michael quiet, a method she only used in emergencies. Julie arched her back, lifted her best features, and let them lead the way back to the bar.

CHAPTER 111

BOBBY

BOBBY LISTENED TO KATIE CLACKING AT THE keyboard as he dug through Michael's file cabinet and bookcase. Cleaning legal and accounting offices over the years had taught him by osmosis what was significant and what was not. So far, nothing had caught his attention, and his back needed a break.

"Are you finding anything?" He stretched his back, then sat in a client chair and waited for Katie to respond.

"Not really." Katie turned away from the computer screen and blinked hard. "Did you?"

"Not yet, but there has to be something." Bobby was stumped. Everything was squeaky clean. "Either we're barking up the wrong tree, or he's a pro at cleaning up after himself."

"No doubt in my mind. He's a pro at hiding whatever he's up to. We just haven't found it yet." Katie's blonde hair swung side to side as she shook her head. She was as disgusted as he felt. "The three of us are not imagining this."

"It's weird, but this just doesn't feel like a normal working office." Bobby was familiar with offices from the nerdily spotless to the utterly chaotic, like Julie's. "It's almost as if it's a showcase."

"A showcase? I don't follow." Katie rubbed her eyes.

"You know, like the showcase units in real estate developments. Everything seems a little too perfect, a little too orderly. It feels like no one lives here. You know what I mean?" Bobby shifted in his chair, hoping Katie understood what he was trying to say.

"I knew something was wrong, but I couldn't figure out what. You nailed it." Katie frowned. "Everything I find goes nowhere. There's no completed or ongoing work, nothing of substance. Even his email. It feels like the computer is waiting for someone to start. Either Michael's done nothing since he's arrived, or he's doing his work elsewhere."

"You said it. The lights are on, but nobody's home. Glad we agree," Bobby said. "But I'm not ready to give up. I still need to go through the desk drawers. Can I disturb you for a minute?"

"Have at it. I need a bathroom break." Katie almost flew down the hallway.

Bobby sat behind the desk and pulled open the right-hand bottom drawer. There was a rack to support hanging files, but like everywhere else, the files were empty. The drawer above was filled with new yellow-lined pads and sticky notes still wrapped in cellophane. He moved to the left side of the desk. Three more drawers waited to be filled.

"Did you find anything?" Katie returned from the bathroom looking a little less pained.

"Not yet, but I need to go through the pencil drawer. You can have the desk back in a minute." Bobby slid open the shallow center drawer designed to hold writing tools. There was one pen and one mechanical pencil, hardly the domain of a busy accountant.

"Dead end." Katie leaned over his shoulder and sighed. "What the hell is he up to?"

Bobby wasn't ready to give up. He slid his fingers into the back of the shallow drawer. As he wedged his muscular hand and thick fingers into the tiny drawer, something grazed the top of his knuckles. He flipped his hand over and tried again. Whatever it was, he couldn't quite reach it.

"There's something stuck in here, but my hand's too big. Can you try?" Bobby moved away so Katie could sit down.

She stuck her hand, wrist, and forearm into the slim space. "You're right. There's something there. It's shoved way in the back of the drawer. Ouch!" She pulled her hand back and rubbed her arm. "I almost had it." She went in for another try.

"Got it." Katie slid her hand out with a packet of papers scissored between her index and middle fingers. She dropped it on the desk and rubbed her arm, now bright red from scraping it against the desktop.

"What is it?" Bobby leaned over, waiting for Katie to pick it up.

"I think it's a lease, dated February first of this year." Katie's smile was triumphantly sinister. "He must have forgotten it was there. We found our smoking gun."

CHAPTER 112

MICHAEL

MICHAEL'S CHEEKS GLOWED HOT AND RED AS he stepped into the frigid air. Cheap booze did that to him. Next time, he'd take Julie to one of Portland's upscale bars with his kind of clientele. The office of Michael Prescott CPA would be an upmarket accounting firm to match Portland's burgeoning high-end population. Julie would need to up her game.

"What a dive! Ready for some class? Let's go barhopping." Michael reached for Julie's arm. She side-stepped his grasp.

"No can do. I'm tired and have a lot to do tomorrow. Can't risk a hangover. Time to be responsible." Julie started walking away. This time, Michael grabbed her arm and pulled her back.

"Come on, don't be a party pooper. The night is young, and so are we!" He leaned in for a kiss. It worked for him the last time, and there was no harm in trying a second time.

A truck, high beams blazing, came barreling down the pier, and halted her response. The silver truck screeched to a stop next to them. The window slid down, and Bobby leaned out. "Everything alright here?"

"Why the hell wouldn't it be?" Michael hated this guy's knight-in-shining-armor act.

"Everything's fine, Bobby. I'm just going to my car," Julie said and continued walking.

Michael followed. She turned around and stared. "No need to go with me, Michael. See you tomorrow." She walked away.

Bobby pulled his truck over to the curb. Michael stared at Julie, then at the truck. He slammed his fist on the truck's hood and staggered around it to find another bar. Bobby did nothing. Smart man.

CHAPTER 113

ELLEN

ELLEN STRETCHED. IT WAS THE END OF A LONG week, and she had finally slept. Whenever her insomnia made her weary enough to allow her to sleep, she always woke up feeling like a new woman. On mornings like this, she faced life with hopeful energy, and her priorities were clear. A contented smile played across her face as she heard whispers, watched the doorknob turn, and her three boys tiptoed in.

"Gotcha!" She pulled back the covers. "I'm awake. Come on in." Ethan and Kevin crawled in on her right, Jack on her left. She spread her arms wide enough to give all three a group hug. "I've missed you guys so much!"

"What're you talking about? You've been back a week." Jack, the pragmatist, needed an explanation.

"I always miss you, even if I just left you. Someday, you'll be a dad and understand," she said, squeezing Jack's shoulder. He groaned in response. Kevin and Ethan giggled.

"So, what do you say we skip Pop-Tarts and go out for breakfast? I'll call school to say you'll be a little late." Her ten o'clock meeting for Sterling's walk-and-talk allowed her a morning of luxury. She wouldn't bother with the office until after.

"Can we go to Uncle Andy's?" all three yelled. Their favorite place had been a mainstay of South Portland for decades. As far as the boys were concerned, their chocolate chip pancakes were a gourmet treat.

Her sons started to wiggle out of bed, and she tightened her triple bear hug to pull them closer. "Hang on there, Uncle Andy's isn't going anywhere. Let's stay and cuddle."

"Oh Mom." Her favorite trio let out a collective groan.

CHAPTER 114

JULIE

JULIE DRAPED HERSELF OVER KATIE'S COUNTER. "Ellen in yet?" Since the flurry of texts sharing the highlights of last night's reconnaissance, Julie was anxious to talk with Ellen. Not wanting her to feel ganged up on, the trio gave Julie the task of confronting Ellen with what they had discovered. Julie hadn't slept a wink since. Damn, Ellen's insomnia; it was contagious.

"I just got off the phone with her; she won't be in until late morning," Katie filled Julie in. "She's taking the boys out for breakfast and then has a meeting with Sterling. I'll let you know as soon as she gets here."

"I need to get this over with. I can't stand this waiting." Julie raked her fingers through her long hair. "At least Michael's not here yet to bother me." She let out a puff of frustration. "Any word on his arrival?"

"Yup, he called too. Has a migraine and will be in later," Katie slapped her hands on the desk and laughed.

"Is that what we're calling it these days? I'll remember that the next time I've been overserved. What an asshole! Can't even hold his liquor. Please make him go away," Julie mumbled back to her office. Katie's laughter followed her.

Julie swiveled her chair to look out her two windows. Watching the few remaining sailboats bobbing and weaving in the wintery waters of the nearby marina calmed her. A relaxed attitude would clarify her thinking. She eyeballed Katie's copy of the lease they had discovered the previous night. She was still confused.

The lease was for office space near the mall in one of the new office parks. What was Michael's intention for it? With all the business opportunities they were exposed to, it was easy for an accountant to have a side hustle, and as long as it didn't compete, it wouldn't violate his employment contract with Hartmann and Associates, but it could distract him from his job responsibilities. Would the lease be enough to persuade Ellen that Michael had to go? Maybe not, but at the very least it would be an opportunity to open the conversation.

Julie watched the resident of the sole sailboat-turned-houseboat climb over his railing onto the dock, swinging his briefcase. Why would a businessperson make life so complicated by living on a boat? And why would a competent accountant need a side hustle requiring office space? Julie's mind whirred at high speed, searching for an answer.

CHAPTER 115

STERLING

STERLING PULLED INTO THE PARKING GARAGE and grabbed a ticket. He hated paying the exorbitant rate, but he was running late and didn't have time to circle the block searching for on-street parking. Besides, it would be less than two hours, long enough to talk and walk with Ellen. He promised his daughters he'd be back for lunch. Everyone but his wife had the day off, and he and the girls were going sledding in Payson Park. The cornflower blue sky above and the warming rays of sunshine reflecting on a new layer of snow from this weekend's dusting should make for a great day of it.

He hustled down the garage's stinky staircase and out the side door onto the plaza. Ellen was waiting across the street at the entrance to his office building, as planned.

"I'm coming," he yelled. Ellen shifted her gaze but must not have seen him and looked down at her phone again.

"I'm here," he yelled, climbing over the concrete lane

divider to get to his building. "Sorry, got tied up playing princess this morning."

"I can see that," Ellen laughed. "Your lips are still ruby-red. Maggie needs to show you how to take off your makeup. You look a bit of a clown."

"It could be worse, I guess." Sterling rubbed his mouth on his sleeve and started walking. He loved this time of year; the tourists were gone, and most locals thought it was too cold to be outside. They could walk side by side on his favorite route and talk.

"So, what do you have to tell me?" Ellen asked.

"You first." Sterling wanted to listen to Ellen's news on the outside chance that she'd tell him the secret he struggled to reveal. "What happened in Nashville?"

"Two words: Sam disappeared." Sterling choked, and it took a while to stop coughing.

"What do you mean? I don't get it," he sputtered. "Sam disappeared? In what way?"

"The only way I know to disappear. Gone. Finito. Kaput." Ellen's voice was unemotional and factual. She must have come to terms with whatever she was trying to tell him.

"Okay, fill in the blanks, please." Sterling's head was elsewhere, but he knew Ellen needed to dump her information to be able to hear his.

"He disappeared without a trace. Henry drove him to a meeting in Atlanta, and that was it. The meeting was a sham. The company he was meeting with didn't exist, and neither Sam nor Roxie was heard from again. They simply disappeared. Even left their poor dogs behind." Ellen tucked her hair behind her ear. She never wore hats, and Sterling longed for the days when his thick hair had kept him warm. He pulled his stocking hat down over his ears.

"Holy shit. I didn't expect that. His mother doesn't know where he went?" Sterling remembered Diane serving lunch to Sam's video crew during their first visit to Nashville.

"She's dead. Fell down the steps the same night they disappeared." Ellen rubbed her eyes and cheeks. He recognized unexpressed emotions from his clients. She was still reeling.

"Damn." It was all he could come up with. "Damn. Do you think her death and his disappearance are related? Seems too convenient."

"I wondered the same thing, but it turned out to be a weird conflagration of events that included Sam's brother showing up. When Sam didn't come home and she couldn't reach him, Diane called David. She didn't want to be alone, but when he arrived the next morning, he was too late. I guess she had a drinking problem, and Henry and I found her the next morning. She had fallen down the steps. It was awful." Ellen wiped her left eye.

"Damn!" Sterling repeated himself. There was nothing more to say. "You picked a helluva time to go to Nashville. You weren't kidding when you said it was your last trip! Holy shit!"

"Amen to that." The color drained from her face. "Sam disappeared, and all our hard work and money was for naught."

Sterling's thoughts ping-ponged through his brain. "Holy shit," he said one last time. His words had disappeared, just like Sam.

Ellen's voice dropped to a whisper. "*The Money Dynamic* is over."

And with its demise, Sterling's last iota of hope for the project that might save him from too many long hours listening to others' problems disappeared. It was all gone.

CHAPTER 116

ELLEN

"YOUR TURN." ELLEN TURNED TO STERLING. THE final chapter of their Nashville story was signed, sealed, and delivered. Like Sterling, she had prayed until the bitter end that something would come of their creativity and hard work. But it was over, and she could let go. Her sons, office, and colleagues were calling, and she must go. John Muir would roll over in his grave for using his quote in vain.

Her Nashville story took them down Exchange Street to Portland's waterfront and up the Eastern Promenade Trail. She was so engrossed in its telling that she hadn't noticed the winter-wrapped boats, the rambunctious pups in the dog park, or even Maine's Narrow Gauge Railroad lining its path. Now, as they turned back for their return, she was ready to listen.

"I heard a rumor," Sterling began. "How or where I heard it isn't important, but what I heard is." Ellen kept walking. She hated rumors. They were based on faulty assumptions and were wrong nine times out of ten. She kept her thoughts to herself.

"Go on. What did you hear?" she asked.

Sterling squinted his eyes and grimaced as if avoiding something distasteful. "They said you were retiring. They complained about needing a new accountant just as the tax deadline was looming."

"Retiring? My clients will never believe that. I'm way too young!" she snorted as her head swung around to look at him. "That's ridiculous. How would that even happen? Did I forget I won the lottery?" She shook her head. Why would Sterling bother to repeat it? He was not a gossipmonger. His years as a therapist taught him how to ignore it.

"I thought the same, but I asked a few questions, and they always gave a plausible answer." Sterling removed his beanie, scratched his head, and put it back on. "They said you were turning over the practice to someone else because you wanted to spend more time with your project. They said you've been gone a lot."

"Well, I hope they said Julie was taking over! Because, in my absence, she has. They're confused." It was the only plausible explanation. She could see how a disgruntled client might spin things this way.

"It wasn't Julie they mentioned. They said some guy named Michael Prescott was taking over the firm, and Julie and other staff were coming with him. Your client even had an appointment to meet in their new office."

"What the fuck!" Ellen hated to use the word, but sometimes, it was the one that best fit the occasion. "That bastard!"

She had to get back to the office to speak with Julie. Was Julie defecting? Had Ellen overused Julie's goodwill one too many times?

Ellen's head was spinning. How could this happen? How could she miss something this big, this crucial? Damn Sam Davis and *The Money Dynamic*. Lost in his promises, she forgot that the dynamic that mattered was here in Portland, not Nashville. Blind ambition and endless hope had clouded her judgment and usurped her priorities, leaving her alone and unsupported. A fear-laced shiver traveled up her spine.

She didn't remember walking to her car, unlocking the door, or getting in. The morning's brilliant blue sky and the street's sparkling snow crystals could not break through the haze that dulled her mind. She sat behind the steering wheel, not sure if it was safe to drive. She was being held hostage by a world she couldn't imagine, one she didn't want to inhabit. Julie played a crucial role in Hartmann and Associates' success. How would it survive without her? How would she survive without her? Julie was her right-hand person, and Ellen knew it from the day she first hired her. She thought Julie did too.

Ellen closed her eyes, looking for clarity. Instead, deep sadness further dimmed her vision, and a trickle of tears carried with it the nightmare of a future without Julie and Katie. Together, they had given Ellen the freedom to pursue her hare-brained ideas. They understood when to set her loose and when to pull her back. It's what they did, what she relied on, but this time, she ignored their concerns and had drifted too far. By thinking of herself instead of those who supported her, she lost the heartbeat of the firm. How would she manage tax season without them?

Tax season, her sons were right. It was always about tax season. She rested her head on the icy steering wheel. Waves of hot, sticky despair spread through the car and fogged the windows. It was easier to worry about tax season, but the depth of her grief wouldn't allow her. Katie and Julie were more than staff; they were her friends. Why didn't they know that? Why hadn't she told them? Their expertise and loyalty allowed her to follow her pipedream to Nashville.

Loyalty. Who was she kidding? If she had been loyal to them, they wouldn't have left. If she had thanked them every day or never taken them for granted, that snake Michael Prescott couldn't have insinuated himself into the firm. But her misguided loyalty to *The Money Dynamic* and Sam Davis put everything at risk. She destroyed their friendship and the firm with her selfishness. The shame she carried from investing the last ten thousand dollars of her family's financial security in Sam's scam was nothing compared to the storm cloud of shame and guilt that now enveloped her.

Ellen's cramped fingers relinquished their hold on the steering wheel, and she lifted her head. She scraped her fingernail down the frosted despair covering the windows and reached for the car's maximum defrost button. Warm air circulated through her vehicle, restoring the visibility of the windshield and her own clarity. She breathed in, shifted the car into drive, and, after looking over her left shoulder, she left the parking space's safety.

It was time. Time to push aside her guilt and shame. Time to part the clouds of her despair. Her spine stiffened with resolve, and her fear dissolved. It was time to take full responsibility for the chaos she had created. She drove through the Old Port and down Portland Pier to face her new reality.

CHAPTER 117

KATIE

KATIE WAS AT THE WINDOW EATING HER LUNCH when she saw Ellen's car pull into the garage. It wasn't a healthy habit, but sitting at her desk or in the windowless kitchen or conference room was even worse. At least here, she could see the great outdoors. It was a breath of fresh air, even if she wasn't out in it. Ellen got off the elevator without a word. Katie waited for her to hang up her coat before speaking.

"Julie's waiting to see you. It might be a good idea to make that your first stop. She's been waiting all morning." Ellen remained unresponsive. She was locked in her mind. Katie waited for her words to click in.

"Any clue what this is about?" Ellen's voice was low, almost shaky. Katie was baffled at her response. Something was wrong.

"Are you all right? What happened?" This was not the Ellen she said goodbye to last night. "Are the boys all right?"

Katie couldn't imagine anything else that would drain Ellen like this.

"Yeah, yeah, they're fine. Just something Sterling told me." Ellen shook her head as if dislodging something distasteful.

"Julie needs your attention, and I'm not sure you want to meet with her like this. Do you want to share?" It wasn't her job, but Katie couldn't help herself. Julie needed Ellen's full attention and a clear head to digest what was about to drop. They all did.

"No. No. I need to talk with Julie first. After all these years together, I owe her that much." Ellen walked away with her head down.

Katie was speechless. Had she heard Ellen right? *After all these years together?* What was Ellen saying?

CHAPTER 118

JULIE

JULIE GLANCED UP FROM THE TAX ARTICLE SHE was reading. Staying current with tax law was the most annoying part of her job, and one that was impossible to focus on when other work waited to be completed. The upcoming conversation with Ellen made it tough to concentrate on anything, and she might as well read some boring crap. She blinked three times to clear her blurring eyes and numbing mind, then scanned the tax journal's table of contents to find something that might hold her attention.

A Federal case about disallowing deductions for cannabis businesses, now legal in Maine but still illegal for Federal tax purposes, caught her eye. With all the pot shops popping up around the state, it might be a new market for their firm to go after. The businesses were bound to be profitable and would need a reputable accountant to help wade through the regulations.

Julie was deep into her research and didn't notice Ellen enter until she had closed the door and taken a seat. "How was your morning?" Julie asked. Ellen didn't respond.

"Good walk with Sterling? I bet he couldn't believe the update on Nashville. I know I still can't." Small talk would help Julie get her head out of the weeds and into the big conversation. She took a deep breath, shrugged her shoulders, and settled back into herself.

"Interesting, to say the least." Ellen's answer was short, without any engaging energy. Julie was puzzled. What did Sterling say that could drain Ellen like this?

Ellen grabbed the arms of her chair and straightened her spine. "Katie said you had something you needed to talk to me about. I'm ready to hear it."

Julie reached into her pencil drawer, a duplicate of the one Bobby searched last night, and pulled out the copy of Michael's new lease. She slid it across to Ellen. "It's about this." Ellen glanced at the document.

"I know all about it. Sterling told me." Ellen's voice was cold and distant. "I want to hear it from you." Julie didn't expect this kind of response. She worried it would be a hard sell, but Ellen had her defenses up already. What the hell?

"Michael's leased a new office; we thought you should know." Julie felt like a little girl confessing to stolen candy. Why did she feel guilty? She was helping Ellen.

"We? Who's we?" Ellen asked. Her face flushed bright red. "I'm confused. You better explain."

"We. As in Bobby, Katie, and me." Ellen's shoulders

stooped over, her head dropped, and Julie thought she saw a tear fall into her lap.

"All of you?" Ellen's whisper was almost inaudible.

"We needed to make a move fast. Tax season is coming, and things have to change." Julie's words jolted Ellen upright, and her eyes searched Julie's.

"But why, I don't understand." Ellen pleaded. "All three of you?" Julie's head went back into the weeds. What the hell was going on with Ellen?

"All three of us, yes," Julie rushed to fill in the details. "I kept Michael busy at J's while Bobby and Katie searched his office and computer. This is all we found. They said his office didn't even look used. I'm not sure what's going on, but we know something is. We have to stop Michael. Now." Her heart pounded, and her mouth was dry. Would Ellen believe them if the lease were the only concrete evidence supporting their suspicions?

The release of Ellen's breath and pent-up energy was palpable. She jumped out of her chair, ran around Julie's desk, and crushed Julie in a giant hug.

"Oh god, oh god, oh god! That's all?" Ellen stepped back, stared at Julie, and bent over to embrace her one more time. "Of course it is!" Her laugh was bordering on maniacal.

Ellen circled back to her chair and glanced over her shoulder three times to look at Julie and laugh. Julie missed the joke.

"Okay, your turn, Ellen. What the fuck is so goddamn funny?"

CHAPTER 119

BOBBY

BOBBY WAS FINISHING THE INSTALLATION OF A keyless lock for the front door of the building, and his knees were starting to ache. The new touchscreen keypad was challenging to install, but well worth it for its ease of denying entry to former employees. Expensive and tedious key replacement was a thing of the past. With a few simple steps, Katie could change the firm's code for the front door and the new elevator lock that Otis Elevator had installed as an emergency. Leave it to Ellen to solve the problem without hesitation. It was good to have her back.

"Guess you wasted your time on the pier last night." Bobby flinched at the sound of Michael's voice. "Or maybe you followed Julie to her car after I left? I should have stayed to rescue her."

Bobby stood up from his crouched position. His knees cracked in protest. "Whatever." Bobby wouldn't bite. This jerk would not get to him. He rubbed his right knee and avoided eye contact.

"Whatever?" Michael bit back. "Is that all you have to say for disrupting my evening?" He puffed up his chest and moved closer. His briefcase swung menacingly at his side.

Bobby smelled stale booze on Michael's hot breath. It was well after lunch, and Michael's morning off had done nothing to refresh his physical or emotional state. The guy had either forgotten to polish his boot-licking smile or thought he had won and no longer needed to charm.

He held the door open for Michael to enter. "Have a great day, Mikey," was all Bobby said. He refused to engage with the asshole.

But he had hit the mark. Michael spun around with the proverbial if-looks-could-kill glare. Bobby met it glare for glare, stare for stare, and added a don't-even-try-it look. To be safe, he decided to stick around in case there was trouble.

CHAPTER 120

KATIE

"THANKS FOR CLEARING THINGS UP, MR. TRASK. I'm so sorry for the confusion. Ellen will see you and Beth next week, here at the office." Katie drew another black line through the list of clients that Ellen had unknowingly passed to Michael for his poaching. Her shoulder-length blonde hair swung forward as she studied the remaining clients to be called. She'd be finished by the end of the day. And so would Michael Prescott.

Katie peeked through her curtain of hair at the sound of the elevator, expecting Bobby to announce he was done securing the office. She was wrong.

"Good morning Katie." Michael bared his teeth. They reminded Katie of a shark, or rather, a shark cartoon. Today would be its final episode.

"Nice of you to make it in today." She couldn't resist one last jab. "Ellen's been waiting for you all morning." Technically, it was two hours, but Michael didn't need to know that.

"This migraine was a killer." He rubbed his forehead.

"Right." Katie offered Michael a fake smile. "I'll let them know you've finally arrived."

She punched the button for Ellen's intercom. "Michael is here."

"Tell her I'm grabbing a cup of coffee, and then I'll be right in," Michael interrupted, and he flashed his signature smile at Katie, hopefully for the last time.

"They'll be waiting in your office. Enjoy your coffee." Katie's mouth contorted as she fought to keep her own smile under wraps. Oh, to be a fly on the wall. Maybe she'd leave the intercom open to listen.

CHAPTER 121

MICHAEL

DID KATIE SAY *THEY*? MICHAEL WAS PUZZLED. WHO were *they*? Julie? And why were they in his office? Last night at J's, although she never said the actual words, Michael assumed she was in lockstep with him. He hinted that an office with better parking would be great, and she agreed that it would be nice. He told her how he loved working with her and that together, they could do great things. She didn't disagree. If she was part of Katie's *they*, what was last night about?

Michael poured the dregs of the coffee pot into his cup. Two sugar packets and a lot of cream might make it tolerable. It was not his job to make the coffee or clean up his spillage. He didn't care if it was Katie or any other lowly staff member, but it wouldn't be him. He juggled his briefcase and coffee in his left hand and opened the door with his right. Coffee dribbled out of his cup and followed him from the kitchen past Katie's desk. He turned away from her disapproving glare and continued to his office.

Ellen was sitting behind his desk, in his chair. Julie sat in one of the client chairs. Michael was confused but wasn't going to let on. "Ellen. Julie. To what do I owe this pleasure?" Stupid comment, but it bought him time to gather his thoughts. He lowered his lanky body into the chair next to Julie.

"I went to a great new bar after you left last night." He reached to touch Julie's hand resting on the arm of her chair. She yanked her hand away.

"I had enough last night." She turned to him with a sinister grin. "Actually, I've had enough for forever." It sounded like a threat.

"Did I offend you or something?" Better to play innocent than to admit that he had been a little too aggressive with his invitation.

"That's neither here nor there," Ellen cut in. He turned to face her.

"Portland is a small city with a tight-knit professional community. Forget about six degrees of separation. Here, it's even smaller. You never know who someone is related to or connected with. Like most small cities, we have an unspoken yet agreed-upon code. I'm sure you're familiar with it. We compete, but we compete respectfully. And, if someone violates that pact, we look out for each other."

Michael listened and waited to respond to Ellen's lecture, sensing his next words needed to be chosen carefully. There was no way she, or anyone else, could have found out already.

"If you'll recall Michael, I hired you for a six-month probationary period," Ellen continued. "I asked for three extra months to see how you'd fit in during tax season. You agreed that was fair." She tucked her hair behind her ear and locked eyes with him. "Unfortunately, you failed the test.

"Excuse me?" Michael's chin jutted forward, and he snarled with righteous indignation.

"There's nothing more to discuss." Ellen didn't blink. Her voice was calm. "This is your last day."

Michael was stunned. He turned to Julie. Her face was emotionless; her eyes were not. They blazed with hatred and a dusting of disgust. She stood and grabbed a small box from the bookcase.

"Not a lot to show for almost six months, Mike." Her voice radiated sarcasm and disdain. What was it with everyone today? Were they too stupid to remember? But Julie's eyes darkened, and he thought better of correcting her.

She dropped a sturdy box devoid of its reams of paper on his lap. "Here's everything from your office, including your pencil drawer." She sat back down.

Michael glanced at the contents. Lying on top was his new lease. Damn, rookie mistake. Why had he taken it to the office in the first place? He lifted his head. An inscrutable Ellen, one he had never met before, was glowering at him.

"The accounting profession thrives on referrals from bankers, lawyers, investment people, and we're a very close network with a very long memory." Ellen's threat came through loud and clear. Michael Prescott was done in Portland, and there was nothing he could do to change it.

Ellen picked up her favorite pen, Michael's contraband, and waggled it in his face. "Good luck in the future."

Michael's lips snapped shut, his jaw clenched, and his teeth began to grind. Then his left eyebrow lifted, and he smiled. No biggie. There'd be other opportunities in other cities. He flashed one last smile and left Hartmann and Associates without another word.

CHAPTER 122

JULIE

"CAN WE GET OUTTA HERE?" JULIE ASKED. "I CAN'T stand being in his office another minute. That goddamn cologne of his is gagging me." She stuck her finger down her throat for emphasis.

"Let's go to my office," Ellen laughed. "And let's get Katie and Bobby if he's still here. I owe all of you a ton of gratitude."

"We're on our way," Katie's voice floated into the room. "Hope you don't mind. We've been eavesdropping."

The foursome reconvened in Ellen's office, where her friendly seagull pecked a round of applause on their arrival. Bobby dragged two extra chairs from the conference room, and Ellen wheeled her chair from behind her desk. They sat in a poorly orchestrated circle.

"Did he say anything on his way out?" Julie's curiosity got the best of her. She leaned forward.

"Not a word. And for once, I didn't need sunglasses to

avoid the glint of his pearly whites," Katie laughed. "I think he kept his mouth shut because Bobby was there."

"I'm a force to be reckoned with." Bobby sucked in his gut, puffed out his chest, flexed his biceps, and burst out laughing.

"Don't underestimate yourself," Julie said, moving closer. "It helped knowing you had my back the other night." She touched his shoulder.

"Me too," Katie joined in. "I would've been a neurotic fool without you."

"Save me, Ellen, save me!" Bobby hid behind Ellen's chair.

Ellen stood up and pretended to shield Bobby. "Enough of this love fest. You are all too wonderful." She glanced at her watch. "It's after four; close enough. Let's call it a day. It's been a helluva long week. Let's blow this pop stand."

Julie wasn't going to argue. She was tired. The intrigue, the confrontation, and the drama of the past months were taking their toll. Last night had added to her overall fatigue.

"But first," Ellen interrupted, bringing Julie's thoughts back to the room. Ellen lifted a round metal tin from the bottom drawer of her desk. "This was going to be my gift on my return, but I held it back because I knew you were all sick and tired of Nashville."

Julie read the white words on the bright red lid: *Nashville's GooGoo Clusters. Since 1912.*

"There are a few missing," Ellen confessed. "I wish I could blame Michael for that." She passed the tin from Bobby to Katie to Julie and waited while each chose their favorite flavor. They unwrapped their nutty, chocolatey confections together.

Julie raised both arms, and they all joined in for an eight-fisted GooGoo salute. "Here's to unraveling the biggest clusterfuck in Hartmann and Associates' history!"

Ten Weeks Later

EPILOGUE

ELLEN

IT WAS APRIL 16, AND TAX SEASON WAS OVER. Ellen adjusted the pillow behind her back and rested her head against the riot of bright flowers covering her living room loveseat. The sun streaming through the antique wavy glass warmed her, and Little Pup lay at her feet, basking in its rays. She loved this room but rarely found time to enjoy it. On weekdays, she came home too late to appreciate its sunny disposition, and on weekends, she was too busy being a mother to sit and do nothing. Today was different. The boys were at school, another tax season was behind her, and she had the house all to herself. She wiggled her toes and picked up the novel she had started in January.

The flap of the brass mail slot in the heavy front door rattled Little Pup awake. His anxiety had improved, although he remained on high alert even as he napped. He trotted off to inspect the day's mail deposited on the floor.

Ellen watched Little Pup nose through the mail. Someday, she'd teach him to fetch it. For now, she marveled at how his sense of smell did the sorting. She saw him nudge an envelope and a couple of flyers to the side. Even from this distance, she could see they were junk mail. So much for the digital world saving paper and trees. How companies found it profitable to send things that went straight to the recycle bin was beyond her.

Little Pup fixated on a plain white envelope. His sniffer went into overdrive, and he pawed the piece of mail until it flipped over. He snuffled some more. When he started to whimper and claw at it, Ellen went over to investigate. What was he smelling?

She reached down to pick it up, and Little Pup snapped at her fingers. "I didn't mean to startle you, Pup. Everything's all right." She stroked his head and returned to the couch with the envelope.

Little Pup jumped onto the sofa and watched as she examined the envelope. Her address was typed, not hand-written, and there was no return address. There was no postmark either; the sender had avoided any identifier on the plain, white business-sized envelope.

Ellen flipped it over and slid her index finger under the flap. The open envelope released more scents, and Little Pup's nose went into high gear. His ferreting paws made it impossible for Ellen to pull out the contents of the envelope. She pushed him off, and he jumped right back. In desperation, she stood up. Little Pup clawed at her feet.

There was one lone piece of paper in it, the same size as the envelope. She slid it out and looked for more. Nothing else. She studied it and blinked. She held it to the light, looking for a watermark or security thread. It was real.

She looked inside the envelope again to see if she had missed anything. She hadn't. She examined the outside of the envelope one more time. Nothing. But there must be a clue, any clue. Then she spotted the USPS Endangered Species Forever stamp. It displayed the picture and name of the Nashville Crayfish. She shook her head in disbelief.

Somewhere, Sam Davis was alive and well. This ten-thousand-dollar cashier's check and Little Pup's sharp nose proved it. She shook her head in disbelief. Somehow, Ellen had connected with the real Sam Davis. She wasn't a naïve rube from the backwaters of Maine who would fall for a huckster's ruse. With this final act of good faith and kindness, Sam Davis restored Ellen's faith in humanity and herself.

Keep Exploring the Mystery...

www.JaneHoneck.com

as mentioned in *Double Entry*

THE MONEY DYNAMIC COURSE

Change your money story. Change your life.

This transformative course offers a fresh perspective
and a powerful new way of being with money.

YOUR MONEY STYLE QUIZ

Take the quiz to discover the patterns that influence your
financial choices. And begin your path to financial clarity.

Still Curious?

www.JaneHoneck.com

MONEY & MYSTERY

Unravel the mystery of money in Jane's engaging, interactive presentations—available in-person or online. With humor and insight, she'll guide you to a deeper, more personal understanding of your financial world.

THE PROBLEM WITH MONEY? IT'S NOT ABOUT THE MONEY!

Internationally published and winner of eight awards, including the 2010 Silver Award for Foreword Reviews Self-Help Book of the Year, this groundbreaking book helps identify your money beliefs across seven key areas. It explains how small, manageable steps can transform your relationship with money, creating lasting, positive changes in your financial habits.

Ellen Hartmann Series

Book #1

NUMBERS DON'T LIE

Next Generation Indie Book Awards
2025 Thriller Finalist

When trusted clients face a double betrayal—personal loss and professional sabotage—CPA Ellen Hartmann suspects foul play. With her sharp-witted associate, she plunges into a maze of secrets surrounding a death at sea to uncover hard truths that blur the line between accident and intent, and awaken a love thought lost.

Coming in 2026

Book #3

UNBALANCED

Grief lingers in silence and in words left unspoken. As Julie tends to her dying father amid her family's unraveling, Ellen fights to salvage a deal fractured by betrayal and absence. Both must navigate heartbreak—not by finding balance, but by embracing grace.